PLAY IT AGAIN?

Everyone deserves an encore

Ever wonder what happened to that old flame? In the wilds of Norfolk, Dylan is mending his broken heart by rebuilding his house. Next door, Ellie gazes lovingly at him over the fence, while her mother Fliss contemplates a school reunion. Should she risk an encounter with her first crush? Meanwhile Dylan's once-famous father Alex, arriving a little late in his son's life, is also recalling the perils of first love – but will Marie return Alex's renewed affection? Can an old rock star capture the magic of his first hit?

PLAY IT AGAIN?

PLAY IT AGAIN?

by

Julie Highmore

Magna Large Print Books
Long Preston, North Yorkshire,
BD23 4ND, England.

British Library Cataloguing in Publication Data.

Highmore, Julie
    Play it again?

    A catalogue record of this book is
    available from the British Library

    ISBN   0-7505-2292-5

First published in Great Britain 2004 by Review

Copyright © 2004 Julie Highmore

Cover illustration © Head Design by arrangement with
Headline Book Publishing

The right of Julie Highmore to be identified as the author of this work
has been asserted by her in accordance with the Copyright, Designs
and Patents Act, 1988

Published in Large Print 2005 by arrangement with
Headline Book Publishing Ltd.

Magna Large Print is an imprint of Library Magna Books Ltd.

Printed and bound in Great Britain by
T.J. (International) Ltd., Cornwall, PL28 8RW

For David

ONE

Dylan's father stood out in the crowd of rail travellers. He was taller than most, still tanned from Jamaica and, as usual, his distinctive fair curls were mildly unkempt. He wore a pale linen suit, one hand in a trouser pocket, the other carrying a brown leather overnight bag. Seeing Dylan, he sauntered towards him flashing the neat white teeth he'd got in the States. In spite of one or two deeply etched lines and little twin peaks of receding hairline, Alex Child lived up to his name and remained persistently boyish.

Dylan chucked his cup in a bin, got up from the bench and gave his father an awkward hug, trying not to spread dried plaster over him. 'How was the journey?' he asked.

Alex eased away and dusted down his jacket. 'Not bad. Well, considering I'm in Britain.'

Dylan laughed. 'Now for the best bit.' He held up a set of keys and jangled them. 'Got my new wheels outside.'

'Great.'

Before they could move off, a middle-aged woman in a colourful dress was beside them, hovering and clearing her throat, and quite red in the face. 'Excuse me,' she wheezed. Her eyes were bulging and her chest bobbed up and down rapidly. Asthma? wondered Dylan. He gestured her towards the bench.

11

'Excuse me,' she repeated, ignoring him and staring intently at his father. 'But it *is* you, isn't it?'

Alex nodded and smiled.

'I thought so,' she said, and a podgy hand flew to her throat. 'Gosh. I saw Blue Plum play here in Norfolk, in ... oh, let me do my sums ... um, around thirty years ago ... ish.'

'Ah, the early days.' Alex put down his bag and took a pen from an inside pocket, ready for the autograph request. 'You must have been very young when you saw us?'

Not that young, thought Dylan. He smiled to himself. What a charmer his father still was, despite being famously prone to putting his foot in it.

'Yes I was, actually. Fourteen or fifteen. My friends and I were all mad about Blue Plum.' She rummaged in a carrier bag and handed Alex a magazine. 'It's Hazel, by the way. You know, as in nutty, ha ha. Just "To Hazel with love" will be fine.'

'One of my very favourite names,' Alex told her as he scrawled flamboyantly over the front-cover model. He handed the magazine back and made warm eye-contact. 'Where was it we played?'

'West Washam Corn Exchange. Do you remember? Absolutely sweltering, it was. I pretended to faint because I'd heard girls got taken to the bedroom ... oh, what am I saying, I mean dressing-room. But instead, they carried me out to this kitchenette where there were all these other fed-up-looking pretend fainters, and we all got given tea and a Penguin – not a real

12

one, you know, the chocolate bar – and ... oh dear, where was I? Anyway, you were *fantastic*.'

'Thank you.'

'I've got all your records.'

'Great.'

'Well, not the recent ones.'

'No?' said Alex. He slipped the pen back into his jacket and picked up his bag. 'It might be worth giving the latest a go.'

Dylan grimaced. Not according to the music critics. *Old rock stars never die,* said one review, *they just run out of ideas and turn to fusion.* He'd read it several times and remembered it well. *I can only surmise that the presence of the didgeridoo on every track of Alex Child's new album* Why? *is designed to distract the listener from his clichéd lyrics (who'd have thought of rhyming 'aching heart' with 'we're apart') and regurgitated melodies. However, with wobble-board, Aboriginal choir and possibly a Billy-can, all competing with Child's still-mellifluous voice – but without, alas, that famous guitar-work – this gets my vote for most apt album title.*

Dylan had eventually binned it, thinking how mean-spirited people could be. He himself had every reason to hate his father, of course, but had inherited his mother's forgiving nature. Alex had not been the best of dads but, as he'd often tried to explain to Dylan, being holed up for recording sessions and having to tour and being so totally out of his head 100 per cent of the time had made fatherhood tricky. Anyway, thought Dylan, just look at him now. Coming all the way from Gloucestershire by train when, twenty years earlier, he couldn't make it across two London

13

boroughs to visit his small son and beautiful young wife, Marie.

'...just done his finals,' Hazel-as-in-nutty was saying. 'Though what you do with an Anthropology and Psychology degree, heaven only knows.'

'This is *my* son,' said Alex, encircling Dylan's shoulders without actually touching him. 'Dylan. Bit of a DIY man, as you can see.'

She laughed in a girlish way that was at odds with her appearance. 'Pleased to meet you, Dylan. That's Dylan after Bob, isn't it? Bob Dylan, as it were.'

'Sort of,' Alex told her.

'That's what you said in an interview. Not that you can believe everything you see or hear in, you know, the um ... oh, what's it called? The um...?'

'Media?'

'That's it,' she said, tutting. She looked Dylan up and down. 'My Greg's a bit taller but just as good-looking, I'd say. Takes after his dad in that respect but got much more up top, thank goodness!'

Alex glanced at his watch. 'Well,' he said, suddenly clasping one of Hazel's hands, as though he really couldn't bear to part from this talkative stranger. 'I'd love to have carried on chatting, only I do have a train to catch home in two days' time, ha ha.'

Dylan rolled his eyes, joined in the hasty goodbyes and led his father to the car park, where Alex stared in horror at his van. 'When I said new, I didn't mean brand new,' Dylan told him. 'Hang on.' He hurried to the back, took out

14

a couple of dustbin liners, blew fine powder off them and draped them over the passenger seat. 'Don't worry, it's not far.'

Alex lowered himself gingerly on to shiny black plastic, placed his bag on his lap and buried his feet in tools. 'So,' he shouted as they began to crawl out of the city, 'tell me about this new place of yours.'

'Well,' Dylan moved up to second gear, which quietened the engine a bit, 'it's still a mess, but this week I've concentrated on the guest room. All painted. Been to Habitat and got you those cotton sheets you like. I think you'll be comfortable.' He turned and grinned. 'So long as you don't want to eat.'

'Oh?'

'No kitchen to speak of. I'm building an extension.'

'Ah. Any restaurants or takeaways nearby?'

Dylan laughed. 'The only thing nearby is my next-door neighbour. Well, and her daughter. We're in a couple of semi-detached nineteenth-century farmworkers' cottages. Bigger than you'd imagine. For some reason they made them three-storey. It's funny, we're surrounded by acres and acres of land – sugar beet fields mostly – but they decided to build the houses tall and relatively narrow. Just the Victorian fashion, I suppose.'

Alex was looking through Dylan's cassettes, picking them up one by one and reading the labels. 'The Flaming Lips. Any good?'

'Very. You'd like them. Here.' He took the tape and put it in the machine. 'Anyway, the farmer decided to sell these two cottages off at the same

15

time. I made a ridiculously low offer for the one that needed the most work, and got it. *So*, as we made a killing on the Finchley flat, I'm in the money at the moment.' He turned and grinned at his father, feeling proud of his independence. Well, semi-independence if you counted the trust-fund payments.

'Why East Anglia?'

Dylan looked back at the road and sighed a very long sigh that couldn't be heard over Flaming Lips and the diesel engine. 'Mostly because it's miles from everything and everybody.'

'Meaning Natalia?'

'Yep,' he said, thinking back to the first few weeks in the house, and how liberated and safe and happy he'd felt, away from Natalia and London and friends who brought her name up in conversation or, worse still, tried not to. He'd therapeutically hammered and wrenched and sawn, filling two skips with old Formica units and the middle wall that his part-time help, Baz, and a local builder had helped him knock down. May had been unusually hot, and most afternoons he'd sunbathed with a beer for a while, playing his guitar or reading. Then, early one morning a removals van appeared, and within minutes a woman with wild blonde hair and a teenage daughter with equally wild blonde hair were knocking on his door; the daughter with a terrifyingly friendly smile. Did he know where their stopcock was?

'Yeah, they're good,' said Alex, pointing at the tape deck. 'Pretty original.'

Dylan nodded and tapped at the steering

wheel. 'Go away!' he'd wanted to tell his new neighbours. Of course, he'd miss them if they left now, but how weird it had felt at first, suddenly having people just inches away through the party wall, surrounded by miles of flat open country-side. Like strangers sitting next to each other in an otherwise empty cinema.

'I thought we could stop for a pub lunch,' he said. 'Fancy?'

'Sounds good.'

Half a mile from his house, Dylan pulled into The Fox, where he hoped proprietor Ken – Sixties/Seventies'-music anorak – wouldn't recognise his father. 'Here, wear this,' he said, feeling behind his seat for his sunhat. 'Let's try to avoid autographs.'

But it didn't work.

'You're a dark horse,' Ken and Wendy told Dylan, before dredging up an old Blue Plum song on the jukebox, taking photos, and insisting they have their lunch on the house.

Why, Fliss wondered, as a taxi pulled away from her front gate, was Hazel Osgood's mother walking up her garden path when she was expecting Hazel Osgood? Had she come with dreadful news of her daughter? Fliss dropped the trowel and yanked off both gardening gloves.

'Hi, Fliss,' called Mrs Osgood from just beyond the laburnum. 'Bloody hell,' she went on, clonking towards her on Queen Mum shoes and lugging a large nylon bag, 'you haven't changed a bit, Felicity Lawrence!'

No, not Hazel Osgood's mother at all, Fliss

17

realised with a jolt, but Hazel herself. It was a struggle not to slap her hands to her face and gasp. How cruel the past thirty years had been to her old friend: puffy face, salt-and-pepper hair growing at right angles to her head, hips as wide as the wheelbarrow she was skirting. In her flowery dress it was hard to tell where Hazel ended and the garden began.

'Neither have you,' Fliss cried, quietly blessing her parents for their genes.

They came together, kissed and made their way past seed trays and jiffy pots into the kitchen.

Hazel looked around and sighed. 'Oh, this is very...'

'Rustic?'

'Lovely, I was going to say. Like something out of a country magazine. I've just had a new kitchen put in. Cost a fortune, but do you know, I can't stand it. Too cold and sterile, but there you go, you never know, do you?'

'No,' said Fliss, not quite knowing what she didn't know. 'Tea?' she offered, taking her friend's bag off her.

'Oh, hang on,' said Hazel, grabbing it back and unzipping it. 'Talking of magazines, you'll *die* when I tell you who I've just had an actual conversation with at Norwich railway station. Go on, try and guess!'

'Um ... Alan Partridge?'

'Nope. And not Delia Smith either. Go back a bit. Think West Washam Corn Exchange. Us, aged fifteen, sixteen.'

'Not Al Green?'

'No, no. Blonder.'

Fliss took the magazine and squinted at an ostentatious signature. She turned it one way, then the other, and pulled a face. 'Alice Chilli? Who's she?'

'Alex,' said Hazel, pointing at the words. *'Child.'*

'No! My God, what was he like?'

'Well...' began Hazel, and by the time she'd finished, her tea had gone cold.

'Then after Mick left, there was another Mick for a while, only he didn't get along with the kids. Talk about intolerant. Didn't like their clothes, their music or their "lip" as he used to call it. Eventually, he decided he didn't like me either and went back to live with his mum in Northampton. No more Micks, I've decided!'

'Right.'

It was 4.20, two hours since her arrival, and Hazel hadn't made a single enquiry about Fliss's life. Fliss, on the other hand, could have drawn a detailed, to-scale plan of Hazel's home and competently taken over her job at Gibbons and Waite, Heating Consultants.

'Do you remember Susie Drysdale?' Hazel asked. 'You know, a year below us. Lanky. Good at hockey.'

'Oh, yes,' Fliss lied. 'Susie. Ha!'

'Well, I managed to get in touch with her through Friends Reunited.'

'Really?' Hazel had found Fliss via her health centre's website; Fliss having reverted to her maiden name after divorce. 'How is she?' she asked, switching off while Hazel told her. A brain

19

could only take so much information about people it didn't recall. She was, however, desperate to hear news of heart-throb Richard Honeyman, and was waiting for an opportune moment – such as Hazel drawing breath – to bring up his name.

'...just to the west of Guildford. Oh, wait a minute, do I mean east?' Hazel pointed at an imaginary map with her right hand, then with her left. 'East,' she decided, then, 'No, west. Anyway, her husband's got his own signwriting business, and they seem to be doing very nicely. When I stayed with them we ate out every night, and I'm not talking Little Chef!'

'Uh-huh?'

Fliss imagined it wouldn't be polite to scream in the living room, so on the pretext of fetching more milk, went to the kitchen and bit hard on an oven glove. Which helped. When she returned she found Hazel admiring Alex Child's signature again.

'*Very* artistic,' she was saying, twisting the magazine then cocking her head. 'Just as you'd imagine, really. Honestly, you could have knocked me down with a–'

'Richard Honeyman!' shouted Fliss, quite surprising herself.

'Sorry?'

'Richard Honeyman. What happened to him?'

'Oh.' Hazel picked up her concertina file again. 'Let me see ... I think he might be... now where is he? Oh yes, I seem to have an emailed photo here.'

Fliss grabbed the piece of paper then stared, uncomprehending, at the printout. Not a trace remained of the person who'd once resembled the young Cat Stevens. What on earth had happened? Too many business lunches? A series of family tragedies? Both? This Richard was puffy and jowly and droopy-eyed, like a large old battle-fatigued cat who now slept a lot. She handed it back. 'I don't suppose there were two Richard Honeymans?'

Hazel shook her head. 'It's funny,' she said, taking the picture and slipping Richard back into the H section, 'how so many of the boys have gone to seed.'

Fliss wondered if Hazel was really one to talk. 'Is that so?'

'Mm, all bald heads and beer bellies. Nothing like Alex Child, I'll tell you.'

'Right.'

While Hazel was back on Alex, her second-favourite subject, Fliss beckoned her out to the kitchen where she sat her on a stool with a slice of cheesecake and got on with peeling and chopping vegetables for dinner.

'He was all over my bedroom walls,' sighed Hazel. 'But you preferred Chas the drummer.'

'Did I?'

'Or maybe that was Jenny. Anyway, do you remember what you were wearing when we saw Blue Plum? You know, I remember my entire outfit.'

'Do you?'

Hazel went on to describe it, while Fliss wondered about doing a few more courgettes. She'd invited her neighbour for dinner, just in case she and Hazel had found nothing to say to each other. Not the case, it had turned out, but how nice it might be to share her guest with another for a while.

Hazel laughed. 'And his name was all over my satchel in that bubble writing. Do you remember?'

'Kind of.'

They'd obsessed about all sorts of people back then: rock stars, film stars, half the boys in the sixth form. Fliss's fantasies – now shattered and forever buried by a grainy printout – had mostly focused on the unattainable Richard Honeyman, who'd occasionally shot her an interested look but, as far as she could recall, only spoke to her once. 'Do you know if Watkins is in his office?' he'd asked in the corridor one lunchtime when they were both in the lower sixth. So stunned was she at finally, and so unexpectedly, being addressed by him that she just shrugged and walked on. Of course she kicked herself repeatedly for the missed opportunity, then about three months later Richard started going out with a girl from the convent and Fliss gave up hope.

While Hazel rabbited on, Fliss thought back to the Blue Plum night, remembering it well, even though they'd been to see lots of singers and groups in those days, when big names were happy to trundle to small venues all over the country. Even out-of-the-way Norfolk. It had been swelteringly hot in the Corn Exchange, and several girls, including Hazel, had screamed, *'Alex!'* over and over at the gorgeous blond singer, dancing and shaking themselves into such a state that they got carried out by large sweaty bouncers in string vests.

'Is there anything you don't eat?' asked Fliss, while Hazel helped herself to more cheesecake.

'Oh, good Lord, no. I eat like a horse. Luckily, I never seem to put on weight.'

Fliss stared blankly. Had Hazel mentioned having any mirrors in her house?

After taking off his linen suit and hanging it in the canvas wardrobe, Alex lay back on the single bed, hands behind his head, and thought about his son, now aged twenty-five, and what an unexpected life he'd chosen for himself. Surely, with his considerable musical talent and dark, brooding looks – not to mention the famous surname – Dylan should be doing what Alex was at that age, i.e. drinking hard and doing lots of drugs, bedding painfully young groupies, trashing hotel suites ... and somehow, through the haze and exhaustion of all that, finding time to write lyrics that make grown men weep and later work their way on to a new-university English syllabus. But no, not Dylan. Here he was, in the back of beyond, building a kitchen extension and getting excited about sunken ceiling lights. Would he ever fathom his son? Or get him to accept any financial help? Well, over and above the trust-fund money.

Alex's eyes grew heavy. God, it was noisy here. He could make out Dylan tap-tap-tapping at something, plus a distant tractor, the bleating of sheep ... and, hang on a minute, was that a woman singing Blue Plum's 'Heaven Came Early'? His eyes grew even heavier. Surely he was imagining it... And, oh dear, she really was horribly off-key...

'You asleep, Dad?' was the next thing he heard. 'Dad?' His eyes jumped open to find the room no longer sun-filled.

'Yes?' he said thickly, easing deadened hands out from behind his head.

'I don't know if you want a shower or something before we go?'

Alex sat himself up. 'Yeah, OK. Thanks.'

Dylan pushed at the door and stuck his head round. 'We've got about half an hour.'

'Right,' said Alex, arching his back and stretching his arms. 'What's the dress code? Black tie? Smart casual? Rural scruff?'

'No pony tail, that's the only rule.'

Alex laughed and rubbed at the back of his neck. 'Don't worry, it's way too short now.'

'See you downstairs then. We'll have a quick beer.'

'OK.'

Alex was slightly reluctant to leave his room, what with the rest of the house being a minefield of missing floorboards and noose-like dangling wires, but he grabbed some clothes and hopped over to the half-done bathroom, where he took a handheld shower in a bath that appeared not to be attached to anything, and wished Dylan would just let him buy him a bloody house. Great towels though, he noticed, when he stepped out: thick, soft, white. Bought especially, no doubt. He rubbed at his hair and his back, and after wiggling water out of his ears, heard it again: a woman singing 'Heaven Came Early'. Badly. Weird, he thought, shaking his head then drowning her out with his electric shaver.

Fliss was enjoying the respite. She lay, legs splayed, head lolled, in an armchair, a large wine glass, containing a large wine, cupped in one hand. Well, it was a kind of respite. Her guest was still audible in the room above, singing away in the manner of that girl who'd always been asked by Mrs Judd to mime during singing lessons – Hazel, in fact. Fliss slipped a finger in an ear, wondering what it must be like to work with such a chatterbox, or be one of her children. People should be given awards for coping with something like that. As a teenager, Hazel had occasionally been irritating, but mostly she was just exuberant, self-confident and something of a leader. Until, recalled Fliss, she was confronted with a boy she fancied. Then she'd get panicky and tongue-tied, or just babble incoherently. They were always teasing her about it.

She and Hazel had eventually grown apart when Fliss started going out with a boy who was into folk music in a big way, and began spending her Saturday evenings listening to Pete Seeger and Ralph McTell in his bedroom in his liberal parents' home. She and Hazel had still hung out together at school, but halfway through A levels, Hazel dropped out to do a building society training scheme. A year later, Fliss went off to study medicine and they eventually lost touch. Perhaps they should have left it at that, Fliss was thinking, just as Hazel appeared at the door in a blue-and-white boldly striped T-shirt only a very thin Frenchman could get away with.

'That's better,' Hazel sighed.

Fliss wondered if she too should change. She was still in her gardening clothes: old jeans and a sleeveless, faded lilac T-shirt. Oh, why bother? It was only Dylan from next door, after all. Mind you, he'd warned her he might have to bring along a weekend guest.

'I thought I'd dress down as it's only you and me,' said Hazel: broad knees beneath mile-wide khaki shorts, heavy leather sandals that were curling with age, hair scraped back in a lopsided topknot. Her florid features were now scrubbed of all make-up and gleaming with moisturiser, and she fanned herself with that *Woman and Home* she was obviously never going to put down. 'Such a warm evening, isn't it? Oh ... was that the door?'

Fliss slipped her shoes back on. 'Gosh, is it that time already? Sorry, I forgot to tell you I'd invited–'

Hazel turned and clomped down the hall. 'I'll get it, shall I?'

Ellie pulled her mother's car up outside Biddle-farm Cottages and compared the two long and narrow front gardens. Dylan's was awash with machines and buckets and sheets of blue plastic, while theirs, owing to the hundreds of pounds and the two hours a day her mother was putting in, was like first prize at the Chelsea Flower Show. Ellie had done her bit too, slapping wood protection on the fence and so forth. Any excuse to linger outside, watching Dylan shovelling sand

and hauling blocks and building up his lovely tanned arms and legs. She gave a little shudder, got out of the car and lifted the latch of the right-hand gate, hoping her mum had cooked enough dinner for two. Ellie was supposed to have been at Rob's all weekend, but she'd finished with him early that evening – something she'd been wanting to do for weeks – and, with a heart and head full of Dylan, and the determination to get him to actually notice her one of these days, she'd set off for home.

'Hi, Mum!' she called out from the hallway. She dropped her things and went to the kitchen. 'Is there any food? I'm–' Oh God, *Dylan*. Ellie felt herself colouring up. Who were these other people? What were they doing there? Her mother never entertained. She always liked to keep her evenings and weekends to herself, just pottering in the garden, reading a novel, the newspapers. In fact, Ellie had often wondered if her mum wasn't a bit dysfunctional in that respect. '–starving,' she said.

'Hi, sweetie. Pull up a chair. Is Rob with you?'

'No.'

'This is my daughter, Ellie,' said Fliss. 'This is my old friend, Hazel, from school.'

'Oh, yeah yeah,' she said, suddenly remembering about the weekend guest. 'Hi, Hazel. Nice to meet you.'

Hazel gave her a brief, wide-eyed nod while her mother waved an arm at the man. 'And this is Dylan's father, Alex.'

'Oh, right. Hello.'

'Hi,' he said back with a big smile. For an old

guy, he had nice teeth. 'Plenty of food left,' he told her. 'Your mother cooked for ten.'

'Yeah, she does that. Luckily for me.' Had Dylan even looked at her yet?

Fliss pointed to the far side of the table. 'Why don't you squeeze in over there, Ellie? Next to Dylan.'

'OK.'

It turned out, to Ellie's amazement, that Dylan's dad was some huge old rock star whose band she'd heard of, and that stunned-looking Hazel, who hadn't yet said a word, and her mum had been big fans of his and went to see him play when they were like twelve or something. Trust Dylan not to boast about having a famous father. You had to admire that.

'Could you pass the salt?' she asked him.

'Sure.'

Their bare arms touched and Ellie quietly yelped, then said, 'How's the house coming along?' She turned to look at him. Had she ever been this close to Dylan before? He had such dark, dark eyes and the kind of lashes you couldn't get no matter how much mascara you used. She loved his hair. Almost black, and short. But not too short. Enough to run her fingers through.

'Oh, slowly,' he said. 'But that's because I'm doing a lot of it on my own. Well, with help from Baz.' He took the salt pot from her and placed it back in the centre of the table. 'How's the fence?'

'Mm, well, I think it might need like one more coat.'

'Really? Surely four's enough?'

He'd been counting! 'Just to be on the safe side,' she told him.

'You should wear a mask, you know. It's quite evil stuff. I've got one you could use.'

'Thanks,' she said, secretly pulling a face. How sexy would that be?

Fliss watched Hazel; the forkful of vegetable curry still poised where it had been for about ten minutes, ever since Alex told her he'd heard her singing.

'Oh Christ, you *didn't!*' Hazel had cried. 'Everyone tells me I'm tone deaf.'

Alex had laughed, and with a bit of a wink added, 'Well, I did wonder if it was an injured tomcat.'

'More wine?' Fliss was now shouting in Hazel's ear, trying to startle her back to life, while at the same time rather enjoying the lack of Hazel-babble that had clouded the first course and sent Dylan's eyes over to the cuckoo clock every two minutes.

'Uh,' managed Hazel.

'*So...*' Alex suddenly directed Fliss's way. She still couldn't believe he was sitting at her kitchen table. 'What made you switch from GP to acu-puncturist?'

She topped up everyone's glass, manoeuvred Hazel's fork towards her mouth and said, 'Drugs.'

Alex shook his head. 'Mm, they can make you do odd things.'

'All those repeat prescriptions I found myself writing out, year after year.'

'Oh, right.'

'The pharmaceutical companies making huge profits. The patients never getting any better.' She stopped and looked again with concern at her old friend. 'Hazel, would you like me to pop your plate in the microwave? Everything must be quite tepid by now. Here, come with me.' She hoisted Hazel and her plate and led her to the other end of the large kitchen where she whispered, 'It was a bit of a shock for me too, you know. Here, give me your arm. I'll try some shiatsu.'

'Oh God,' Hazel whispered back, while Fliss firmly applied pressure to the first and then the second of five points along her plump forearm. 'Alex Child called me a tomcat.'

'I'm sure he didn't mean it. But anyway, we can't all have great voices. Just try to remember how beautifully you played the violin.'

'Did I? That's nice of you to say so. I've taken it up again, you know. Taught my youngest and now we play together. Mostly classical but also some folk and jazz. We even did a little recital for charity at the local primary school. Went down a storm.'

'Did you?' People can be so surprising, thought Fliss, now at the fifth point. She pulled Hazel's striped sleeve down. 'Breathe deeply,' she told her, 'and go and join the others. I'll bring your food over.'

By the time Fliss got back to the table, Hazel was chatty again but not hyper.

'Majorca, did you say? I *love* Majorca. Do you know the Hotel Alfonso? That's where we stayed last time with Sunrise. Discoing every night. Fabulous.'

'No, I don't think I've come across it,' said Alex. 'My villa's in Deya, in the north-west of the island. Beautiful area. But rather popular with the rich and famous, unfortunately. Always tripping over other musicians when I'm there.'

'Hazel plays the violin,' announced Fliss, before anyone – i.e. Hazel – tried to wangle a Deyan holiday. 'Used to be really good.'

Ellie turned to Hazel. 'Hey, I've got my old violin upstairs. You could maybe play it for us, yeah?'

'Oh no, Ellie,' jumped in Fliss. The thing would need a good tuning, and what if Hazel had lost her touch? Or inadvertently hummed as she played? 'I really don't think–'

'I was total crap on it,' laughed Ellie, 'so it'd be nice to hear it played properly.'

She'd pushed back her chair and was halfway up the stairs before Alex chuckled and said, 'You wouldn't believe how many times that happens to me. Someone produces this warped acoustic guitar from a damp cupboard and wants you to do every Blue Plum number.'

'You'd better play it if Ellie insists,' Dylan said to Hazel. 'She's just told me she's got a black belt in judo.'

'Blimey.'

Fliss laughed. 'Well, not quite black, but she has been doing it for years. Since she was ten.'

'Here,' said her daughter, flying back into the kitchen with the speed and agility of an eighteen-year-old judo queen. She wiped at dust and handed the violin over to a scarily serene Hazel, who thanked her, gave it a couple of twangs and

31

said she'd love to have a go on it later.

'What an honour it'll be to play in front of the great Alex Child,' she added.

Fliss smiled encouragingly at her old friend and wondered how she could snap the bow in two without anyone noticing.

TWO

On her birthday the previous October, Marie Child had come out of a long sleepwalk; one in which she'd lived a very easy life with Geoff, in Guildford, in the house she'd bought for herself and Dylan – with a little help from Alex – some fifteen years before.

Geoff had been seven years older than Marie. An auto-parts middle manager by trade and by nature, he played golf, knew a lot about World War Two, and started the newspaper with the sport and worked his way forwards. She'd met him at Beginners' Spanish, where he was very attentive towards her and mildly humorous and, as she'd been going through a bit of a low patch, she gradually took up with him.

He moved in after Dylan left for university, and although they'd rarely quarrelled and had spent many a nice evening with Pauline and Len at number 17, Marie suddenly realised, as two tickets for *Phantom of the Opera* fell out of Geoff's birthday card to her, that this wasn't the life for a former wild child with an Open University degree and the soul of an artist. Geoff was a gentle, giving kind of person, and Marie felt just terrible as she wrote him an apologetic note and a large cheque – later returned to her in shreds – while he was at work, but she knew one more night with a man in two-tone pyjamas would kill her. She moved out that day, stayed with her cousin Kathleen in Wimbledon for a while, then rented the top half of an Edwardian house in Peckham. Once Geoff had found another home, she put Guildford on the market and looked for somewhere to buy.

Marie changed her diet, exercised and shed almost a stone, then had a bit of Botox and, after a week of intense shopping, gave all her drab former-life clothes to Help the Aged, which seemed appropriate. She decided to grow her dark and curly hair and had Kit at Mahogany erase the one or two grey bits with lowlights.

'You look a lot like Cher,' he'd shouted above a high-pitched dryer. 'Only more, you know, *real.*'

'Thanks,' she yelled back and kept quiet about the Botox.

Once settled in her nicely done up red-brick South London terrace, she'd retaught herself the guitar, listened to recent Linda Thompson, Emmylou Harris and Nanci Griffith albums and, for the first time in decades, wrote music; this time alone, rather than with Alex, and this time for herself, rather than for Blue Plum. Several of those dozen songs she'd co-written back in the Seventies had become minor classics and were now bringing in steady royalties, thanks mostly to car ads and recent teen-band covers. Marie was thrilled to discover she could still write a good tune. However, words were always a headache, as she tended to go for deep and didactic and could never get anything to rhyme, so she'd enlisted Dylan's help. With his live-in relationship lurching from crisis to crisis, he'd come up with lyrics of the romantic, heartrending kind before, puzzlingly, buggering off to Norfolk.

Marie did experience the odd qualm about what she'd done, sometimes missing Geoff's handyman skills, for instance, or Pauline and Len's merry fondue-and-whist evenings. But, ten months after giving all that up, at 9 p.m. on a sticky July Saturday, she was feeling pretty contented, if a little pissed off with Dylan for not being home.

'Damn,' she said, putting the phone down. What on earth could he be *doing* in the middle of Norfolk? She tried again, in case he hadn't got to the phone before Callminder kicked in, and this time left a message. 'Hi, darling. Ring me back?'

'Who was that?' asked Gavin, emerging from the bathroom, damp and luscious, with a small towel round his hips.

'Never you mind,' she told him. From where she lay half-dressed on the bed, she chucked her pad and pen aside and crooked a finger at him. Like the obedient young lover/drainer-of-her-resources that he was, Gavin threw himself down beside her.

'I'm dead jealous,' he said, beginning an oral massage that immediately had her catching her breath and clutching at the duvet. It was at times like these Marie knew she'd done the right thing *vis à vis* Geoff and Guildford.

Later, they sat and watched TV for a while and, later still, Marie packed him off home, or to whichever bar he'd end up in. She didn't mind. She hadn't invested emotionally in him – he was thirty-two, for heaven's sake – plus she did rather value her space these days, after all those years of 24/7, or so it had felt, togetherness with Geoff.

'I'll ring you,' she called down the path after him, then lay on the bed, took up the pad again and chewed on her pen.

In the hot, candlelit kitchen of 2 Biddlefarm Cottages, everyone sat transfixed by Hazel 'Call me Grappelli' Osgood's jaunty rendering of 'Ain't Misbehavin'. A stunned silence greeted the end of the tune, before Alex began a round of applause. The woman could really play!

'*More*,' called out Fliss.

'Really?' asked a glowing Hazel, and without waiting for an answer she threw herself into something Celtic.

Terrific, thought Alex, feet tapping away. He looked around the large but cosy kitchen with its old-pine this and its old-oak that, its vases of wild flowers and original floor tiles, and felt he could almost be in a Galway pub, drinking Guinness and enjoying the craic. Hazel even looked the part of an Irish minstrel, with her high colouring and unselfconscious dress sense.

Before long, Dylan was returning from his house with a guitar for Alex and an old tambourine for himself, and the three of them began to jam haphazardly. Hazel would say, 'Do you know this one?' and plough into something Alex wasn't always familiar with but could easily accompany. To everyone's delight, he did a couple of Blue Plum songs, with Hazel then accompanying him. Very well, actually. Fliss and Ellie kept topping up glasses to the point where

36

Alex was hitting the odd bum note and Dylan wasn't fantastically in time with his tambourine, but a jolly evening was had by all until Fliss's cuckoo clock told them it was midnight and they decided, reluctantly, to call it a day.

'That was great,' Fliss told Alex and Dylan as they were leaving. 'Thank you so much.'

'No, thank *you*,' said Alex, wondering if he should kiss all three women goodbye. Maybe not. Everyone was pretty hot and damp. He cradled Dylan's guitar and gave his hosts a bow of the head.

'It was absolutely brilliant,' panted Hazel.

Alex said, 'Wasn't it?' and wondered why Fliss's daughter was hiding the tambourine behind her back.

'Night, Dylan,' the girl sighed, all puppy-eyed, and Alex thought: Ah.

Back home again, Dylan went off to pick up phone messages while Alex stayed in the kitchen-cum-building site and managed to make himself a hot drink without personal injury. He thought back over the evening and shook his head. Who'd have thought it possible to have so much fun at the end of a dirt track in East Anglia?

At ten past twelve Marie's bedside phone rang and made her jump.

'Hi, Mum. Thought you'd still be up,' said Dylan. 'You called?'

'Mm, I was working on some lyrics earlier and got stuck. That was all.'

'Oh yeah?'

'I need something to rhyme with "mass

37

destruction". Well, "destruction" at least.'

Dylan laughed. 'I take it it's not a love song, then?'

'Oh, everyone's gone political again these days, darling. All those landmine records and Steve Earle and so forth.'

'Destruction...' pondered Dylan. 'Hang on, I'll ask Dad.'

'Your *father's* there?' she said, but Dylan had gone.

Marie felt pangs of guilt while she waited. Of course she'd go and see Dylan's new place soon. It had just sounded so horribly primitive when he'd described it to her. She heard him clonking back to the phone over bare floorboards that didn't sound even vaguely varnished.

'Dad says how about "suction"?'

She frowned and jotted it down. 'OK. The other one was "diaspora".'

'Blimey,' he said. 'Hang on.' And off he went again.

Maybe she'd go and see him next weekend. First she'd have to find out where Norfolk was, of course. She heard Alex's familiar laugh in the background, and before she knew it he was on the phone with a deep and throaty, 'Hi, Marie.'

Hell, she thought, how did he still do that to the pit of her stomach after all these years? 'Hi, Alex. I hope you weren't laughing at me?'

'Not at all. But I do know how you always struggled with lyrics. I have the same problem these days, unfortunately. Diaspora, eh? You might have me stumped there. What's the song about?'

'Ireland ... Cromwell, potato famines, the issues of contraception and abortion...'

'Right. Are you sure you want to be going down this road, Marie? I mean, I don't see the teen bands snapping it up.'

She giggled. 'No, I don't suppose they will. I'm just doing it for my soul, really. My Irish roots and all that.'

'Of course.'

'Anyway,' she said, 'how are you? Still seeing Annabel?'

'No, not really.'

'Oh? What happened?'

'We ... um, we've been having ... well, difficulties.'

'Hey, how about Viagra?' asked Marie.

Alex went quiet on her, then said, 'What's Annabel been telling you? I mean, good grief, it's a very personal–'

'No, I meant *Viagra* to rhyme with *diaspora*. Loosely.'

'Oh, I see.'

He was plainly relieved, no doubt thinking he'd given nothing away, while Marie herself felt inexplicably happy at the idea of an impotent Alex. But then she thought, Oh, poor chap, because she was actually terribly fond of him, and guessed he'd simply worn the thing out over the years.

'Sounds like one hell of a song,' he said.

When Fliss dropped Hazel off at the railway station on Sunday afternoon, after the longest twenty-three hours on record, she said, 'It was great seeing you, Hazel. Thanks for coming. I really enjoyed it.'

'Oh, me too. Brilliant. But next time I think I might drive.'

'Good idea,' said Fliss with resignation. There'd be no shaking her off now.

Hazel hugged her goodbye. 'But anyway, I'll see you at the reunion do at my place before then?'

'Definitely!' said Fliss. Unless she happened to contract dengue fever, of course. She could say she picked it up on the Norfolk Broads. Hazel would never know.

After waving her friend off with an enormous sense of release, Fliss headed back to Biddlefarm Cottages to resume her life's work of turning a clinker-ridden wasteland into something in which you could sip Pimms and – should it be your thing – share travel stories with fascinating globetrotting friends.

Which was more or less the scene she found on arriving home, but without the Pimms. Ellie and Dylan were at the table in the front garden with a can of beer each, listening to Alex, also with a beer, but sprawled, shirt half-undone, on her new lawn.

'...in the Blue Mountains,' she heard him say. 'It's an amazing country. Oh hi, Fliss.' He sat himself up and flashed her a smile. 'I was just boring them with tales of Australia. Have you ever been?'

Fliss's heart semi-sank. Alex might be a nice man and a bit of a VIP, but she really had to get the *ceanothus* planted before the day was over. There were those seedlings to prick out, too. But then she told herself she mustn't turn into a reclusive old gardening bore, and that it wasn't every day you got a rock star helping your new squares of turf settle in, and that she should try to make an effort.

'No, but I'd love to one day,' she managed.

On the other hand, when would she get the *ceanothus* in? Perhaps she could leave the three of them to amuse themselves for an hour or so. Get those little jobs done. After all, she saw people day after day, person after person, at the centre. People, people, people... Plus, verbally incontinent Hazel had quite put her off the human voice for a while. Solitude was what she wanted. Blissful aloneness. Not another soul for a ten-mile radius. Or just her garden all to herself would do.

'Oh, you *must* go, Fliss,' insisted Alex. 'You'd love Australians. They're just like you. Incredibly sociable and hospitable.'

Was Ellie sniggering behind her hand?

'Shall I rustle us up some lunch?' Fliss asked, all of a sudden wanting to live up to this persona.

'Oh, no, no,' said Dylan, looking at his watch. 'If we hurry we'll make it to The Fox before they stop doing food.' He smiled and scanned the group. 'Come on. My treat.'

Ellie jumped up. 'Great!'

Alex nodded enthusiastically and quickly did up his shirt. Fliss guessed he'd not had much to eat since last night.

'Coming, Mum?' asked Ellie. She had a kind of pleading edge to her voice.

Fliss cast a nervous eye at the *ceanothus*, resting against the fence in its tight plastic coat, and told

41

herself to get a grip. She smiled at Dylan. 'Love to. We'll all go in my car, shall we?'

'You know,' said Alex, brushing grass off his trousers, checking for stains and then running both hands though his hair. 'I was praying you'd say that.'

THREE

On Monday morning Alex was trying to read Paulo Coelho's *The Alchemist* on the train. Dylan said he might like it and had chucked it in his bag at the last minute. A novel could often last Alex a good six months, but this was a slim volume with nice short sentences and he aimed to get through it before Mr Farthing met him at Gloucester station. He'd found himself a quiet corner in a half-empty carriage, where no women of a certain age might accost him, and although his eyes went back time and again to page four of the book, his mind was on other matters. Dylan, for example, and how much more relaxed he seemed now, away from Natalia. Troublesome Natalia. She'd even come on to *him* once. Extremely flattering, of course, having a top model proposition you, but not somewhere Alex had wanted to go.

He went back to *The Alchemist*, which seemed to be all about following your dream. Alex stared at the page. If Dylan had a dream he'd never shared it with him. All his son seemed to want at the moment was a bit of peace and a good night's sleep. Days spent working on the house no doubt knocked him out. Where Dylan got all his DIY skills from was baffling. Geoff maybe? Alex himself had never built a wall. Or used an electric drill, or even a paint roller. Now why was that making him feel a little inadequate? There was no rule said real men should be able to change a washer. It just wasn't an area of life he'd ever ventured into. No role model for a start. His father had been a concert pianist who, despite insuring his hands for a fortune, always refused to take risks with hammers and saws. And then, of course, success came early for Alex – still at his public school when Blue Plum first hit the charts – and the money started rolling in and, well, there'd never been the need to lift a tea towel, let alone knock up a breakfast bar.

Ridiculous! he told himself and went back to the book. Of course he was a real man.

He raised his eyes and watched the passing countryside, gradually becoming less flat as they whizzed towards London. What a rural spot Dylan had got himself. And so isolated, though not totally. She was a bit of a conundrum, the neighbour. Not the daughter, Ellie. Perky little blue-eyed thing. She was very bouncy and open and so transparently nuts about Dylan. But then what girl wouldn't be? Fliss, though, he found puzzling. What had he got to know about her? Very little. Mind you, that friend of hers had been a bit of a talker. But even over Sunday lunch in the pub Fliss had been fairly guarded. More or less answering each of his questions with one of her own. Mid-forties, he guessed, and attractive, in a pale English-rose sort of way. Was there a boyfriend? he wondered. Not that he was drawn or anything. Always gone for brunettes for some reason. No mention was made of a former husband, or why she'd bought a house in the middle of nowhere. Perhaps he'd find out more

44

next time. He was sure to visit Dylan again soon. Anything was better than spending an entire weekend all alone in a rambling seventeenth-century manor house with tennis court, games room and recording studio. Well, not quite alone if you counted full-time Mrs Farthing ... dear old Mrs F.

At Liverpool Street, Alex got off the train and made for the exit, intending to hail a taxi to take him to Paddington for the train home to Gloucester. But then he stopped on the platform, took out his phone and called Dylan to ask for Marie's number. How long since he'd seen her? Two years? Three?

'Hi,' he said when he got through to her mobile. 'Me again. I'm passing through London. Fancy meeting up?'

She told him she'd love to, that she was in Bond Street shopping and how about meeting at the British Museum for coffee in the Great Court.

'Sounds good,' said Alex. 'In, say, half an hour?'

'OK.'

'Oh, and mine's an espresso if you get there first.'

If he'd been in a Tom and Jerry cartoon, Alex's eyes would have popped out on springs. She looked so amazing, so different, so like the Marie of twenty-two or -three, that he had to steady himself on the nearest person.

'Sorry,' he told the elderly woman, who tutted and no doubt thought he was drunk. 'So sorry. Lost my balance.'

He composed himself and approached the table.

45

'Marie?' he asked tentatively, though of course it was.

'Alex, hi,' she said, still carrying that trace of Irish.

She stood up and kissed his cheek and he could smell something wonderful. How trim she'd become since their last meeting. She was in red, a colour that had always suited her: a sleeveless dress in a soft-looking material that managed to cling in all the right places, beneath a solid gold necklace that brought out the olive in her skin. He leaned back, holding both her hands, and took in the dark, now much longer, naturally curly hair, and that strong-but-sweet face with – incredibly – barely a line upon it. Wow, he thought. *Wow*, and his stomach did a little flip and his knees went weak. He couldn't make out if this was love at first sight with someone he'd known for decades, or if he just needed lunch after three hours of travel.

'Don't you just love this Great Court?' she asked him, letting go of his hands. Her eyes wandered up to the glass-domed ceiling and his followed.

'Absolutely. First time I've seen it.'

'Really? You should come to London more often. I got you an espresso, by the way. Hope it's still hot.' She sat and patted the metal stool next to her. 'Here, come and sit beside me,' she said, and he did.

They talked about Dylan, and Marie's new house and Alex's last record and his exploratory trip to Jamaica. How easy it was, chatting with her. Had it always been so? He couldn't

46

remember. But then, what could he remember of his twenties?

'I'm just not sure about incorporating reggae into what I do,' he told her. 'It all tends to end up sounding like UB4O. Which is fine but, you know, it's been done.'

Marie nodded thoughtfully. 'Let's face it, Alex, there isn't much that hasn't been done. We were so lucky when we were writing all those songs. There was still room to be original back then. Also, we had the drive and determination. Do you remember how we used to hole up for weeks and just go at it?'

'Mm,' he said. 'I can't do that now. Too many distractions. Emails to pick up, twenty-four-hour news channels.' He smiled. 'Plus, it would completely upset Mrs Farthing's regime.'

Marie laughed and rolled her eyes. 'Ah, yes. Mrs Farthing. Once met, never recovered from.' She dropped the teaspoon she'd been playing with back in the saucer. 'Come on, let's walk down to Covent Garden and have some lunch.' She was suddenly up and hooking her bag over her shoulder.

Alex had forgotten how Marie's impulsiveness could completely throw him. She'd always hated planning, and if anything had even a whiff of becoming a plan, she'd completely go off the idea. They'd never have married if Marie's very Catholic mother hadn't first insisted upon, then totally organised the Kingston-upon-Thames wedding. Alex remembered how beautiful Marie had looked, and how his hands had shaken uncontrollably. Had it been an attack of nerves, or just a day without drink and drugs taking its toll? He drained his coffee cup and caught up with her on the far side of the Great Court.

'I know a fabulous Italian place,' she told him. She put her arm around him and slid her hand into the furthest of his back trouser pockets, just as she used to. 'Their gnocchi dishes are simply orgasmic.'

'Sounds wonderful,' Alex said, and just stopped himself adding that it'd been a while since he'd had anything orgasmic.

Dylan and Baz were on their lunch-break. Dylan was stretched out on the sunbed, surrounded by bags of sand and cement, while Baz, bottom spread over an upturned bucket, was launching into a Lion Bar and talking about what he'd done over the weekend: Friday got pissed with his mates and had a Chinese takeaway, Saturday got pissed with his mates and had an Indian, Sunday watched DVDs, played computer games with his mates and had a pizza delivered. More or less the same thing he did every weekend.

'Don't you sometimes get tired of one another?' asked Dylan.

Baz frowned and thought about it for a second. 'No. Mostly we just have a right laugh.'

'Hmm.' Dylan wasn't sure he really understood. Baz and his friends were twenty, twenty-one. Surely there were a few girls on the scene. 'Listen, I've got to go and do one or two things this afternoon. I'll have to leave you with that wall.'

'Thass ookay,' said Baz in the soft Norfolk accent that was rapidly growing on Dylan,

48

especially when it came from Emma, part-time barmaid at The Fox.

'I shouldn't be more than a couple of hours. Three at most. Just lock up and go home if you're finished before I get back.'

'Will do.'

Dylan could trust Baz not to cheat on his hours. He was an honest sort of bloke. Well, if you overlooked the fact that he was working and signing on.

Great Banwell School of Art turned out to be less of an institution and more of a cottage than he'd expected.

'Welcome, welcome,' said one of two identical women in navy fisherman's smocks. 'I'm May and this is my sister, Fay.'

'Twins?' Dylan asked and they nodded and smiled pleasantly and led him through a chintzy living room to a large and airy conservatory where four women and a wan-looking young man were copying a central display of cauliflower, carrots and onion.

'This is Dylan,' said May, or maybe Fay. 'Who's going to join our class.'

'Hello,' the bolder amongst them called out.

'Hi,' said Dylan.

'Did you bring any materials?' he was asked.

'No, sorry.'

'Don't worry, we've got everything you'll need. There's a spare easel by Dot. Paper, paints, pens, charcoal, over there. Choose your medium and get stuck in. Either May or I will come and check on you in a while.'

Dylan wasn't quite sure what he was expecting from Great Banwell School of Art. A little tuition, hopefully. He did as he was told, grabbed a sheet of paper, chose a soft black pencil and settled himself at the easel.

The problem was, he hadn't actually done anything like this since dropping Art at the age of fourteen. He'd doodled, of course, and felt some of his doodles to be pretty good, in a kind of graphic-comic sort of way, but he really wasn't sure how to approach the cauliflower now before him. Was he about to make a complete arse of himself?

'Hello,' said the sweet white-haired lady beside him.

'Hello,' he replied, taking a peek at her effort and suddenly feeling a lot more confident.

Dylan got going and found it wasn't all that hard to draw a cauliflower, after all. His lines were thick and confident, just as in his doodles and, not long into the activity, he got up to find himself a piece of charcoal for added boldness. On the way back he stopped by the only other bloke in the group and saw that he was going in for a far more abstract interpretation of the vegetables: his cauliflower was made up of square florets; his carrots were Scud missiles. When the pale young man turned and squinted long and hard at him, it occurred to Dylan that it might be short-sightedness rather than Cubism. 'Mm, interesting,' he said with a wise nod before taking his seat again.

Dylan hadn't told anyone he was doing this. He'd reached a point in his life when any inclination to follow in his father's footsteps had all but disappeared. Yes, he had a modicum of talent, and he certainly enjoyed playing and singing and writing songs, but how often did the offspring of rock's big names make it in the music business? Almost never. Of course it had been tempting to try, and he'd thrown together several bands over the years, more for fun than to go platinum or anything. But, probably better to find his own thing, he'd decided some time ago, or at least have something to fall back on. However, after a History degree, a year travelling, a computer course and a spell working in Natalia's uncle's restaurant, Dylan was still waiting to see what his 'thing' was. Could property enhancement and the odd 'still life' be it? He sat back and admired his drawing and heard a sharp intake of breath behind him.

'*Super*, Dylan,' said a twin in hushed tones. 'Have you trained, dear? It always shows, you know.'

'Well, no, I–'

'Fay,' she called across the room. 'Do come and inspect.'

Dylan noticed he was getting odd, worried looks from his female classmates. One of them came and joined May behind him, as did Fay and the shortsighted Cubist. Now he began to feel self-conscious and rather wanted to be back at home hearing about *Grand Theft Auto* from Baz.

'Excellent,' someone said.

'You should be teaching us!'

'Hold it up, Dylan, and let the others see.'

He did so, reluctantly, and a murmur worked

its way through the three women opposite. 'I haven't done the onion yet,' he told them, just for something to say.

'Ah yes, onions are tricky,' said one of the twins. 'Beware.' And the crowd dispersed.

Well, this was turning out better than he'd expected. Of course, praise from the Great Banwell School of Art wouldn't be in the same league as praise from, say, Anish Kapoor, but Dylan felt pretty pleased with himself. Until, that was, he finished drawing the onion and realised it looked more like an apple, or a very round potato. He fetched some white chalk and spent a good ten minutes trying to give it a soft oniony sheen, but then it just looked like a peeled but muddy potato. The more he did to it, the messier it became.

'Oh,' said a voice behind when the others were washing out brushes, whipping off aprons, snapping shut boxes of pastels and looking anxiously at their watches, *what* a shame.'

Dylan turned. It was May, or Fay.

'Why not spend time this week practising your onions?' she suggested, and Dylan found himself promising he would.

Marie felt quite nervous singing in front of Alex after all this time, but worse still was playing the guitar to him. A swift vodka and tonic before she'd got going was helping to a degree, as was the way he said, 'Fabulous,' or 'Terrific,' after each new song. She was hoping she could trust him to be honest with her.

She was sitting on a stool in the middle of her

satin-finished wooden floor, while Alex was stretched out on her big cream sofa, stocking feet up on one arm, just, well ... just staring at her. It was like being in front of a scary audience again, but somehow scarier. This, after all, was *Alex* – former love of her life and guitar legend – in his lovely dark shirt and slightly crumpled cotton trousers with a glass of wine in his hand and a strange look in his glorious blue eyes which, all-in-all, was doing very odd things to her insides.

'Dylan wrote this next one,' she told him as she tightened a string. 'Dedicated to Natalia, he said, and to be sung in the style of Hank Williams.'

'Can you do that?'

'Well, I'll give it a shot.' She cleared her throat and quietly strummed. 'It's called "I Understand You Leaving, Honey, but Did You Have to Take the Fridge?"'

Alex laughed. 'I can't wait to hear what he rhymes with fridge.'

'Let me see.' Marie looked down at the song sheet. '"Now I'm living on Doritos, warm Coke and nuts, and the odd sand*wich*".'

'Ha! The boy's a genius.' He took a sip of wine and gazed tenderly at her. 'An angel in red,' he said with a sigh.

'Sorry?'

'That's who you remind me of this evening. That gorgeous *Angel in Red with a Lute*. Do you know it? By one of those Renaissance guys.'

'Leonardo,' she said, returning his smile. 'Well, an associate of.' She'd done 'those Renaissance guys' as part of her OU degree. 'You're too kind,' she told him, then strummed a bit more and

53

broke into Hank Williams.

After the fifth song, Marie slipped out to the bathroom with her phone and sent a text. *Gavin d'ling. V busy. Don't call or call in. Heaps luv.* She sprayed some perfume on, redid her lipstick and went back downstairs to seduce Alex. Impotent indeed.

After about fifty minutes Alex gave up. Poor guy, thought Marie as she lay in his arms with her back to him. She remembered their early heady days of round-the-clock lovemaking, when Alex and his joystick had been inexhaustible. The chemistry had been so powerful – right from that first night in the band's Dublin hotel – and Marie could feel it still. But now ... well, she'd seen more stick, and even joy, in a used teabag.

'I'm sorry,' he said into her hair.

'Don't be.'

'They all know, I'm positive.'

'Who?' Marie asked. 'Knows what?'

'I'm sure Annabel's been blabbing. You should see these emails I get all the time.'

Marie turned over and saw Alex's eyes were teary. She stroked his head. 'What emails, sweetie?'

'Things like, *Alex, she believes bigger is better!* Or, *Herbal Viagra. We promise next day delivery, Alex!*'

'But darling, we all get those.'

'I know. But it just feels so ... well, like they know so much about me.'

Marie ran the back of her finger down his cheek. 'Hey, hey. You're just being silly.'

'I mean,' he went on, 'how would you feel if you

were bombarded with emails for nose jobs? Hm?'

Marie stiffened. 'What do you mean?'

'Well, I know you've always had a complex about it.' He kissed the end of her nose and smiled lovingly at her. 'But I've always thought of it as strong rather than huge.'

'Huge!' She flung back the duvet and sprang from the bed. Bloody hell, she thought, sliding into her kimono. Coming back into her life after all this time, only to insult her.

'Marie?' said Alex plaintively. 'Oh Marie. Please. I didn't mean...'

But she already had the phone in her hand. 'Yes, we'd like a taxi as soon as possible,' she said calmly. She gave her address and Alex's name then added, 'Paddington,' before replacing the receiver and going off for a long shower.

Alex was crestfallen, particularly when, as the train pulled out of the station, he all of a sudden remembered that it wasn't Marie who'd had a thing about her nose, but Brenda. 'It's *huge*,' she used to say. 'I *hate* it.'

Brenda! Not Marie! How could he have made such a stupid mistake, and was he going to be able to make up for it without blundering again? *I'm so sorry. Marie, I got you confused with your successor.*

'Damn and blast and buggery,' he murmured, then wondered what had happened to Brenda. How had she suddenly vanished from his life? They'd all done that. All the women. Just sort of dissolved. There must have been reasons and incidents. He did recall a large hotel vase being

55

hurled at him, one or two vicious handwritten notes, someone sobbing on the end of the phone. Actually, lots of them sobbing on the ends of phones.

A man of around forty-five was giving him I-know-you looks from across the aisle, so Alex held *The Alchemist* aloft and pretended to be engrossed. God, what a stupid thing to say. Just when things had been going so well between himself and Marie. Well, apart from the technical problem. Hell, hell, hell.

'Excuse me, but you *are* Alex Child, aren't you?' asked the man, who'd now transported himself to the seat opposite. He wore a bright yellow and black T-shirt and black-framed glasses.

'No, I'm not,' Alex told him with a curt smile. He'd never done this before. Perhaps, for the first time ever, he was wishing he wasn't Alex Child? Or maybe he just couldn't talk at length to someone resembling a wasp. 'But people often mistake me for him.'

The man said, 'Oh, I ... er,' and shook his head and went back to his seat. 'Sorry,' he called across.

'No problem,' Alex told him, returning to his book and reading a few lines. *Listen to your heart*, the boy in the story was being told. Alex looked up and watched back gardens shoot past. The good thing about Marie was that she was never mad for long. She might even have calmed down already and be feeling stupid for overreacting. He took out his mobile, tapped at it and held his breath, but he just got her message. *If that's you calling to apologise, Alex, you can go boil your head.*

Hmm. Maybe she held grudges for a little longer these days. He ended the call and was about to put the phone away when he wondered why she'd recorded a special message for him if she wasn't expecting him to call. Even hoping he might?

He rang the number again and this time laughed at her greeting. 'Hi, Marie,' he said warmly. 'It's Alex. Listen, sweetheart, I'm–'

'Ha!' he heard from across the aisle.

FOUR

The invitation could only have come from Hazel. She'd somehow managed to lay her hands on one designed especially for reuniting friends. *We'll Meet Again!* it said above jolly middle-aged cartoon figures wearing school uniform and popping champagne.

Fliss groaned and opened it up to find Hazel had filled the left inside page with details of the venue (her house), the fare on offer ('Buffet and barbecue but please B-a-B') and the lengthy guest list. An arrow directed her to the back of the card where there was a hand-drawn map of most of Bedford beneath a list of directions. How Hazel found time to eat or sleep, Fliss would never know.

She propped the card on the kitchen table. No way was she going to the party, but there was still a week and a half to excuse herself.

'What's that?' asked Ellie, who'd made a salad and was laying the table. She wore jeans and a top, with around a mile between the two.

'It's an invitation from Hazel to a sort of reunion at her house. You know, old schoolfriends.'

'Are you going to it?'

'I don't think so.'

'*Mum*, you're so predictable. Socialise. It's fun!'

'Hmm.'

'Maybe she'll have music, and you can all

dance in a hilarious way to Marc Bowling.' She wiggled her bare midriff and waved her arms around, hippy style.

'Bolan,' said Fliss. 'And we never danced like that.'

Ellie laughed and picked up Hazel's card. 'Bedford. Not too far. And, you know, she did like make the effort to come and visit you.'

'Mm.'

'I thought she was really nice.'

'Yes, me too.' Fliss had actually warmed more to her old friend after she'd departed. And to go to all this trouble to get everyone together was bordering on heroic.

'Oh *go* on. Go to it. Even if it's just to find out how brilliantly you've done and how great you look for your age and how fantastic your daughter's turned out compared to theirs.'

'I'm not sure my ego's that fragile.'

'Aren't you dying to know what they're all like now?'

Fliss pulled a face and told her about the change in Richard Honeyman. She didn't say she'd once been nuts about him.

'Yeah well,' said Ellie, 'it can go the other way too. Some bloke who was like spotty and geeky at school might have turned into a total hunk over the years. Hey, we could go into Norwich and get you something drop-dead to wear, yeah?'

Fliss was slowly coming to the conclusion that Ellie was trying to get rid of her for a weekend. She took the card off her and looked down the list of guests. Most of the names were familiar, but she could work up no enthusiasm to go and hear about their place in Gascony or their son's GCSEs. And how dispiriting it would be to see how everyone had aged or, perhaps worse, how the women still had tiny waists and taut upper arms.

Mind you, she'd quite like to see how Trudy had turned out. Hazel hadn't been very forthcoming about her at first. 'Oh, Trudy?' she'd said, when Fliss enquired a second time. The three of them had been close friends for years. 'Well, we met up for a coffee...' At this point Hazel had looked over both shoulders, even though she was only in Fliss's living room, and lowered her voice until the final word of her sentence was merely mimed. 'Only I'm not too sure about her sex-u-al-i-ty.'

'Oh,' Fliss had replied with a nod. Had she always known? She thought back to the time Trudy had asked if she wanted to practise snogging in the bus shelter. What were they, fifteen or sixteen? 'So we can do it properly with boys,' Trudy had added, somewhat unconvincingly.

'So?' Ellie was saying. 'Are you gonna go?'

'I'll think about it.'

'Good.'

'Only I'd be a bit worried about leaving you here on your own all weekend.'

'Oh, don't be silly,' said Ellie, her eyes dancing like lottery balls. 'I know self-defence, remember?' She placed the big wooden bowl of smoked salmon salad on the table next to crusty garlic bread. 'Shall we have some wine?'

'OK. But just a little for me. Work tomorrow and all that.'

Actually, she didn't have that many clients the following day but there was tedious admin stuff to do, plus tidying cupboards and so on. Things that had been much easier to keep on top of when she'd been working from home in Norwich. On the whole though, Fliss was far happier leaving her acupuncture practice behind her each day and heading for the country. No chance of bumping into clients in the street who, when she asked, 'How are you?' would actually tell her: the sciatica, the depression, the recurring headaches...

'Oh, that's far too much,' she said to Ellie.

'No, it's OK. They're like really narrow glasses. Look.'

'Is it my imagination,' asked Fliss, after they'd eaten, 'or do you keep filling my glass when I'm not looking? Hm?' She leaned across the table and picked up Hazel's card again. Oh, what did she have to lose, she thought, her spirits now considerably raised.

'Here,' said Ellie, handing her the phone.

'All right then.' She giggled and rang the number on the card.

'Great!' screamed Hazel down the line. 'You're the first "definite".'

'Well...' Fliss could feel her feet turning cold. It wouldn't be much of a party if everyone else declined. 'I'm not sure about *definite*.'

'Richard Honeyman rang and he said he'd try and make it but would have to rearrange things. He asked after you, by the way. Wondered if you'd be coming.'

Fliss was astounded. And also distressed by the unfairness of life. All that time she'd dreamed of eloping with him he'd barely noticed her. And now ... well, now she found herself slowly reverting to the dengue fever idea.

'Tell you what,' she said to Hazel. 'I'll call you nearer the time. Just to confirm one way or the other. Put me down as a maybe, bordering on yes. OK? Yep. Bye then. Bye.' She put the phone down and looked up at her scowling daughter. 'What?' she asked.

On Thursday, deep in a slough of despond, Alex picked up the phone and heard Marie's sweet voice.

'So you never lost that knack of saying the wrong thing, then?'

'Unfortunately not. I'm sorry, Marie.'

'You got me muddled with someone else, didn't you?'

'Uh-huh.'

'What are you doing next week?' she asked. 'I thought I'd come and see you.'

'Sorry?' There she went again, catching him offguard.

'Annabel's definitely history, is she?'

'Oh yes. *Yes*. Definitely. Yes.' He hoped he wasn't overdoing it. 'Got herself a new man.'

'Ah. Anyway, I'm visiting Dylan this weekend and thought I'd tootle over to you afterwards.'

'That would be great,' said Alex. Norfolk to the middle of Gloucestershire was hardly a 'tootle' but he thought better of mentioning it. Didn't want to put her off. 'How long were you planning

62

on staying here?'

'Planning?' laughed Marie.

'Ah, yes, of course. I'll expect you when I see you, then. Um, listen,' he added. 'About Dylan's place...'

'Mm?'

'You might want to think about a hard hat.'

'Oh dear. Well, I've got my old riding hat?'

'Perfect. Come to think of it, Marie, you wouldn't be able to say *roughly* when you'd be arriving? Only Mrs Farthing might like a bit of notice.'

'Oh, I'd guess either Sunday, Monday or Tuesday.'

'Right.' He decided to give up. 'Well, see you Sunday, Monday or Tuesday. You remember how to find me, don't you?'

'Think so. I'll call you from Norfolk anyway.'

'OK. Have a good weekend, then. Oh, and drive safely.'

'Huh!' cried Marie. 'I'm not the one who has a glass of champagne too many, rolls my car over on the motorway and loses my licence.'

'Oh,' said Alex, cringing. 'You heard about that?'

'Dylan told me. Plus it was in the papers.'

'So it was. Anyway, I wasn't drunk. Only a touch over the limit. I just didn't see the turn-off in time and took a last-minute sharp left. Could have happened to anyone.'

'Thank God you weren't hurt, anyway.'

Alex was strangely touched by this last remark and, after hanging up, felt like doing one of those jumps where you click your feet to one side but, what with Marie coming to visit, he chose not to risk it. Instead he punched the air and asked Mrs Farthing to ask Mr Farthing if he'd be able to drive him into Gloucester for a spot of shopping.

Mrs F – four foot ten but a human dynamo around the house – said, 'Well, I'll ask him, but you know what he's like.'

Curmudgeonly was what Mr Farthing was like. 'Would you?' asked Alex nicely. 'Only I've got a guest coming next week and I'd like to buy a few things. Make the house look decent for a change.'

Mrs Farthing's jaw dropped. Her arms folded themselves and her eyes bored into his.

'No no, don't get me wrong,' he said. 'It always looks fantastic. You do a *wonderful* job. I just meant, you know, I'd get a few more plants and things.'

Mrs Farthing gave a quiet, 'Huh,' and went down the lane to have a word with her husband.

Was it him, wondered Alex, or had the whole world become reactive?

Mr Farthing was eighty-one and really should have been retested years ago, or at least been reminded that oncoming traffic has priority when you're turning right.

'Godalmighty,' said Alex, not for the first time, his arm flying up to cover his eyes. Luckily, the old chap was deaf on his left side.

How Alex would have loved to hire a chauffeur for the period of his licence deprivation – someone who could spot in good time when brakes should be applied – but he just couldn't bring himself to do so. Mr Farthing had, when needed, run Alex and his house guests to and from places for the past fourteen years and might have been terribly hurt if he and his Austin Princess were usurped. Not that Alex ever got the impression Mr Farthing *liked* driving him around. He was a man who derived little merriment from life, believing as he did that everything, and everybody, was out to give him grief. 'Confounded car!' he'd snap when he noisily cocked-up a gear change. Or, 'Bloody women drivers!' when he'd meandered over the central white line and elicited a honk. Mr Farthing wasn't big on self-awareness.

Once in the city, he careered into a car park and into a space, all in fourth gear, the engine then switching itself off by stalling. People often put Mr F's singular driving style down to his gliding around in a milk float for forty years.

'Well, here we are then,' croaked Alex, hurriedly letting himself out.

'God knows what I'm going to find to do all afternoon,' said Mr Farthing, one eye on the bookmaker's he'd conveniently parked near.

'Actually, I'll only be an hour or so.'

Mr Farthing attached his Krooklok then went round and carefully secured all the doors of a car you'd have to pay someone quite a bit to steal. 'Now don't go buying too much,' he instructed Alex as he patted the roof affectionately. 'The old girl gets bloody sulky when she's weighed down.'

'No,' said Alex, resisting a salute. 'Wouldn't dream of it.'

They rarely found a lot to talk about, Marie being interested in politics, the arts and the world in general, and Gavin being mostly concerned with his wardrobe, getting his hair right and motor-bikes. Although from a middle-class background, Gavin had left school at sixteen, spent many years drifting, and was currently a motorcycle courier. Which was how Marie had met him. 'Oh, come *in*,' she'd told the handsome young guy in leather. He was a bit James Dean-like, only with a bead necklace and blonde highlights. She'd wanted a birthday present delivered to Dylan but hadn't quite finished wrapping it. She hadn't quite fin-ished dressing either, and when he offered to hold the ribbon in place while she tied the bow, Marie noticed he had one eye on her rear and the other on the expensive décor, so she seized the moment and offered him a cup of coffee. And, well, here they were four months later, discussing his new shoes over lunch in Knightsbridge, Marie stifling a yawn and itching to get to the National Gallery.

'Yes, they're a really good shade of black,' she said again.

'You think so?' he also said again, a long leg stretched into the aisle so they could both admire one of the expensive but terribly ordinary-looking shoes she'd just bought him.

'Really good.'

Gavin hadn't finished his dessert but Marie nevertheless motioned to the waiter for the bill. She took a couple of twenties from her purse and said, 'Here, sweetie. I'm going to have to dash.'

'Oh. OK.'

'I'll see you later, though, won't I?' she added. It was more of an order than a question.

'Sure.'

Marie had always been seen to have a bit of an artistic bent. Friends in Guildford would tell her she had a flair when it came to décor, for instance. However, as she had little confidence in her current ability to draw well, she held the pad fairly close to her chest as she sat and copied *An Angel in Red with a Lute* in the National Gallery. Well, tried to copy. Just a rough sketch really, she'd colour it in at home. When no one was nearby, she held it at arm's length and decided it wasn't too bad at all for an amateur. Had she missed her vocation? At seventeen, her parents had been encouraging her to go to art school but she'd then got herself caught up with Alex and her life took an altogether different trajectory. Over the years she'd done the odd drawing of Dylan, and had once gone on a watercolour weekend in Dorset, but she'd never really put her skills to the test.

Marie looked up again at the real thing. How sweet it was of Alex to say she resembled this beautiful young angel. When he wasn't being thoroughly tactless, he could be a darling. She packed up her things and headed for the shop to see if they had a postcard of it.

Was this what she wanted, Marie asked herself later: having sex with someone who had to get his hair right before coming to bed? Gavin was staring into her dressing-table mirror, knees slightly bent, as he delicately arranged and rearranged his multi-shaded, semi-spiky hair with both sets of thumb and forefinger. He must have been at it for five minutes now. Young men just weren't what they used to be, she decided, as she drummed fingers on the pillow. But then he suddenly came at her with a disarming smile and superb body and she forgot all about his foppishness.

'Listen, I'm going to be away for a while,' she told him afterwards, while she lazily stroked his thigh. She was pleased she'd never given him a key. Didn't want him dossing there in her absence, running up her phone bill. 'I'll have the mobile switched off, so no point in texting or anything. Lots of work to do, you see.'

'Yeah?'

She knew he wouldn't ask 'What work?' She turned towards him. 'I expect you'll miss me like crazy.'

'Of course,' he said. 'Call when you're back? We'll go for dinner. Mario's maybe?' Gavin's sentences rarely ran to six syllables.

Marie rolled towards the alarm clock. 'Gosh, it's eleven fifteen already,' she said with an exaggerated yawn, and within ten minutes he was revving up his bike and gone. Perhaps forever, she thought, if things went well next week.

Alex, having well and truly overloaded Mr F's car, then spent the evening placing new pot plants, rugs and lamps around the place. Annabel had always complained about the lack of cosiness in his house. 'All those overhead lights,' she'd say, bringing in her own candles. And she'd been right. Lamplight gave the place – especially the sitting room with its high ceilings and original wood panelling – a sumptuous and seductive ambience.

But if he wanted to completely win Marie over after his blunder he'd need a little help, so he was now on the internet, trawling through a million websites and wondering if they could get the stuff to him by Monday or Tuesday. Jesus, so many products to choose from. He went from site to site. Side effects were mentioned, which was slightly off-putting. As was the term 'erectile dysfunction', bandied about all over the place. Somewhere in London promised next-day delivery so ... well, no hurry then, Alex decided, before logging off and leaning back, hands clasped on his chest. And who knows, maybe it would happen of its own accord.

He surveyed his study, with its AppleMac and its fancy printer and brand-new scanner, and that digital camera he had no idea how to use. What a waste it all was. Wasted on him, anyway. Even if he knew where to begin he wasn't sure he'd have the inclination. Sometimes he thought of donating it all to the village primary school and getting himself a little laptop. But then he had bought them a new gym recently.

FIVE

Ellie was on the sofa when she heard a car pull up, a door slam and someone call out, 'Dylan?'

She chucked the newspaper to one side and turned to look out of the bay window immediately behind her. It was a woman: slim, glamorous and slinking along in sunglasses, shorts and a skimpy top. She had dark curly hair and wore gold jewellery with her casual outfit. Ellie felt her insides slowly freeze, even more so when Dylan wove his way down his cluttered garden and gave the woman a kiss and a long cuddle. He took her bag off her and as they began wandering towards his house arm-in-arm, Ellie quickly ducked down into the sofa, hugging her stomach, suddenly close to tears. Dylan had a girlfriend. Fuck.

'What's the matter, Ellie?' asked her mum, who'd come to get the other bit of the Saturday *Guardian*. 'What? What is it?' She sat down beside her. 'Are you worried about your exam results? I'm sure they'll be fine.'

Ellie shook her head. 'Dylan's got a girlfriend!' she blurted out. Her mother looked dumbfounded, just as Ellie guessed she would. She'd not once mentioned how much she liked Dylan, not to anyone. She pointed at the window. 'You should have seen them kissing and cuddling.'

'Well ... you know, it might not have been a

good idea, Ellie. You'll be off to university soon, and–'

'*If* I get the grades. I know I messed up. I *know* it.'

'No, you didn't. Anyway, Dylan could be just a little bit old for you?'

'Yeah, yeah. It's just that he's so, you know...'

'Devilishly handsome?'

Ellie nodded and let out a small sob. 'And like really good on the guitar. And he's got a lovely voice. I listen to him at night.' Ellie had the attic bedroom, as did Dylan. Sometimes she held a glass against the wall.

All of a sudden a woman's laughter – deep and sexy – could be heard through the living-room wall. And then again. And then Dylan laughing, and then silence. Ellie crossed her fingers and willed them to say something to each other, but the silence continued and two more tears fell from her eyes, while her mum was asking her if she wanted some soup.

'I could quickly heat some up for both of us?'

Ellie shook her head.

'A sandwich?'

'No, thanks.'

'Hey, I know. Why don't we go into Norwich and find me something to wear to Hazel's party? Something daring that knocks twenty years off me.'

'What?' sobbed Ellie, dabbing at her wet cheeks with a cushion and presenting her mum with the most miserable face she could manage. 'You're not gonna leave me here all alone for a weekend, are you?'

Fliss thought it better if she went next door to find out who this woman was, what with Ellie's face looking exactly as it had the day her father moved out, nine years ago.

'Won't be long,' she said, putting her sensible shoes on to negotiate the rubble.

Dylan's door was ajar, and opened further when she knocked on it. 'Anyone home?'

'In here!' he shouted, and Fliss made her way down the hall and into the big knocked-through living area, where Dylan and his friend were sitting at the table at the far end of the room by the wide-open, recently installed French windows. They had their backs to her.

'Hello,' she said, but neither of them turned around when they called out, 'Hi!' back.

'Come and join us,' said Dylan. 'We're drawing.' At this point he did turn and face her, as did the woman, who was older than Fliss had been led to expect, but stunningly attractive, with long wavy hair the colour of Bourneville chocolate.

'Have you ever tried drawing onions?' the woman asked her.

As far as she could recall, it was a question Fliss had never been asked before. 'Not much of an artist,' she said. 'Actually I just came to scrounge some teabags.'

'Oh right, help yourself,' said Dylan. 'This is Fliss, by the way,' he told his friend. 'From next door.'

The woman smiled. 'Hi, I'm Marie. Dylan's mum.' She held up her sketch which, to Fliss, looked a brilliant replication of the four onions in the middle of the table. 'What do you think?' she asked with a wink. 'Better than Dylan's, wouldn't you say?' She had a slight accent, Scottish or Irish.

Fliss could now see the family resemblance, but if asked to bet would have said older sister or young aunt. She had Dylan's eyes and colouring but otherwise was quite different: high cheekbones and a strong nose and chin. Dylan had inherited Alex's softer, rounder features plus those dimples when he smiled. Poor Ellie. What bad luck to end up next door to such perfection. 'They're both good,' she told Marie. 'I didn't know you were artistic, Dylan?'

Marie said, 'He's multi-talented, my son. Have you heard him singing, Fliss?'

'No, but my daugh ... no, I haven't. Heard him on the tambourine, though. Excellent.'

Dylan smiled at his mother, stretched out a hand and stroked her arm. 'I'm nowhere near as gifted and accomplished as you, and you know it. Listen,' he said, turning to Fliss, 'we were thinking of eating at The Fox tonight. Would you be able to join us? And Ellie, if she's free? I could book a table.'

Fliss stalled. There was that Atwood she was dying to start. Quick, think of an excuse, she was telling herself while her mouth said, 'Mm, love to. And I'm sure Ellie would too.'

'Great.'

'Well, I'll leave you to your onions,' Fliss said and went home without the teabags she didn't need anyway.

'It's his mother,' she told Ellie in a loud whisper. *'What?'*

Fliss nodded. 'Yes, really. And Dylan's invited us to The Fox again this evening. I said yes. Hope that's OK?'

Ellie jumped off the sofa, said, 'Oh God, my toenails!' and flew across the room and up to the attic.

Dylan was surprised when Wendy and Ken recognised his mother the moment she walked in. They started quoting some of the songs she'd co-written and saying how she'd really added to the band when accompanying them on stage for those couple of years. They truly were aficionados of thirty-year-old music. Dylan could see even his mother was taken aback.

'Thank you,' Marie said. 'But I was very peripheral. Just strumming a guitar at the back of the stage.'

'And you sang,' said Ken, screwing his hands together. He had that awed, deferential mien of a Big Fan. 'Wonderfully.'

'You *heard* me? I'm amazed.'

'Ken always thought you could be a star in your own right,' said Wendy. 'But then he did have an enormous crush on you.'

'Yes, well...' said Ken. He rubbed his palms on the seat of his trousers and said maybe he'd go and get the camera.

'What'll you have?' Dylan asked his mother. They stood at the bar while Fliss and Ellie settled themselves at a table with a couple of menus.

'Just mineral water, please. Still.'

Dylan gave her a look. 'Oh, come on.'

'No, really. I'm having a semi-detox day.'

'And a still water, please,' he told lovely Emma, who was looking exceptionally nice in her short black Saturday-night gear. Once he'd got Natalia completely out of his system...

'Here we are then,' said a breathless Ken as he handed the camera over to Dylan. 'Would you mind? Now, where's Wendy?'

Dylan paid Emma, took a couple of photos to join the ones of his father, now framed and hung above the bar, and carried three drinks over to the table.

'We couldn't help overhearing all that,' Fliss told Marie. 'I didn't know you'd played with Blue Plum on stage. Must have been after I saw them, maybe when I was going through my folky period. I expect it was fun, wasn't it?'

'Yes and no. Some of the other band members were a bit, you know, disgruntled.'

'Oh, right,' nodded Ellie, who Dylan thought could easily slide a bit further along the padded bench they were both on. Give him a bit more space. 'Like Paul, George and Ringo hated Yoko, yeah? We did that in History.'

Marie laughed and tossed her hair back. 'History. Goodness. Well, I'm not sure they *hated* her, but yes, it was a bit like that. Anyway, I kind of bowed out of everything once I became pregnant with Dylan. Mostly because I felt like shit for nine months.'

'Sorry,' Dylan said, pulling a face.

Marie stretched diagonally across the table and cupped his hand. 'I forgave you the moment I saw you, of course. Such delicious big brown eyes.'

'Mm, yeah,' said Ellie, turning to look at him. She was still way too close. The thin wooden arm of the bench was digging into his waist.

'You wouldn't like to just inch along a bit, would you?' he asked her politely. 'Er ... no, not that way.'

'Oh, sorry.'

Once they'd all chosen their dishes and Emma had taken their order, Dylan chatted with Ellie about going to uni, but also found himself half-listening to the conversation going on between Fliss and his mother, and catching just the odd word.

'...acupuncturist...'

'Friend...' his mother was saying '...problem ... down below ... help?'

'So *if* I get the grades I need, and do this Psychology degree,' Ellie was telling him, 'then afterwards, I'd be able to take this like conversion course ... Dylan, are you listening?'

'Yes, of course. Conversion course.'

'An advanced something or other in Psychology, it's called. It'll all take *ages* to do. I just hope it's worth it.'

'...holistic,' said Fliss. '...make an appointment?'

Marie leaned towards Fliss and whispered something. 'Oh,' said Fliss, wide-eyed. '*Him?*'

'So what's it to be, Dylan?' asked Ellie.

'Oh ... what? Yep, definitely do the advanced thingy. If you're really sure you want to be a psychologist, that is.'

She stared at him with a confused and puzzled look. An almost pained expression. Poor kid, he thought. So hard to know what you want to do when you're that age. Well, any age really. And so easy to find yourself on altogether the wrong track. Look at how he'd got stuck in Natalia's uncle's restaurant as a trainee manager. Which was a joke. Although he *had* learned how to make a top-rate omelette.

'I was offering to get you a drink,' said Ellie.

'Ah, sorry.' He gave her a great big smile to make up for his rudeness and touched her arm. 'Just a half this time. Thanks, Ellie. Need a hand?'

Her eyes quickly smiled back at him. 'No, it's all right.'

'He needn't know, need he?' Marie was asking Fliss.

'No, I suppose not,' Fliss replied. 'Oh, lovely, yes, another white wine for me, Ellie. Have you got enough money, love?'

'Mum, *please.*' Ellie's eyes darted Dylan's way, then she picked up the empty glasses and made for the bar.

'But will it be terribly painful for him?' Dylan heard his mother whisper.

Both women giggled.

'Don't worry, there wouldn't be too many needles, you know … *there.*'

'Ah good. Listen, I'll pay. It's his birthday soon. An early Leo. But more of a pussy cat than a lion – especially now. What better present could he wish for?'

Ah, thought Dylan, that reminded him. It was his dad's birthday soon.

SIX

Marie Child lay on a lounger, taking in the sun with as much exposed flesh as she could manage without embarrassing Dylan's sidekick, Baz, perched on two upturned buckets not that far from her. Dylan had gone off to some art school, Baz was taking yet another break with yet another half-melted chocolate bar, and Marie was thinking about Alex, Gavin and even Geoff, and which one of them she might turn to in a variety of situations. Certainly, in a broken-down vehicle in the middle of the desert, she'd want Geoff and his Swiss Army knife to be there. For someone to mull over the Middle East with, she'd go for Alex. And Gavin ... well, that was easy. Images of his smooth, honed body began to fill her head. That chest, those undulating buttocks that reminded her of Cumbria when he lay on his front.

'Anyway, it's dead hilarious,' Baz was telling her. 'You should get the video.'

She opened one eye behind her shades and stopped herself telling him not to eat so badly. She'd noticed earlier he was the same shape as the breeze blocks he'd been laying all morning, and now... God, that huge roll of naked stomach was making her queasy. 'What was it called again?' she asked out of politeness.

'*Goldmember.* You know, Austin Powers?'

'Ah yes.'

'You see, Dr Evil decides he's going to kidnap Austin Powers' dad, who's Michael Caine. I love kidnapping films, me. Anyway...'

Oh no. Marie didn't want to hear the whole plot of this one as well. 'I used to worry about someone kidnapping Dylan,' she said quickly.

'Yeah *right*,' sniggered Baz. 'Why would anyone want to do that?'

Marie sighed. He really wasn't terribly bright. 'Well...' she said, 'because of who his father is.'

'Oh yeah? Who's that then?'

'Alex Child. You know, singer and lead guitarist of Blue Plum. Huge in the Seventies. Surely Dylan's told you that?'

Baz stopped mid-chew, as though he couldn't digest this information as well as the Yorkie. His eyes rolled here and there and then he swallowed. 'No kidding?'

Marie cursed herself. Had she put her foot in it?

'Fuck,' continued Baz. 'Oops, 'scuse my French. He must be loaded then – Dylan.'

Oh Christ, now he'd be wanting to up his hourly labouring rate. Dylan would surely kill her. 'He doesn't like to take money from his father,' she explained. 'He's always been like that. Wants to make his own way in the world, which you have to give him credit for.'

'Jesus, what a twat. I know what I'd do if my dad was rich and not a plumber.'

'I thought plumbers *were* rich.'

'Yeah well, he has the three holidays a year but there's never any spare for anything else. Like me, for example.' He laughed and chucked his chocolate wrapper on a stack of new guttering. 'So you're not still married to Alex Child?'

'No, I'm not. But we're on good terms.'

'Where does he live, then? Round here, is it?'

'No, Gloucestershire. Got a lovely place. In fact, I'm going there. Tomorrow perhaps.'

Baz shook his head. 'Huh, wait till I tell Jamie and Wes.'

He then went silent and stared into the middle distance, grinning to himself, while Marie squeezed more sun cream on to her leg and began thinking of Alex. How would the visit go? Last time she'd called in on him she'd been with Geoff; they'd been passing through on their way to the Lake District. She remembered Geoff had taken a particular interest in the old wartime air-raid shelter by the tennis court. Standing staring at it with chin in hand, then poking around inside for a while. Alex said, 'I expect you spent many a miserable night in one as a boy, didn't you, Geoff?' and Geoff had replied tartly that he was born in the Fifties.

Marie chuckled to herself. It was quite an endearing trait in Alex, so long as it wasn't directed at oneself.

'Anyway, where was I?' Baz asked. He tapped his feet and drummed on his bare knees. 'Oh yeah ... Dr Evil thinks up this time-travel scheme to take over the world, and to do that he has to kidnap Austin Powers' dad who's a famous English spy, right?'

Marie lay back and closed her eyes again. 'Uh-huh.'

If anyone had asked Dylan to name his current favourite sexual image it would have been that of Emma from The Fox, stretched out naked, apart from those couple of bangles she almost always wore. That long blonde hair tumbling over a shoulder and a slightly mischievous twinkle in her dark brown eyes. So, to actually come across this vision in the warm conservatory of Great Banwell School of Art was quite a shock. No, more than that, for it had been Emma who'd told him about the school, who said she sometimes 'helped out' there. Dylan had thought she meant guillotining paper, cleaning paintbrushes. He began to feel slightly set up, but in a rather nice and surprising way.

'We're life drawing today,' said a twin, unnecessarily. 'Emma's our favourite nude.'

Mine too, he thought, trying not to stare. He hoped he wasn't going to embarrass himself by getting turned on, so lowered his pad full of onion sketches, just in case, and made his way to a spare easel. 'Emma,' he greeted her with a nod, almost as though he'd just walked into The Fox, a place he might now find difficult to go back to.

She smiled and retained her pose: horizontal and facing the 'artists', her head resting on one hand, the other arm slung over a long, lightly freckled thigh. Her knees were firmly together, which was something of a relief, but he could nevertheless see she wasn't, after all, a natural blonde.

Once he'd gathered assorted items from the materials corner, he sat down, collected himself, savoured the finer details of the model and, after considerable thought, decided to start with an arm and make his way up to the more interesting features. He took his time. God, this was the most fun he'd ever had drawing. She really was a delight, clothed and unclothed. He'd try to get everything just right, he decided. Be respectful. No exaggeration, no thick bold lines. The last thing he wanted was to offend her. Just the opposite, he decided, as he set out to wow her with a fantastically flattering portrait.

He'd chosen a fine pencil, and by occasionally rubbing at his work with a finger, felt he was portraying her softness, her beauty and that vaguely ethereal quality quite well. It was all a matter of getting the shading right really. And proportions, of course. It was strange, but he found that by concentrating on the technicalities, it wasn't long before he began to see Emma as less delicious temptress and more ... well, cauliflower.

After half an hour or so, one of the twins came and gave him a little finger-perspective advice. 'Hands are always difficult,' she told him.

'Like onions?'

'Mm?' She cocked her head. 'No, they look nothing like onions.'

'I mean...' he began, but she'd already floated off.

At the end of the session they were asked to stand and hold their work up for the others to see. The easels had been arranged in a semi-circle opposite the model, and when they all obligingly stood with their drawings against their chests, facing outwards, Dylan felt sure either Fay or

May, or perhaps even Emma herself, would declare that he was indeed the weakest link. But then he saw that the artistic-looking woman in kohl and heavy earrings opposite couldn't draw for toffee, and that the pasty young man had put one of Emma's eyes on her knee and a breast where the eye should have been – the guy should really get some glasses – and guessed he wasn't in for humiliation.

'My, what a talented lot!' cried a twin, generously.

Dylan watched, disappointed, as Emma slipped her arms into a handy robe, flicked the back of her hair out of it, and stood up. She then padded over to the pale young man and said, 'How was I?' She gave him that fabulous smile of hers and touched his scrawny neck.

'Gorgeous,' he said, kissing her forehead, then running a hand a bit too far down her back to be her brother or anything.

'I think *you* did me really well, Joe,' she told him, looking round at everyone else's efforts then giggling and making eyes at what was evidently Her Bloke.

Dylan was surprised, faintly upset and more than a shade jealous. Plus, all confidence in his artistic abilities drained away into the quarry-tiled floor and he lowered his drawing behind his easel, then found himself folding it in two and then four and then, with some difficulty, eight.

'But,' he heard above the group's mutterings, 'Fay and I believe first prize today should go to Dylan. *Do* let us have another look, dear.'

When he arrived home with carrier bags of fresh, already cooked delights, exciting breads and a variety of salad ingredients, his mother was swinging her suitcase into the back of her black Mini. 'Thought I'd head off to Gloucestershire,' she said.

'What – *now?* I've bought food and everything.'

'Sorry, love.' Her eyes wandered over to Baz. 'Just suddenly felt like the right time to leave.'

Dylan guessed she'd been plotted to death. He said, 'That's a shame,' and thought about all the things they hadn't done: that long walk they'd talked about, a drive to the north Norfolk coast.

'I'll come again soon, though,' she told him with a peck on both cheeks. 'Promise. It's been fun, hasn't it? All those onions!'

'Yes,' he said suspiciously. Was she just being nice? 'Drive safely, won't you. Got your road atlas?'

'Of course. Bye, darling.' She gave him a final hug. 'Bye, Baz!' she called out, and with that roared off in the direction of Norwich, leaving Dylan with way too much fresh food for one person.

'You and your mates couldn't take some of this off me, could you?' he asked Baz.

'Ookay.'

'Great.' He put it all down on some plastic sheeting, but as Baz poked around he began scratching his shaved head.

'Oo-er,' he said. 'I dunno. It all looks a bit foreign.'

'But you live on foreign takeaways.'

'Yeah well, there's foreign and there's *foreign.*

Know what I mean? Anyway, you can just chuck it, can't you? It's not like, you know, you're down to your last penny.' He chuckled to himself and wandered off.

Had Baz been rifling through his bank statements? Dylan went into the kitchen and dumped everything on a half-demolished worktop. He'd never even thought of hiding all his papers and things.

'Now,' he said out loud after emptying his bags. 'Only one thing for it.'

He went next door.

'Yeah, I'd love to,' Ellie told him, propping herself against the doorframe. 'Only I can't speak for Mum. She sees patients till quite late on Mondays, you see.'

Just Ellie. Oh well. 'Eight o'clock?'

'OK,' she said. 'I'll really look forward to it.' She slowly pulled a strap back on to her shoulder. 'Just the two of us, yeah?'

'Well, it needn't be,' he said, beginning to make his way back home. 'Got *loads* of food. Bring some friends along if you like.' He turned and grinned. 'The prettier the better!'

Fliss got home knackered just after nine. *I'm next door having dinner,* said the note. *Dylan says to come round. (But no need to rush.)*

Actually, there was a need to rush. She was famished. Fliss made herself a cup of coffee and took it with her.

It was a very warm evening and Dylan had gone for almost al fresco: the table as close to the French windows as it could be, overlooking his builder's yard. He jumped up when she walked in.

'Fliss, hi,' he said, looking overly pleased to see her. 'Are you hungry?'

'Ra*ther.*'

Ellie was chewing the inside of her mouth and twisting a fork over and over. Something was amiss, but Fliss had been sorting people out all day and just wanted to dive headfirst on to the table and consume all the little Provençal tartlets and stuffed peppers and cheeses and salad and mixed olives in one go. But, because she was a woman not a whale, she took the plate he offered and daintily helped herself to one of everything.

'Where's your mother?' she asked Dylan.

'Gone to Dad's. Just sort of took off. She does that.'

'Oh?'

'Mm. Anyway, lucky you came. I've been pouring my heart out to poor Ellie about my ex.'

'Natalia,' said Ellie, stabbing at something on her plate that looked as though it had already been stabbed quite a lot. An artichoke heart? 'She's half-Italian and a model,' she added. 'You know, as in practically *super.*'

'Oh?'

'Absolutely ravishing,' chipped in Dylan.

Fliss wondered about changing the subject but her mouth was full.

'Highly intelligent,' said Dylan.

'The wittiest woman he's ever known,' said Ellie, flipping the thing on her plate over.

Dylan sighed and refilled his glass. 'Just can't get her out of my system. In many ways we were such a perfect match, you see. Four years we were together.'

Fliss nodded. The tartlets were very good. She took another and saw her daughter's bottom lip wobbling.

'You know,' Fliss began, unclear about where her sentence was going. 'You know,' she began again. Dylan had his eyebrows raised, waiting. 'I had a patient today with one leg really quite a bit shorter than the other. Almost an inch. All muscle tension. Everything had kind of shrunk on one side of her body. Squeezed together, as it were. I referred her to a chiropractor.'

'Ha, fancy that,' said Dylan

This was all he needed: to have his mind taken off his old girlfriend. 'It's amazing,' she carried on, 'the different effects prolonged tension can have on the body.'

'Yeah? I suppose some people have breakdowns and others find their legs shrinking?'

'Quite!'

They both laughed.

'Natalia's legs are forty-four inches long,' said Ellie quietly.

Fliss took the last tartlet. 'Is that right.'

Alex woke with a start when something went *zing* on his window. He'd fallen asleep with the light on, *The Alchemist* in his hand, open at the bit where the boy has all his money stolen in Tangiers, which he'd actually been quite gripped by only a nanosecond ago. He looked at his alarm clock. Eleven fifty-eight. OK, maybe twenty minutes ago. Something cracked against the window pane again, making him jump. Thoughts of George Harrison's attacker whizzed through his head, and his heart began to pound. But then he heard, 'Alex! Your bell's not working. Let me *in*.'

Marie? Or, alternatively, someone impersonating her, with a freshly sharpened knife up his sleeve? So much for the security system on the gates. That hadn't been much use to George, either.

'For Christ's sake, Alex. Wake up, you dozy *twit*.'

Ah. Marie, after all. The only person who could still make 'twit' sound horribly insulting.

'Coming!' he shouted. He jumped out of bed in his T-shirt and shorts and headed straight for the half-open window, which he was wary of sticking his head out of, owing to the missiles. He thrust an arm through. 'Don't chuck any more stones,' he yelled. 'It's the original glass. Please.'

'OK. But hurry up, would you? I'm desperate for a pee. I'd go in the garden only I expect you've got rats.'

'Hang on.'

Alex ran down the stairs and opened the front door. 'Where's your car?' he asked as she flew past him.

'Outside your bloody locked gates, of course.' She disappeared into the cloakroom and slammed the door shut.

'But how did you get in?' he asked when she reappeared.

Marie laughed. 'Oh Alex, your fence is full of gaping holes. It's just a case of finding them in the privet. Now, are you going to offer me a drink, or not?'

'Let me bring your car in first. Got the keys?'

'They're in the ignition.'

Alex tutted, remembering how cavalier Marie could be about such matters, and slipped into a pair of shoes. 'Help yourself to a drink,' he told her. 'You'll find tea, coffee, cocoa ... er, somewhere in the kitchen.'

'Cocoa?' said Marie. She seemed to be laughing at him again. 'I was thinking more of booze. It's taken me seven hours to get here.'

'Seven!'

'Thought I'd pop home first.'

'Ah.'

Now she was winking at him. 'You know,' she said with a smile, 'it's quite sweet to find Alex Child tucked up and fast asleep before midnight.'

'I was reading,' he told her, wishing he wasn't sounding quite so defensive. He sighed and grabbed the torch from the hall table. Oh dear, he thought, still a bit groggy, not the best of starts to her visit. And why did he have to be wearing that old ripped T-shirt and moth-eaten boxers when he'd bought all those new clothes last week? 'Back in a tick,' he said, returning her smile and suddenly noticing how tired she looked. That must have been quite a journey. 'Then I'll crack open a bottle.'

'And something to eat would be good.'

'Sure.'

Alex thought about this all the way to his gates, and in her car, and then as he crunched over gravel back to the house. Something to eat, something to eat. If he'd only known Marie was coming he'd have got Mrs F to have a wholesome dish waiting for her. With some heating instructions.

'OK, give me a clue,' Marie said, when Alex entered the kitchen and chucked the keys down. She was standing with her hands on her hips, surveying the panorama of Scandinavian units. 'Which one's the fridge hidden in?'

Alex scratched his head and looked around Mrs Farthing's vast territory. 'Um...'

The following morning, at her three-days-a-week job in a city-centre café, Ellie was trying to stop herself feeling gloomy by imagining the celery stalks she was slicing for the Stilton and celery soup-of-the-day were Natalia's forty-four-inch legs. Chop, chop, *chop*, chop, *chop!* Ah yes. She reached for another and began again. Forty-*three*. Forty-*two*. Forty-*one*. *Forty!*

'Actually, that's enough celery, Ellie,' said Janet the manager. 'More than enough. Goodness, look at that pile.'

'Oh sorry. Got carried away.'

Janet cocked her head. 'You OK?'

'Yeah,' Ellie sighed. 'Just, you know, *man* trouble.'

She knew she was exaggerating. Dylan was hardly her man, and you couldn't say he was any trouble.

'Rob, isn't it?'

'Uh uh. Different one. Rob and I finished.'

'Oh, that's a shame. He seemed really nice. And dead hunky. Tell you what, if I'd been fifteen years younger...'

'Yeah?' Ellie had never seen Rob – skinny with

big ears that wouldn't lie flat – as someone other girls might want to pull. Except when he was doing his Friday-night dee-jaying, that was. DJ Robo. Rob said he thought a set of headphones was definitely a babe magnet, but Ellie wondered if it was just that they hid his ears.

'So, what's the new one called?' asked Janet.

'Dylan,' said Ellie before she could stop herself. Shit. 'Shall I get the Stilton out and start making the soup?' she asked, heading for the big fridge and humming loudly.

'Dylan, eh? Nice name.'

Change the subject, Ellie told herself. Quick. 'Sorry, what are the other ingredients, Janet? I've completely forgotten, ha ha.'

'You know, if he's treating you badly, just send him in here and I'll sort him out.'

Ellie wasn't sure what that meant, but Janet *had* been in the Army for twelve years and had loads of upper-body strength and a short fuse. She'd once, literally, thrown Terry Kelly – well-known gang leader and breaker of many legs – out of the café for being ill-mannered.

'Thanks,' Ellie told her boss. She smiled and tried not to look such a miserable loser. She also wanted to appear appreciative. 'I'll let you know if things get any worse.'

'Good. I don't know why so many men these days are such complete bastards. Now ... you want butter, milk, garlic, seasoning.'

'OK,' Ellie said cheerfully, while inside she felt like the most horrendously disloyal next-door neighbour ever.

91

SEVEN

The estate was littered with cars. Each house seemed to have three or four outside, and mostly new ones at that. Had these people never heard of the Kyoto Protocol? Or buses? Hazel's house had eight or ten vehicles gathered around it, nose to bumper which, thank God, meant Fliss wasn't the only guest. She parked behind one that had *Warning! Driver applying make-up* in the rear window, and for a while toyed with the idea of going home. But she got out, locked up and purposefully strode along a path lined with miniature fir trees to Hazel's carriage-lamped, frosted front door, where she stood with a bottle of New Zealand white and a fixed raring-to-go smile.

'Fliss! Great!' cried Hazel blindingly. She was in dazzling pink – totally wrong for her ruddy complexion – and the satsuma hallway carpet wasn't helping.

'Hi,' said Fliss, blinking hard and now feeling drab in black sleeveless top with what she hoped was a flattering neckline, and boot-leg jeans but without the boots; it being July.

'Almost everyone's here now.' Hazel took the wine and thanked her. 'Did you bring an old school photo for the board?'

Did she hell. 'Oops, sorry. Completely forgot.' What sane person shows others their school photographs?

'Oh well, never mind. Come on through. Excuse the chaos, I had to move all the furniture around. This is Greg, my oldest, by the way. Just finished uni and getting under my feet, aren't you, love? This is Fliss, my best friend from school. Would you get her a drink? What would you like, Fliss? There's a non-alcoholic fruit punch for the drivers. Got banana and coconut in it.'

'Mm. Yes, please.'

'And oranges, apples and some mint leaves. Look, here are all the photographs. That one of Jenny's hilarious! Most people are in the garden. Come through. I thought, what with it being such a lovely evening. How was your journey? And this is my daughter, Naomi. This is Fliss. No Trudy! Don't eat that. It's the uncooked chicken for the barbecue!'

Was it their old friend Trudy? Hazel rushed off to save a woman in a man's shirt – oh yes, definitely Trudy – from salmonella poisoning, leaving Fliss on the patio, drinkless and alone, but quite pleased to be away from the gruelling pink for a while.

'Felicity Lawrence?' asked someone.

She spun round to face a woman who was cotton-bud thin with short autumnal hair. 'Yes,' she said, returning the woman's smile and trying to think who the blazes it could be. Was she going to have an entire evening of not remembering people? Why hadn't Hazel super-efficiently handed out name badges?

'Joanna.' The woman raised her eyebrows. 'Joanna Brown?'

Ah yes, of course. 'Joanna Orange' they used to call her. She was a real carrot top back then, with so many freckles she looked tanned all year round. The hair had faded now, as had the billion freckles that still covered her exposed arms. As a girl she'd had skeletal legs and thick glasses, and actually looked far more attractive now.

'Joanna!' said Fliss. 'Didn't recognise you without your glasses.'

'Got contacts.'

'Ah. Well, how nice to see you. How *are* you?'

'Very well, thanks. And you?'

Hazel's son approached with a glass of driver's punch. He was a good-looking boy and towered over most of the crowd. 'Here you are,' he said, handing it to Fliss. 'Take it easy, though. The bananas are so old they're fifty per cent proof.'

Fliss laughed and thanked him and wondered who he got his sense of humour from. She turned back to Joanna Orange and, with the smile she hadn't dropped since the front door, said, 'I'm fine. But tell me all about you.'

While Joanna said she lived in somewhere and was married to someone and had three children called something, something and something, Fliss sipped her drink and managed sneaky glances at the crowd over the rim of her glass. So many people. Twenty-five or thirty perhaps? Where were all their cars? Trudy was staring at Fliss and half-smiling. Fliss discreetly bobbed her head at her while Joanna Orange told her she'd been working as a ... something or other. Jesus, how could Hazel have *not been sure* about Trudy's sexuality? For a start there was the severe, elderly-lesbian, did-it-with-the-shears-and-two-mirrors haircut: chunky and irregular and vaguely shaved at the back. If you missed that clue, there were the thumbs hooked in the combat trouser pockets...

'And how about you?' Joanna was asking.

'Mm? Oh. Well, I was a GP for twelve years.'

'Wow, a GP. You always were clever, though.'

'Not really. Anyway, a year after qualifying I became pregnant with my daughter. Luckily, I was able to work part time as I was married to a GP too. Colin. We ran a surgery from home.'

'Sounds perfect.'

'Yes. Yes, it was in a way. Only after a while I became disillusioned with conventional Western medicine and decided to train as an acupuncturist. Which took several years and led to one or two ideological rifts between Colin and myself.'

'I can imagine.'

Fliss couldn't make out why she was telling this relative stranger her life story. She sniffed her drink and wondered if it was true about the bananas. 'Ellie, my daughter, is eighteen now and hoping to study Psychology,' she continued. 'Anyway, that's about it.'

'And where are you living?'

'Still in Norfolk. I've got an old farm cottage between Norwich and West Washam.'

'Oh, not too far from me then. You know, half the people here still live in East Anglia. If we'd known, we could have booked a coach to bring us all.'

'Oh well, next time!' said Fliss before scanning the garden again. She was looking for Richard

Honeyman in the vain hope that the emailed image had been a cyber-distorted misrepresentation of him. But no, there he was close by, looking just like his photo. He smiled and bobbed his eyebrows, then beckoned Joanna and herself over.

'Shall we?' asked Fliss, and they went and joined him.

'Hello,' he said and kissed her cheek. 'How lovely to see you. And Joanna.' Kiss kiss, he went again while Fliss simply stared. She recalled Richard Honeyman reaching six foot plus in the sixth form, and now here he was, worn down by life and weight to around, oh, five ten? She sipped at her drink as he introduced them to a pneumatic blonde in boob tube, leather trousers and heels. 'Margaret,' he said. 'Remember?'

Hazel swooshed up behind Fliss. 'Mousey Margaret,' she whispered.

'Blimey.'

'I'm Maggie now,' the woman said, as though that explained the transformation.

Hazel had a tray of canapés. 'Fliss,' she said. 'Would you like some?'

'Yes, please. Quite peckish, actually.' She took a couple and the tray moved round.

'Joanna?'

'Mm, thanks.'

'Margaret? Sorry, *Maggie*.'

'Oooh, no.' She patted her ironing-board stomach. 'Got to watch this.'

'I'm so pleased I don't have that problem!' said Hazel, moving the tray on to Richard Honeyman. 'You'll have some, won't you, Pete?'

Pete?

'Thanks,' he said.

Fliss frowned and turned to Hazel. 'Don't you mean...' She looked back at the man and an odd sensation worked its way down her spine. Hadn't Richard's eyes been blue? His nose total perfection? His mouth plump and full of promise? This wasn't him, it was *Pete Hooper*. Hooper ... Honeyman ... probably side by side in the H section of the concertina file.

She wheeled Hazel away from the group and towards the house.

'Is Richard Honeyman here?' she asked her.

'Mm, yes he is. And just as dishy as ever, believe me. He's inside somewhere. Why don't you go and say hello? Tell him you've always had the hots for him.'

'As if I would,' said Fliss, her knees suddenly losing strength, all her insides turning funny. 'Has he brought, you know, a wife or a girlfriend or anything with him?'

'No, no, he's here on his own.'

'Great!' Fliss giggled and knocked back the rest of her punch. 'Mind you, that doesn't necessarily mean he's not attached. Hard to imagine him not being, though. God, I feel *so* nervous.'

Hazel tapped at her chin. 'Now, did he mention a wife or partner? Or children? Oh crikey, I'm sorry. There's only one thing for it, you'll have to go and ask him yourself. Be brave! Seize the day!'

'Actually, I'm divorced,' said a lovely deep voice. 'No children.'

Fliss and Hazel slowly turned to the open kitchen window a couple of feet behind them, through which a tall man with blue eyes and a perfect nose was propped against a cupboard, arms folded across his chest, a drink in one hand. He seemed to be finding something amusing – the colour of Fliss's face maybe.

'Well, it's been lovely,' Fliss rasped at Hazel, handing over her glass. 'But I really must be off now. Long journey ahead of me and all that. Do come and visit again.'

'Hang on a minute,' called Richard Honeyman to her retreating back, and before she knew it they were colliding in the conservatory. 'I thought you had the hots for me?' he said, grinning.

'Past tense,' she told him.

'I never knew. You were always so standoffish.'

'I was not.'

Something lovely was emanating from him. Probably pheromones. He wore a charcoal shirt. He still had his hair: thick and dark brown with the odd stray grey. He was how Cat Stevens might have looked, had he not found Islam.

'Anyway,' she continued, with a flick of her hand, 'I had crushes on everyone. You know what teenage girls are like.'

'Really?' He sounded almost disappointed. 'Listen, why don't we find a corner and catch up?' He leaned towards her till she felt his body heat. 'Got stuck with a caravan bore in the kitchen. Goes to conventions. He's even brought photos along.'

'Why did you come?' she whispered, moving just a touch closer.

'Thought you might be here.'

'Oh?'

'I'm so pleased you are.'

'Really?'

'And looking so good.'

'Well, thank you.'

'What are you drinking?' he asked, pulling back.

'Let me think,' she said, composing herself She'd had her fill of fruity punch. Bugger it, she'd get a taxi to the B&B. 'White wine, please. But not a rubbishy one. Thanks.'

In the two minutes that he was gone, Fliss breathed deeply, told herself she'd wriggled out of the eavesdropping incident well, and wondered why the hell Richard Honeyman had come to see *her*. She also pretended not to notice Trudy winking at her from afar.

'Happy birthday, sweetie,' said Marie, and they clinked glasses over the upmarket-Cotswold-pub table they'd almost not got. When Alex had finally mentioned his name over the phone, the proprietor all of a sudden realised he did, in fact, have one table free. Then when they arrived it was 'Mr Child' this and 'Mr Child' that, and they were given a choice of tables. They took the one in the window and Marie thought, yes, she could get used to all this again. Several people stared at him, but Alex had developed a way of screening that out. 'If you avoid making eye-contact,' he told her, 'they don't, on the whole, bother you. Mind you, sometimes it's quite nice to be bothered. Not tonight though, eh?'

'No,' Marie agreed.

Actually, she could get used to the whole package she'd been enjoying over the past five days. The fabulous house, the tennis, messing about in the recording studio with Alex. If she could add sex and delete Mrs Farthing it would be perfect.

Ah, that reminded her. She bent down and delved in her handbag.

'Here,' she said, handing him an envelope. 'One more present.'

'Another? *Thank* you.'

He put his wine glass down, took his reading glasses out, opened the envelope and read the contents. 'Felicity Lawrence?' he said with a puzzled look.

'Dylan's neighbour?'

'Oh, Fliss. Right.'

'It's a token for an acupuncture session. She does massage too, but–'

'Can I use it for a massage, then?' He looked anxious. 'Never been keen on needles.'

'Neither have I, but they absolutely don't hurt. Promise you. And the benefits can be enormous. Acupuncture can relax you, or give you more energy...' Should she bring the word 'libido' in here? 'I've often had it.'

'A great ad,' he said, eyes smiling. 'Maybe I'll plump for the acupuncture then. Next time I'm visiting Dylan. Or...' his hand came across the table and covered hers, 'perhaps when *we're* visiting Dylan?'

'*Peut-être*,' she crooned, just as their food arrived.

While the waitress fussed over the table, a man in his late forties, who looked as though he might still enjoy pulling legs off insects, hovered behind Alex, clearly waiting for the girl to finish.

'Uh-oh,' Marie whispered. 'Fan alert.'

'Damn.'

'Or else someone canvassing for the BNP.'

The waitress walked off and the man homed in behind Alex. 'Excuse me,' he said, in a gruff voice. He wore a sleeveless T-shirt and had a dragon tattoo the length of one arm. His hair was short, grey and spiky and he didn't exactly blend in with the restaurant crowd.

Alex, who couldn't see him, replaced the fork he'd only just picked up and hooked a pen out of his jacket pocket. Marie guessed that any moment now he'd turn on the charm and give the impression he didn't mind at all having his birthday meal interrupted.

'But you are Marie Child, aren't you?' continued the man, thrusting a serviette and a pen at her over Alex's head. 'Ju mind...?'

'Not at all.' She coughed back a chuckle while Alex sheepishly returned the pen to his jacket. 'What's your name?'

'Rocky,' he said, casually scratching at his chest in alpha-male baboon fashion.

To Rocky, she wrote. *With all best wishes...*

The man bent forward, forcing Alex's head towards his plate of food. 'You know, my mates and me always thought you was far too good for that useless, drug addict, hippy dipstick you was married to.'

Alex's hand slowly rose to shield his face from view, while Marie hurriedly wrote her name. She smiled pleasantly and handed back the serviette.

101

'How very nice of you to say so.'

Dylan put down EXCITED, which was not exactly how he was feeling. Unfortunately, the x went on a double-letter square and the whole word was a double-score one, which took him up to 238, compared to Ellie's 76.

'Sorry,' he said again. He could have just put CITE. Why hadn't he?

'I'm rubbish, aren't I?'

'No, no. It's the luck of the draw. We could scrap this game and start another one?'

'But we've already done that twice.'

'I know,' he sighed. 'If it's any consolation I'm useless at mental arithmetic.'

'Oh, I'm really good at that.'

'Well, there you go,' he said with what he knew was a patronising smile. Why wasn't she out with her mates in Norwich? Pissed on cocktails and getting off with a fitness coach, then shagging herself giddy while her mum was away? He watched her place her next word.

'Actually, if you put that over here, horizontally,' he told her gently as she laid the S of JOKES, 'you'll have the J on the triple letter.'

'Oh yeah ... cool.'

'Great word. Well done.'

He'd always thrashed Natalia at Scrabble too, but somehow it had felt less like having teeth pulled and more like fun. Probably because the loser had to perform a sex act of the winners choice. He'd sometimes wondered if Natalia lost on purpose, exhibitionist that she was. God, he missed her.

'OK, my go,' he said. He swallowed a yawn behind his hand and his eyes meandered from kettle to cuckoo clock and back to kettle. Might a coffee help? And could it really only be twenty-five past nine?

Back at The Manor, Mrs Farthing had, yet again, put out one mug with hot-chocolate powder in it, so that Alex need only boil the kettle. Alongside, on a plate, sat two custard creams wrapped in film. Marie wasn't sure what she was most cross about: that the woman did it at all, or that, for the fifth night in a row she, Marie, had not been left this sad little nightcap. But because it was his birthday, she tried hard not to feel angry with Alex for allowing these ridiculous rituals to continue.

She put the biscuits away and chucked the mug in the sink, then went to the fridge for the champagne she'd slotted between Mrs Farthing's Sunday leg of lamb and a cracked pudding basin of leftover tapioca. But it wasn't there. 'Sodding woman,' Marie hissed, kicking the door shut again. She checked the food cupboards and found the Bollinger amongst the cordials, warm and useless.

Ice, she thought, heading for the freezer. Every jug of Mrs F's lemon barley had come laden with ice all week, so there was bound to be a good supply. She opened the door. No ice trays either. In fact, there they were, over in the dish rack. Empty and stacked. Mrs Farthing had thought several moves ahead.

Marie stuck the bottle in the freezer and took two glasses back to the sitting room. 'We just need to give the champagne ten minutes,' she told Alex, who pulled her down to where he lay stretched on the sofa.

'Oh Marie,' he said quietly. 'Was I really such a shit back then?'

She snuggled up to him and nuzzled his chest. ''Fraid so.'

'I'm sorry. You know, I honestly don't remember much about those years. There were gigs and hotels and booze and drugs and–'

'Yes, I know, the endless stream of girls. But let's not dwell on the past. I *never* do that, haven't you noticed? I can't bear those "If only I'd..." type of people. The present is what counts, Alex, and it's *great*. You and I are close again. Dylan's doing well. As far as I can see there's only one fly in my ointment, and that's your bloody housekeeper. Sweetie, isn't it time you pensioned her off? Mm?'

Alex went rigid in her arms and checked his watch. 'That must be ten minutes, now. Don't you think?'

Acutely aware that she'd spent the entire evening talking to just one person, Fliss gave Hazel an over-the-top, '*Thank* you! It was *terrific* catching up with everybody,' as she left the house at ten to eleven, three minutes after Richard Honeyman. The taxi was idling, so she ran for it with a big backwards wave and another 'Thanks!' and when she jumped in and slammed the door and the driver moved off, Richard pulled himself upright beside her, put his arm around her and said words she would have killed her cat for, aged sixteen: 'Your B&B or mine?'

104

EIGHT

On Tuesday, Alex was trying to choose a dog. He'd been thinking about getting one for a while, but with Marie suddenly departing the day before and leaving a gaping emotional hole that had taken him by surprise, he decided to ask Mr Farthing to drive him fifteen miles to the animal sanctuary, and to maybe chuck an old blanket on the back seat just in case.

If he'd had work to do, Alex would no doubt have been feeling more cheerful and less needy, but the flurry of album-release publicity engagements and the British and Australian tours were now behind him, and the only reason his manager phoned him these days was to ask how the songwriting was going for the next solo album. It wasn't, but Alex didn't let on. Some of the reviews for his last one had been real kneecappers, leaving Alex vaguely shattered, slightly perplexed and wondering – particularly after his fruitless trip to Jamaica – if the world would be a better and less cluttered place without more Alex Child records.

Mind you, *Why?* seemed to be selling fairly steadily, which was comforting and one in the eye for the reviewers. Blue Plum's fan base had expanded enormously with the digitally remastered re-releases of their old albums throughout the Nineties. New, younger CD buyers got into them and, a few years back, the record company talked the band into re-forming and giving it another shot. Bad idea, it turned out. Old grievances still simmered and halfway through recording what might have been a great comeback album, Rick announced he could no longer stomach the same studio air as that fucking girlfriend-stealing, royalties-swindling arsehole Chas, and went back to plumbing in Barnes. Chas himself had, by that time, become a chronic back-pain sufferer and could no longer stretch to the furthest drums without tear-filled eyes and the odd howl.

Alex laughed at the memory and shook his head. Why was he thinking of Chas? Perhaps it was the 'oh please, please take me home with you and throw me your toast crusts and let me sit on the sofa' look of the large, doleful, floppy-eared hybrid of a dog in the metal cage in front of him. He was a strange Identikit of a creature, long-legged and pug-nosed with floorcloth-coloured dull fur, but Alex was rather taken with him. He wasn't barking rabidly and relentlessly like the others for a start, and he looked sensitive and intelligent and far too refined in nature to be in with this hoi-polloi. Like Oscar Wilde in Reading Gaol, or Brian Sewell in a Hallmark shop. Alex was tempted to rescue the endearing, if scruffy little soul, but found himself shallowly concerned about the 'owners growing to look like their dogs' thing. Well, there was Marie to consider now. Would she be so keen to share his bed if saliva dangled from his lower jaw? He wandered around and checked out the others but kept returning to the quiet sad-eyed one.

'I think I'd like him,' he eventually told a

woman who looked as though she might have a corgi at home.

'Fluffy?'

'Oh, surely not?' said Alex.

'Nothing to stop you changing his name. Anyway, I've just a few questions to ask, if you wouldn't mind stepping into the office.'

'Certainly.'

Twenty minutes later Alex was feeling thoroughly grilled and confounded, having learned that it was far, far easier to have a child in Britain than to give an unwanted mongrel a home. No, he didn't have any children under sixteen. No, children under sixteen almost never visited his home. No, no cats or any other pets. Yes, he worked at home. And yes, he did sometimes have spells abroad.

'Oh,' the corgi-woman said at this point. 'Oh dear.'

'But I have a live-in housekeeper.' It was almost true. 'Who adores dogs.' Not true.

There'd been a bit of a running battle between Mrs Farthing and himself about the getting of a dog. Hairs everywhere, apparently. Muddy paws all over the floors and furnishings. 'They smell,' she said. 'Show me a house with a dog and I'll show you a house that pongs.'

Marie was of the opinion that Mrs Farthing wielded way too much authority for her position, not to mention her stature. 'She's your cook/cleaner, for heaven's sake, Alex. If you want coffee for breakfast, insist on it!' Mrs F believed in tea with breakfast and coffee mid-morning, and Alex had always gone along with that. There

107

was something nice and comforting about routine, he'd discovered, when his hedonistic days finally came to an end and he'd settled in the fold of a Cotswold village and let Mrs Farthing structure his days.

'Garden?' asked the corgi-woman.

'Twelve acres,' Alex said proudly.

'Mm, that sounds a bit big. We don't want Fluffy getting lost. Does any hunting take place on your land?'

'Certainly not!'

'Dangerous sports?'

Alex sighed and ran a hand through his hair. 'Yes, I set fire to six buses then try to clear them on my Suzuki. I was thinking Fluffy might like to ride pillion.'

The woman placed her pen on the table and folded her arms. 'Our animals have often been *terribly* abused, Mr Child. We think it only right and proper that prospective owners are thoroughly vetted to prevent further heartbreak.'

'Yes, of course,' said Alex, feeling a little ashamed before this Good Person. 'Sorry. Um, no dangerous sports. No.'

She picked up the pen again. 'And how's your health?'

'Excellent.'

'No mobility problems?'

'No.' He guessed she wasn't referring to the smaller parts of his anatomy or the fact that he'd been forced to hand back his driving licence.

'Well, everything seems to be in order,' she finally said. 'That'll be a hundred pounds, then.'

Alex was stunned but took out his chequebook

and pen.

'We also insist that new owners come along for a training day here at the centre before they take Doggy home.'

'What?'

'Oh yes. People often tell us they found it invaluable.'

Alex couldn't help feeling this was all turning into a terrible idea. 'Look,' he said, twisting his chequebook round. 'How about if I add another nought on to this hundred? Mm? Could we forget the training day?'

The woman's eyes widened. 'That's extremely generous, Mr Child. Thank you. We'll have Fluffy all nice and ready for you on Friday morning.'

Alex wondered what that meant. Showered, suitcase packed? 'Once the cheque's cleared,' she added.

'Yes, of course.'

It had rained earlier in the day and Dylan had sent Baz home and taken himself off for a circular walk; along footpaths that took him past vast fields of sugar beet, through a beautifully damp and dripping wood and back down a narrow almost traffic-free road. Warm rain was definitely his favourite walking weather. All those earthy smells. He saw no one en route but a distant farmworker – possibly the farmer himself – who'd waved, then got back to his solitary chores.

As much as Dylan loved the country, he could never grasp the appeal of farming: the hours, the huge tracts of land you're responsible for, everyone thinking you live on EU subsidies. He could see himself with a smallholding, though – chickens, organic veg, rosy-cheeked wife and children, and maybe some goats. Norfolk or Wales? he wondered. East or West? He had friends in Wales who'd done the whole back-to-basics thing, but Norfolk was beginning to feel like home now. Perhaps Emma could be his rosy-cheeked smallholder wife ... when she wasn't busy stripping off for all and sundry.

On arriving home, the weather had changed to dry and sunny – it never seemed to rain for long in these parts – and so the plastic sheeting came down and Dylan was soon on the phone asking Baz to come back.

'Ookay,' Baz said. 'Only it costs, you know. All this coming and going.'

'Yeah, yeah, I'll pay your petrol. Quick as you can, eh?'

When Baz arrived in his battered old Fiat they got the cement-mixer going and by five o'clock had managed to finish the back wall of the kitchen extension.

'Yes!' Dylan cheered before waving his helper off again and collapsing on to plastic. All that was needed now was a roof and windows, which he was hoping Baz might be good at. He seemed pretty capable in most areas, but the last thing Dylan wanted was rain seeping through his sunken ceiling lights. He pictured the house all done. Lots of chrome in the kitchen. Warm wooden flooring everywhere. His Bang and Olufsen set off nicely against white walls. His rosy-cheeked, golden-limbed beauty draped over

110

an outrageously expensive white sofa. No – dark blue sofa. OK, one of each.

'You all right?' asked a voice over the fence.

'Fine thanks, Ellie.' From where he lay he turned his head towards her and shielded his eyes from the sun. 'And you?'

'I dunno. I'm a bit worried about Mum.'

'Oh?'

'Mm. She's been in this trance-like state since the weekend. Honestly, I can't get through to her. Last night she just sat and watched the phone and chewed her nails for like an hour. She doesn't bite her nails, you see, and she hates people phoning her in the evenings … so that was *really* odd. And when I say like, "Mum, are you all right?" or, "Mum, do you know you're pouring orange juice in your tea?" she just goes, "Uh? Did you say something, love?" with this scary stare, and God, Dylan, it's totally spooking me.'

'Oh dear. What did she say about that party she went to?'

'When I asked she just said, "Fantastic," really quietly and sort of did this funny thing with her eyes and smiled like the Mona Lisa and went off for a two-hour bath.'

'I see. Is she eating?'

'No. Hardly anything.'

'Right. Sighing a lot?'

'Er … yeah.'

Dylan grinned to himself and sat up. He'd been exactly like that when he first met Natalia. 'I'm sure she'll be fine, Ellie. Don't worry. I expect she's just tired.'

'Uh oh. That sounds like her coming back now.

111

Some bloke called Richard's just rung and I'd better go and find where I wrote his number.'

'OK. See you later.'

'What,' she said, turning back, 'do you mean like later this evening?'

'Um, no. Just, you know ... *later.*'

'Oh right. Sorry.'

Dylan lay back again and wondered what kind of a psychologist Ellie was going to make if she couldn't put fantastic party, plus dreamy mother, plus calls from a man together. Still, she was just a kid, he thought, drifting halfway towards sleep and wondering whether to spend the evening working on that new song or finishing off his drawing. 'We're having what we call a free session this week,' he'd been told by a twin at yesterday's class. 'Do whatever takes your fancy.' He'd sat and pondered for a while then began drawing Emma again. From memory, of course, but her naked body was pretty well etched there.

Of course, he didn't *have* to draw or work on his song this evening. He could nip down to The Fox and win the barmaid away from her truly weedy boyfriend. He was missing sex quite badly, and with Emma being the only candidate for miles...

'Oh yeah,' said Ellie, sticking her head back over the fence and making him jump. 'Let me know if you fancy another game of Scrabble some time. It was fun, wasn't it?'

Dylan didn't think Ellie did irony, so simply lifted his head and nodded.

As Richard Honeyman had left it two days to call

her, she'd leave it two hours to call him back. At least. She may as well start as she meant to go on. Playing games, some might call it. Not appearing desperate was how she saw it. He'd ask to see her again, she'd be at her coolest, checking her diary. 'Now let me see ... I'm free for lunch on September twentieth...'

But, around four minutes after Ellie had given her the message, she was dialling and holding her breath. Why was she feeling so jittery? This was someone she'd shared a single bed with three nights before. Disastrously. Tumbling on to the floor at 5 a.m. and hurting her shoulder. It wasn't a thing middle-aged people should be doing.

'Hello,' he said and her heart thumped.

'Hi, it's–'

'Fliss, hi. How are you? How's the injury?'

'Fine.' She was rather hoping he'd forgotten. The one good thing about the incident was discovering that Richard could laugh uproariously when rudely woken in the night.

'Fine,' she repeated. It wasn't actually, but euphoria had somehow numbed the pain. None of this had really sunk in yet. Apparently, he'd been as keen on her as she'd been on him at school. Unbelievable. 'But you were so aloof,' he'd told her. 'And so bloody clever. You scared the life out of me.' For the past few days she'd imagined what might have happened if they'd got together back then. Two or three years then a messy break-up that would have taken her ages to recover from? That 'first love' thing that people carry heavily around with them forever? One advantage in marrying Colin had been that she'd

113

never actually fallen in love with him, or even fancied him that much. She'd liked him a lot and still did. Divorce had been painful only on a practical and legal level. The shared surgery, and so on.

'I'd love to see you again,' Richard Honeyman was saying.

'Me too.' She wondered where her planned coolness was, and why Ellie's multi-coloured toenails were standing perfectly still behind the half-open kitchen door.

Of course she'd love to see him again. OK, he wasn't the flawless beauty he'd been at seventeen, eighteen. The mouth was slightly more set. Small frown lines now fanned out above the bridge of his nose. His neck could have been smoother, his stomach a little flatter, but *my God* he was an attractive man. What's more he was a landscape gardener, so they had masses to talk about. Had his own – thriving, by the sound of it – business. He played tennis, he told her. Loved the theatre.

'How about this weekend?' he said. 'You could come here?'

He lived in Chiswick. Had bought a small flat there with his wife when prices were still sane. They decided to start a family, so traded up to a nearby three-bedroomed house that needed a lot of work. But the babies didn't happen – Richard hadn't told her why – and he bought his wife out when they divorced.

'Great. Love to,' said Fliss, barely recognising herself. A whole weekend. Was she mad?

They made arrangements, flirted a bit, then hung up, and while Fliss sat and smiled at the fridge, she heard Ellie's toenails creak their way back to the living room.

Of course it would be nice, but at the same time Marie felt she'd somehow be diminished by it. Possibly.

'Look, Gavin,' she said. He'd just undone the last shirt button. 'No, keep the trousers on. Please. In fact, let's go out to dinner, mm? You choose.'

'Mario's?'

'OK.'

'You see,' she expanded over her coffee and his dessert, 'I'm kind of getting back together with my ex.' Was she really? True, she'd been reluctant to leave Alex's place, but at the same time she'd experienced a sudden and overwhelming need to go home and think about things. Plus, Mrs Farthing had been doing her head in. Marie was unsure of what was going on emotionally or even professionally between herself and Alex – they'd arranged and recorded several of her new songs – but nevertheless thought she'd better clear the way, as it were, and send Gavin packing. Regretful as that might be.

'Geoff?' asked Gavin.

'Christ, *no*.'

Gavin and Geoff had once bumped into each other. Geoff had come to collect a few things he felt he was entitled to as he'd bought them – the antique-style globe and other nightmare items she'd hidden in the loft – and the two men had passed on the front garden path, both clearly startled by the other's appearance and giving each other the merest of nods.

'Alex,' she told him.

'The old rock star?'

'He's not that old.'

'So, are you saying...?'

'Yes, I am. Sorry, Gavin. It's been–'

'Will I still be able to get stuff on your store-cards?'

'Let me think about that one.' Maybe the kindest thing would be to wean him off them.

He was quiet while he finished his meal, then Marie paid the bill and they left the restaurant.

'I need to come and get a couple of things,' he said with a look that suggested he was already in mourning. For the lifestyle rather than the sex, Marie guessed. 'There's a jacket and some shoes. And, you know, my wash stuff.'

'Of course, sweetie. Come on.' She hooked her arm through his and they strode off.

Once inside the house, he turned and smiled at her and ran a finger down her front. 'How about one last shag?' he asked.

Had he been reading her mind? 'Why not?' she said before clamping her mouth on his.

NINE

Alex turned to look at the dog, whose eyes were firmly fixed on the road ahead while the poor thing swayed from side to side and occasionally lurched forward on the back seat of the Austin Princess. It was almost as though Fluffy were taking note of the route and watching out for hazards to warn Mr Farthing about. Yes, there was something very bright and perceptive about this unkempt creature. If given the power of speech, Alex felt sure the dog would pronounce intelligently on the issues of the day in an understated but nevertheless compelling way. Like Nelson Mandela or Noam Chomsky.

When they finally came to an abrupt halt outside the house, Fluffy threw Alex a 'thank Christ that's over' look and jumped from the car on to the drive. But instead of haring off into the twelve-acre garden as Alex was expecting, the dog sat himself on the gravel and quietly contemplated the frontage of his new house. 'Woof,' he said approvingly.

'What's its name again?' asked Mrs Farthing. 'Fluffy, did you say?' She was walking backwards, laying sheets of newspaper across the kitchen floor.

'No, it's Chomsky,' said Alex, suddenly deciding.

'Oh dear. You'll have to write it down for me,

I'll never remember.'

'Chomsky!' called Alex, trying it out. 'Here, Chomsky!' He slapped his thighs in encouragement but received no response from the dog, who was obligingly standing on one sheet of the *Guardian* while appearing to be reading the next one. 'Chomsky!' tried Alex again.

Mrs Farthing laid the last page, straightened up and looked at her watch. 'Time for your elevenses,' she announced.

'Jolly good.'

'No, not you,' she tutted. 'This one.' She went to a cupboard and took out a box of bone-shaped biscuits. 'Come on then, Fluffy,' she sang and the dog trotted over.

Well, it was bound to take time, thought Alex. 'You've remembered Dylan's coming tomorrow?' he asked.

'Of course. Made his favourite, I have. Jam roly-poly.'

Mrs F loved to spoil Dylan, to almost the same degree that she enjoyed rubbing Marie up the wrong way. Not that Marie had been totally blameless: asking Mrs Farthing if she had shares in Bisto as it seemed to come with every meal. Alex wondered if he might one day have to choose between the two women. A painful thought that he immediately put out of his mind.

'Right then, Fluffy,' said Mrs Farthing when the dog biscuits had gone and she'd rinsed out the bowl. 'I'll show you what to do about your mucky paws when you come in from the garden, and where you're allowed to go and where I'll have your guts for garters if you so much as venture.'

The dog glanced Alex's way questioningly, and Alex gave him a better-do-as-she-says nod. It just made life easier.

Ellie unravelled a tape measure and let it fall down the outside of her leg. It was only a rough guide as the tape was all crinkled, but the high heels seemed to make her legs forty-one inches long. Almost forty-two! Wearing short shorts and the tiniest strappy top she then tottered out to the back garden with a tin and a brush and began slapping wood preserver on the fence.

'Hi, Dylan,' she called over to where he was sawing something, bare-chested and tanned. 'What are you doing?'

He stopped, said, 'Floorboards,' and carried on.

Ellie was a bit disappointed that he hadn't turned to see her long, long legs through the gap in the greenery she'd placed herself directly opposite. Oh well, he'd have to look some time. She carried on painting the disgusting stuff on the wooden fence that she now recognised every inch of. Her feet were hurting like mad in her mum's size fives, but she wasn't going to change the shoes till Dylan had noticed her.

It had to happen this weekend. *Had to*. Her mum was going to be away again, the weather forecast was brilliant, and for once in her life she didn't have a single spot. She moved along to the next panel. *Ouch*. The slingback was really digging into her left foot. Maybe she'd offer to cook for him this time. She'd got to know quite a few soup recipes at work. Or a salad, if it was

119

going to be hot. They could eat in the garden, light candles when it got dark. He'd say, 'I expect you feel I'm too old for you, Ellie, but since seeing those long, long legs of yours yesterday, I've thought of nothing else.'

'Ellie?' he called across. The sawing had stopped.

She swivelled round quickly and almost lost her balance. 'Yes?'

'Did you know your foot's bleeding? There, at the back.'

'Oh.'

He put the saw down, and with a, 'Hang on,' hurried into the house and returned carrying several items. 'Here,' he said. 'Mum's walking boots. She left them when she came to stay. I'd guess she's about your size.'

He knelt down and eased the shoe off her left foot while she clung to the fence. Next he pulled a plaster from his jeans and put it over her wound, rubbing it gently into place. In other circumstances, Ellie might have found it quite erotic.

'Slip into this,' he told her and she did. He laced up the colossal brown boot and tied a double bow. 'OK, now this one … that's it.' When he'd finished, he stood upright and shook his head, dangling her mother's shoes from his fingers. 'What possessed you to work in these things?'

She stared down at her legs, which now looked more like Baz's than Kate Moss's. Don't cry, she told herself. Don't. Cry.

'Oh, and here,' he said, handing her a big bulbous white mask on elastic. 'You'd better put this on. I worry about your lungs, you know.'

'Thanks,' she managed, her throat thickening.

'Let me do it.'

He placed the monstrous clown-like thing on her face and hooked the strap over the hair she'd spent ages ironing. She felt like she was about to be anaesthetised and her head began swimming.

'Listen,' he continued. 'I've been meaning to say I'm going to be away this weekend. Visiting Dad. It was his birthday last week, and, well ... if you and your mum could keep an eye on the house, that would be great.'

Ellie produced a muffled, 'Sure,' and turned back to the fence before he spotted her eyes welling up.

'Hi, Dad,' she said, after she'd tugged off the boots and limped to the phone. 'It's me. Yeah, yeah, fine. And you? Good. Um, I was wondering if I could like come and stay with you and Gillian this weekend? I know it's short notice but I haven't seen you for ... oh, cool. Yeah, yeah. I'll be ready at one tomorrow. Bye. OK. Bye.'

Phew. She really didn't want to be alone at night out here in the middle of nowhere with no car, thank you. You'd have thought her mum might have checked that Dylan would like *be there*, but she was still floating around in zombie mode and being dead mysterious about that Richard guy. 'I'll have my mobile, love. Don't worry,' was all Ellie got. Mind you, this was the first time she'd known Dylan go away anywhere. She sat back with her eyes closed, rubbed her sore foot and thought about him down on his

121

knees forcing her into combat boots. A bit odd when you thought about it. It hadn't occurred to her before, but could it be Dylan liked his women a bit butch?

Fliss watched her daughter hobble over with a baked pasta dish and said, 'What have you done to your foot?'

'Oh, I borrowed those old slapper shoes of yours and they were *way* too small.'

'What do you mean?'

'Well, you know – I take size seven and you take a five.'

'By old slapper?'

Ellie laughed. 'I was just testing you, Mum. You know you've been like *so* not present this week. I could have said anything and it wouldn't have registered. Anyway, I meant tarty, not old slapper.'

'Tarty? Oh dear. I was thinking of wearing them this weekend.'

'No. Tarty's cool.'

'Is it?'

'He-*llo?* Haven't you heard of reconstructed feminism?'

'Actually, no.'

'Oh right, well I read about it in this magazine. Anyway, it's like it's become *compulsory* to wear Wonderbras and fishnets and things to show you're an empowered, like, rejoicing-in-her-sexuality woman.'

Fliss nodded. 'I see. Nothing to do with men liking all that? And there being armies of desperate women in their twenties and thirties and a dearth of available men?'

'*No.*'

'You don't think all this "let's go clubbing in our skimpiest underwear" is in any way connected with finding a mate?'

'Uh uh. We've moved way beyond that now. Honestly Mum, you're *so* Seventies. Women are just dressing to please themselves now. Right? You wouldn't catch me pandering to men's fantasies, or whatever you old bra-burners in your dungarees used to call it. No! Way!'

'OK, calm down,' said Fliss. She stuck the spatula into the bake and served herself up a large portion. 'God, I'm starving.'

Ellie sniggered. 'I'm not surprised. You haven't eaten all week.'

'Really? No wonder I got into a size ten skirt today. Mmm, this smells good.'

'Thanks.'

'So, you think it would be fine for someone as old as me to rejoice in her sexuality and wear those stilettos?'

'Of *course*. It's not like you're Granny's age or something.'

'Well, I'm not far off it.'

'God, Mum, you've got such a hang-up. Madonna's way into her forties now, you know. It said in this article she was like the original reconstructed feminist. Anyway, tell me about this Richard bloke. Was he the one who looked gross in his photo?'

Fliss explained about the mix-up but didn't want to build Richard Honeyman up too much. 'I'll let you know what I think after this weekend.

Will you be all right here on your own again?'

'Dylan's away, so I'm going to Dad and Gillian's.'

'Oh, right.'

'Even though Gillian's a bit...'

'Oh, I don't know. She's just so *nice* to me. I suppose I'm not used to that.'

'Why, thanks.'

Ellie sighed. 'I wish all my old friends weren't doing Thailand and stuff. I could be having the *best* parties.'

'I'm sorry.'

'What for?'

'That you're stuck here working in a sandwich bar and not swanning around Thailand. You know your father and I could always pay for a flight so you can go and join your friends.'

Ellie shook her head, then nibbled on her bottom lip and frowned and fiddled with the spatula. Her nose was reddening, her eyes grew watery and her throat made a strange sound.

'Yeah, I know. But I'd rather you helped me when I'm at uni. And anyway, I love being here, next to...' She grabbed some kitchen roll and blew her nose. 'But I don't think he likes me,' she continued with a small shudder. 'You know, I was out in the garden today doing the fence and looking *dead* glam especially for him and,' she lifted her head and blushed. 'I mean...'

'Chomsky!' yelled Alex through cupped hands. Where the devil was he? 'Chom-*sky!*'

No. No sign. He plodded on towards the spinney, hoping the dog wasn't trying to make his way back to the sanctuary with a list of complaints. They make me walk through a trough of water every time I come in the back door! Then over a towel. And I'm not even *allowed* to use the front door. They want to give me this pretentious name but they're treating me like a tradesman!

'Chom-*sky*.'

Alex put two fingers in his mouth and attempted a whistle, but he'd never really been able to do that. 'Chom-sky? Here boy! *Please?*'

He'd seen him just three minutes ago, disappearing into the distance, happy as a ... well, as happy as a dog on a walk, basically. He couldn't be far away, but with such a lot of unfamiliar land to explore he could have been lost or got stuck, or escaped from the garden, and it was beginning to get dark and, oh Lord, why had they ventured out quite so late in the day?

'*Fluuu-ffeeee...*' Alex tried, and within seconds the dog was bounding to heel.

'Right,' said Alex, attempting a stern look but no doubt displaying utter relief not to say defeat. Perhaps he could try morphing Fluffy to Chomsky. Begin with Fluffsky, say for a week... He attached the lead and the two of them jogged their way back to the house where, as Mrs Farthing had gone home for the night, they let themselves in through the front door.

TEN

It was about an hour after her mother had gone belting off in the direction of London, and Dylan in the direction of wherever his dad lived, that Ellie thought she heard noises coming from next door. The odd quiet thud, feet on the stairs, a cough. Her whole body began to tingle, her stomach tightened and she swallowed hard. Shit, what should she do? Dylan had asked her to keep an eye on the place, after all. She wished her dad would suddenly arrive an hour and a half early, but that wasn't likely as he was on Saturday-morning emergencies at the surgery. Which meant she couldn't even phone him. It was down to her to do something and, hey, maybe if she stopped Dylan's place being burgled or vandalised he'd have a whole different opinion of her. Especially if he really did like his women a bit macho.

She looked around the living room for a weapon. Nothing. She tried the kitchen and decided on a big heavy saucepan – part weapon, part shield – then picked up Dylan's keys and went round the back, squeezing between the bushes and unlocking his French windows, all on tiptoe, teeth clenched.

Was the saucepan such a good idea? It could, after all, be snatched off her and bashed on her own head. She put it down on Dylan's table, very slowly and quietly, then crept through the living room and round the corner into the hall where a stocky man in a baseball cap, leather jacket and cut-offs was bending over Dylan's phone table with his back to her, humming to himself. He was flicking noisily through pages of something. A magazine? The telephone directory? Did it matter? He surely shouldn't have been in Dylan's empty house while he was away.

Right, she thought, taking a running jump. In a flash the man was over her shoulder and pinned to the floor on his front in the confines of the narrow hallway, saying, 'Let go of my sodding arm before you pull it out, will you?' in a familiar voice.

'*Baz?*' she asked.

'*Ellie?*'

'Sorry. Oh God, sorry. Here, let me help you up. Did I hurt anything? I thought you were a burglar, you see. Didn't recognise you. Is that a new jacket? It's very nice.'

'More like *was* very nice.'

Baz heaved himself up with the aid of the banisters, his shorn, now hatless head completely flushed, his bare knees a matching red from the harsh landing. Ellie stepped back, ready to be verbally beaten up, but instead he turned and grinned at her. 'You're shit hot, you are, Ellie. Like something out that *Crouching Tigers* film. Wicked.'

'Thanks. But are you all right?'

'Yeah, yeah. I don't feel pain, me. It's generic. My dad doesn't either.'

Should she correct him? Not the best time,

127

maybe. 'Anyway, I'm sorry. Dylan didn't say you'd be here, that's all.'

'Didn't he?' Baz scratched his nose and said, 'He ... er asked me to come in and ... er finish off the floorboards. You know, in the kitchen.'

Ellie could tell this was a lie. In the past few days she'd been learning about body language and eye-contact from her *Introduction to Psychology* book. She glanced over at the telephone table and thought she'd try him with something else. 'Were you looking for something in Dylan's address book?'

Again, his eyes avoided hers. 'No.'

'Well,' she said. 'I'd better, you know, be going. Things to do and all that.'

'Right.'

'I'll let you get back to the floor.'

'Eh?'

'Kitchen floorboards?'

'Oh yeah. Yeah.'

She let herself out the back, locked up and returned the saucepan to its place. For a minute or two, Baz made a pretence of working – bang bang bang, bang bang bang – before slamming Dylan's front door behind him. Ellie watched him hurry up the front garden. Where was his car? Parked out of sight? Why?

Marie was bored and restless and missing Alex. She'd given the house a good going-over, washed all her clothes, weeded her compact garden, done a food shop and tried to write a new song. And it was only twelve thirty-five. She phoned an old friend who said she'd love to meet up but was busy all weekend so how about next week some time. She tried Kathleen, her cousin and only family in London, but they had guests. She called Alex and got Mrs Farthing.

'He's out walking the dog,' she was told.

'What dog?'

'Fluffy.'

'Oh, *that* dog.' No way was she going to let on she didn't know.

'Great lolloping thing.'

'Yes, so I've heard.' She'd spoken to Alex on Wednesday. They'd emailed each other on Thursday. Why hadn't he told her? 'Could you say I called?' she asked.

'Well, I'll try to remember.'

I'm sure you will, thought Marie. After hanging up she went back to working on her song, but it made her miss Alex even more, so she gave up and called Gavin. 'Hi, sweetie,' she said. 'What are you doing? Oh, are you? Oh, OK. No ... no reason.'

How completely out of character this was. And all so unreal. Driving through London on her way to spend an afternoon, an evening, a *night*, and then maybe another half-day with Richard Honeyman. The weather was glorious, her spirits were high and she'd made good time. Just after one o'clock. Would he be pleased that she'd arrived early? 'You can park in a residents' spot,' he'd told her. 'I'll give you a visitor's ticket.' So, when she found his house, that was what she did.

Fliss sat still while the engine died down, then checked her face in the rearview mirror, hauled her bag from the back seat, locked up, walked along his short, tastefully tiled front path and pushed the bell. Number twelve. She liked that. The house was Edwardian and bigger than she'd expected; half-covered in Virginia creeper, original sash windows.

There was no answer, so she pressed it again, this time for a little longer.

Perhaps he was in the garden. Or the bath. He'd no doubt appear any minute in a short towelling robe that was the perfect colour for him. She rang the bell again, twice.

Nothing.

Fliss checked her watch. She was earlier than she'd said. One more try, she thought, but the house just gave off a deathly quiet.

Oh. What to do?

She knew she couldn't leave the car where it was, so went back, chucked the bag on the passenger seat and drove around the mad Saturday streets for a full ten minutes until a car pulled out of a pay-and-display space right in front of her. She pumped coins into the machine, stuck the ticket in the window and went off to find a café. She wouldn't tell him she'd arrived way too early. Embarrassing for both of them really.

By one-fifty, Fliss was back in the residents' parking space outside his house, but this time she didn't bother lugging her bag up to his front door.

No answer.

This was roughly the time he'd been expecting her and she was beginning to feel a shade pissed off. She took her mobile from her handbag to check for missed calls. No missed calls. She didn't have his mobile number with her, but knew she could get it by dialling his land-line message. Seemed like desperate measures, though, so she thought she'd just wait in the car for a while. Shoot off if a traffic warden came along.

But then a taxi pulled up and Richard jumped out. 'Fliss!' he shouted over its engine. 'So sorry!' He paid the driver and hurried towards her, dishevelled and clearly flustered. 'I'm *really* sorry. Had to go and see a garden. Give an estimate. It took forever. Have you been waiting long?'

'No, no. Just arrived.'

'Oh good.' He tugged his house keys from a trouser pocket and something fell on to the path. 'Come on in,' he said with a peck of her cheek.

While he unlocked his door, Fliss picked up a pair of theatre tickets. 8 p.m. Yesterday's date. Oscar Wilde.

'Lovely to see you,' he went on, pushing open the door and bending down for his mail. Beyond him, the hallway was cluttered with shoes and wellies, jumpers and jackets, free newspapers and a racing bike. 'I might just take a quick shower, if that's all right? But I'll put the kettle on first. What would you like? Tea or coffee?'

'Oh, a cup of coffee, please.' She'd already had two in the café, but knew she wouldn't be drinking this one. 'I'll just go and fetch my bag.'

'Hang on,' he said, disappearing into a room. 'Let me give you a ticket for the car.'

'Oh, no need,' she called out, and an hour later she was in the Ladies of a motorway service station, desperate to get the smell of stale perfume – Chanel? – washed off the cheek he'd kissed.

The last thing Dylan expected when arriving at The Manor was to be almost mown down by the Hound of the Baskervilles.

'No, Fluffsky!' shouted Alex and the dog stopped in its tracks.

'Hello there, Dylan,' called out Mrs Farthing, wiping her hands on her apron as she approached. 'I've made your favourite. Jam roly-poly.'

'Great,' he said. Some time back, his humour had completely missed Mrs Farthing and she'd ended up thinking he actually liked that evil stodgy dish. When the diminutive housekeeper reached him, he bent right over and lowered his knees to kiss her. 'You're much too good to me, Mrs Farthing. And looking as gorgeous as ever.'

'Ooohh,' she giggled, flicking him with her tiny hand. 'Get away with you.'

'No, really.'

'Come along, then,' she said. 'Let's get you fed and watered.'

She turned for the house, the dog following her, while Alex shook his head and scratched at it. 'I'm never sure if it's the dog she's talking to or what. Anyway, come on in. You must be hungry and thirsty driving all this way in that jalopy. Not to say half-deaf.'

'Pardon?' said Dylan and they laughed.

A late lunch was served outside on the terrace which, although he had absolutely no appetite, pleased Dylan. He adored his dad's garden with its Capability Brown-style layout and its view over the stone village, nestled in the valley. He guessed he'd inherit it all one day. He couldn't imagine his father uprooting himself now. The wrench from Mrs Farthing alone would be too much.

'Chocolate ice cream,' she was now announcing over the top of an ornate silver tray which shook in her hands, making everything tinkle. 'I know you like chocolate flavour best, Dylan.'

When he was twelve, yes. Dylan was stuffed, but what could he do? 'Yum-mie,' he said with a heavy heart. He might be able to slip some to the dog, who seemed to have developed something of an attachment to him and had already helped him out with his soup and half a Coronation Chicken baguette. If only he hadn't stopped for that burger en route. Mrs Farthing retreated and Dylan prayed she wasn't off to prepare a fourth course. He put his bowl of chocolate ice-cream balls with fanned wafers on the ground, and Fluffsky, with some initial trepidation, wolfed the lot.

By five o'clock, after a walk around the grounds in blazing sunshine with a boisterous dog, Dylan and Alex had settled themselves into the recording studio for a bit of a session. It would be a good two hours before Mrs F sent oceans more food their way.

'Fliss?' said the phone message. 'It's Richard. Where on earth did you go? And why? Your mobile isn't switched on. Please let me know you're all right.'

Ha!

She topped up her glass.

Men! Jesus. So obvious. So careless. So couldn't-give-a-fuck.

He rang again. 'Fliss, please. I know I was a bit late and well, not quite prepared for you. Oh dear ... I can explain. Please, please call me.'

It was after his third call – this time he didn't leave a message – that she rang him back. With a glass and a half of Chardonnay inside her, she felt tanked up enough to speak her mind.

'Richard, you were so obviously wearing yesterday's clothes.'

'That's because I stayed overnight at my aunt's house. In Epsom. I was just too exhausted to get home last night. Then I had to go straight to this prospective client this morning.'

His aunt's house? Pathetic. 'You were at the theatre last night.'

'Yes. *Lady Windermere*. Aunt June loves Oscar Wilde.'

Oh *honestly*, thought Fliss. She took another fortifying gulp of wine. This really was too limp of him.

'You reeked of perfume!' she blasted.

'Ah, yes. Aunt June does tend to pile it on. Chanel No. 5. I have to carry her a lot, you see. In and out of taxis. She's in a wheelchair.'

Fliss was beginning to come over a bit strange. 'You said you needed a shower?' she said, rather less forcefully.

'Aunt June's bathroom is all set up for a dis-abled person. Hard to use, so I thought I'd grab one at home before you arrived. But then this

134

client asked a million questions about what I might be able to do for her garden, and I stupidly didn't have your mobile number in my mobile, and well ... I can see how it must have looked.'

Fliss breathed out slowly. 'Oh Richard, I'm sorry. I just thought–'

'I know, I know. Anyway, what shall we do? I was so looking forward to the weekend. You don't want to get in your car and come back, I suppose?'

'Can't. I'm a bit drunk.'

'But it's only twenty past five.' He chuckled. Deliciously. 'Is this something you make a habit of?'

'Only when I'm dealing with love rats.'

'Hmm, tell you what. Why don't you sober up and I'll be with you in, oh ... three hours?'

'I look like the fag end of a jumble sale.'

'I don't care.'

She put the phone down and sank into the armchair. What a day it had been. And such a long one. She'd woken at dawn all buzzy with excitement. Then those hours and hours of practically continuous driving, there and back. All that loathing and utter disappointment she'd felt on the way home. Bloody hell, she was knackered, not to say feeling foolish. But Richard was on his way, which was great – heart-warming, in fact. She closed her eyes and pictured him driving round the M25, up the M11, then thought maybe she should tidy up a bit. Change the sheets at least and ... what was that noise? *Bang, clonk, patter patter patter...* It was coming from next door. But surely Dylan was away? There was no van

135

outside. How odd. Was she hearing ghosts? She opened one eye, squinted at the more than half-empty wine bottle on the coffee-table and shook her head. Had she really told Richard Honeyman she looked like a jumble sale?

'Marie!' exclaimed Alex.

'Dylan?' said Marie.

'Mum?' said Dylan.

There was all-round surprise and delight when Marie turned up on the doorstep of The Manor just before eight. She'd had no idea Dylan would be there. 'Goodness,' she said, 'when was the last time the three of us were together? And who's *this?*'

'Fluffsky,' said Dylan. 'Dad's new dog. Only he's convinced I'm his long-lost Siamese twin.'

'Oh, he's adorable. Aren't you, Fluffsky?' A rather silly name, she thought.

Alex came over and put one of his strong arms around her shoulders, drawing her to him. 'Are you hungry?' he asked before kissing her brow. 'We're about to eat.'

She stared up into his face and rubbed her nose on his slightly rough chin. How solid and reassuring he was – something that came with age, perhaps. Gavin was tall and nicely covered and beautifully toned, but leaning on him wasn't something you'd risk. 'Famished,' she told Alex.

'Er... ex*cuse* me?' said Dylan, his mouth hanging open.

Marie and Alex clung to one another and laughed. 'Ah yes,' said Alex. 'Something you should know perhaps, Dylan.'

Over by the dining-room door Mrs Farthing cleared her throat loudly. 'Dinner's ready,' she announced. 'Only I'm afraid there won't be enough for three.'

Marie clenched her teeth and smiled brightly.

'Oh, that's all right,' said Dylan. 'I'm still full from that delicious lunch. Mum can have mine. And she loves jam roly-poly, don't you, Mum?'

'It's my absolute favourite,' Marie shouted across to the little demon. 'How splendid.'

They made their way into the dining room where, of course, there was plenty of food. Mrs Farthing fetched another plate and more cutlery, then departed with a, 'Goodnight, Mr Child. Goodnight, Dylan.'

This was great, but also a little weird: sitting around one end of his huge dining table with his ex-wife and his son, chatting away about the past. Well, mostly it was Marie and Dylan talking about it.

'Who was Tom?' Alex had to eventually ask Dylan. His name was coming up a lot.

'Only my best friend for years and years.'

'Oh yes, that's right.' Had he ever seen Dylan with a friend?

'Hospital?' he enquired, some time later.

'You know, when I had my appendix out.'

He nodded. 'Remind me again of how old you were?'

'Seven.'

Alex caught Marie smirking. 'That's right,' he said. 'I was on tour, I believe.'

'Actually,' said Marie, and Alex braced himself,

137

'you were in a hotel a couple of miles from the hospital, but after I rang you, you went back to sleep for three days.'

'Ah.' He looked at his son and said, 'Sorry.'

Dylan shrugged as though he'd heard the story a million times. He even managed a chuckle, and Marie joined in. Had the poor boy been fed a diet of your-father's-negligence tales, over the years?

'It became something of a joke,' Marie explained. '*You* became a joke, Alex. It was the best way of dealing with it.'

Alex suddenly couldn't eat any more. He put down his spoon and thought back to his own absentee father, who was always off on some concert tour himself, or shut away in the 'music room' endlessly practising his pieces. Even when he'd made himself available, there was an indifference and coldness that had cut to young Alex's core.

He felt a hand on his shoulder. 'It's all right, Dad,' Dylan was saying, and Alex lifted his head from his hands. 'Water under the bridge and all that.'

'Sorry,' said Alex desolately. What a wonderful young man Marie had produced. And what a waste of space he, Alex, had been. His only saving grace was that, somehow, he'd managed to amass a fortune – there for anyone who wanted to dip into it.

'Let's have a game of tennis before it gets dark,' suggested Marie, pushing her half-eaten pudding aside and leaping to her feet. 'Son versus parents?' She laughed as she bounced over to the door. 'Or should that be youth versus wisdom?'

138

Alex heaved himself and his weighty heart up off his chair, feeling far from wise, and also rather too full to be hurling himself around a tennis court. But he reminded himself he was New Alex, so with mind over body he set off to let his neglected – but remarkably unscarred – son give him a good thrashing.

ELEVEN

First she heard the clomp, clomp, clomp of sturdy heels through the open bedroom window. Then came the, 'Hi-*ya!* Anyone home?' and a hefty couple of knocks.

Fliss froze for a few seconds, then unhooked her body from Richard's and looked at the radio/alarm. 11.24. She couldn't believe how late they'd slept.

'I'm having this weird dream,' murmured Richard, eyes still closed. 'That our friend Hazel's walking up your path and battering at your door.'

'Fliss?' sang Hazel. 'Are you there? I've been visiting Jenny in Cromer and thought I'd drop in. Is your phone switched off? I did try it several times. Perhaps it's faulty. Oh. Maybe you're round the back? I must say, the front garden's looking lovely.'

'Shit,' said Fliss. Why were the gods conspiring to ruin her weekend? She grabbed her cotton dressing-gown and stuck her arms in it. 'Sorry about this. I'll try and head her off. Say I've got flu or something.' She stood and tied the belt, looked in the wardrobe mirror and fluffed up her hair.

'Fliss?' they heard again. This time it was accompanied by creaks on the stairs. 'Where are you? Ellie? Is everyone OK?'

Hell, she'd forgotten to lock up last night. All

the excitement of Richard turning up. Before Fliss had time to shout, 'Don't come in!' Hazel had pushed the bedroom door open and stuck her florid face around it.

'Oh,' She said. 'Oh, blimey. Sorry. Oh dear, trust me! Look, I'll just go down and put the kettle on, shall I? Um, anyone for tea?'

'Please,' yawned Richard, the duvet mid-navel. 'Milk, no sugar, thanks.'

The three of them went for Sunday lunch at The Fox. It seemed like the easiest thing to do in the circumstances, there being very little in the way of food in the house. But as the meal went on, and the whole 'fancy you two getting together and it's all down to me,' thing had been exhausted, Hazel grew unexpectedly quiet and gloomy.

'You all right?' Fliss asked her when Richard went to the bar.

'Not really.'

Fliss waited for her to expand but she didn't. 'What's the matter?'

'Me. That's what's the matter.'

'What do you mean?'

'I know I'm annoying and overbearing—'

'No, you're not.'

'—but I just don't seem to be able to help it these days. I didn't used to be like this, did I, Fliss? You know, when I was a girl?'

'You were ... ebullient. Still are. Now finish your apple pie and don't be silly.'

Hazel shook her head. 'My kids find me an embarrassment, I know they do. My youngest says she's running away from home if I play my

141

old records one more time when her friends are round.'

'You don't sing along, do you?'

'Well, yes, sometimes. But only quietly.'

Could Hazel do anything quietly? 'I'm sure your children love you to bits.'

'Greg's been seeing a girl from uni, Karen, for eighteen months now and he won't bring her home.'

'Oh, they're all like that. It was *ages* before I got to meet Ellie's boyfriend, Rob.'

Well, two weeks, but it had felt like ages.

'Thing is,' whispered Hazel, 'I'm always happier when there's a man in my life. Much calmer. Must be the sex.'

'Right.' Why was Richard taking so long? Once he returned they could get back to the neutral subjects they'd been on before: public transport, soft furnishings. 'Anyway, you're great fun, Hazel. Everyone thinks so.'

'Oh, you're just saying that.'

'Here we are,' sang Richard, putting three soft drinks down on the table and sliding Fliss her change. He'd managed to come out without cash or credit cards. 'Just popping to the gents,' he said.

'Can't you wait?' Fliss asked nicely. *Please*, she mouthed.

'Um, yeah. I suppose so.' He sat down and handed round the glasses.

'But you know,' said Fliss, not quite believing how her weekend had turned out, 'I've always found you can't beat Debenhams for good-value bedding. Although–'

'I don't suppose you know any available men?' Hazel was suddenly asking Richard. She gave a weak little laugh. 'Looking for an ebullient woman?'

'Hhm, let me think.' He sipped at his juice and looked pensive. 'There's Dunstan. About our age. Lives with his mother and keeps reptiles. Wears bicycle clips, even when he's not cycling.'

'No thanks.'

'Probably to stop the snakes going up his trousers,' said Fliss.

'I hadn't thought of that.'

'Any others?' asked Hazel.

Richard furrowed his brow. 'I suppose you'd want heterosexual?'

'Please.'

'Actually...'

'Yes?' demanded Hazel.

'There is Hal.'

'Oh?' Her face lit up and she wiggled in her seat. 'Tell me more.'

'Can I go to the toilet first?'

Ellie waved at her father pulling away and wondered whose cars they were, parked by their gate. When she got to the house the phone was ringing and she ran for it.

'Hello?'

'Hello, Ellie.'

'Oh hi, Dylan.' Her tummy did a flip. 'How are you? Are you having a nice time at your dad's?'

'Yeah, I am actually. So I'm going to stay on a while. Just a couple more days. Mum's here too and we're doing a bit of recording.'

'Are you?' She had a sudden vision of Dylan moving in with his father and tried not to panic. 'Must be fun.'

'Yes, it is. And such a fantastic spot. It's peaceful, the scenery's magical. You should see it.'

'Oh.' Ellie wasn't sure what to say. Did he mean he'd *like* her to see it? It wasn't what you'd call an invitation, though.

'I'll bring some photos to show you.'

'Great.'

'Anyway, I take it everything's OK with the house? No burglars or vandals?'

She thought she wouldn't bother him with the Baz business. She'd maybe got it all wrong anyway, and didn't want to sound like she was grassing on the guy. 'I wasn't here last night and neither was Mum, but if you want I could like pop round and check?'

'Would you? And if you could put out the rubbish too? Oh, and Natalia's plant could do with a water. I forgot to do that before I left. It's the big umbrella plant in the front window.'

'Natalia's, did you say?'

'Mm, she's going to come and pick it up soon. Before it chokes on all the building dust, hopefully. She'd definitely never speak to me again if that happened.'

'No?'

'Absolutely loves that plant.'

'OK, I'll take care of it.' Too right she would.

'Thanks, Ellie,' he said almost tenderly. 'I'll make it up to you when I get back. Treat you to dinner or something.'

'Yeah?'

'We'll go somewhere other than The Fox for a change.'

Had the sight of her in those walking boots done something for him? A lovely warm feeling spread through her. 'That'd be nice.'

'It's a date then,' he said. 'Whenever your mum's got a free evening, yeah?'

Five minutes later she was searching Dylan's kitchen for something toxic that didn't smell. She didn't want the thing dying immediately, just sort of giving up the ghost slowly, over like a week or so. Washing-up liquid? That might do it. She squeezed some into a big glass jug, counting to ten as she did so. Then she topped up with water, gave the whole thing a shake and went into the living room. It was quite a plant. Almost reaching the ceiling. But not for much longer, she thought while she watered it. The soil ended up covered in bubbles, but she guessed they'd soon disappear.

After rinsing out the jug, she scooped up a dustpan full of sawdust from a corner of the kitchen and took it to the living room, where she flung it all at the plant, just so Dylan would put the deterioration down to atmospheric conditions. That was when, through the dusty haze, she saw her mum and Hazel and a strange man walking up their garden path.

'Oops, forgot to lock up again,' she heard, her mother say in what Ellie could tell was a fake-cheerful way. 'Would you like a cup of coffee for the road, Hazel?'

Excellent tune, thought Dylan. Shame about the cheesy hook. They were listening to their fourth recording of the song, all three of them on acoustic guitars – his father brilliantly, of course – Dylan sometimes switching to keyboard, and all three singing the chorus.

'How I long to be wed to my angel in red...'

While Dylan squirmed – hardcore gangsta rap it wasn't – his mother was practically swooning. Afterwards, she disappeared upstairs and came back unrolling a small painting.

'I copied the original,' she told them.

'Oh Marie,' sighed Alex. 'You remembered.'

'Do you like it?' she asked him. 'I did it for you. Finished it last week.'

'It's brilliant. I love it. Come here.'

Dylan couldn't help thinking he was missing some information, but while his parents held hands and chatted in the corner, he strummed on his guitar and tried out one or two things. Fluffsky was by his side, listening with his head cocked. What a heartwarming scene they all made.

'How about this?' he asked after a while.

Alex and Marie turned their attention to Dylan and he sang, 'What's in your head, my angel in red...' It was hardly revolutionary, but his suggestion was greeted with silence. 'It's just a bit less, you know – sentimental?'

His parents looked at each other, raised their eyebrows and, to Dylan's relief, agreed.

'Cool.'

They recorded the song again with the new lyrics, then played it back.

146

'Excellent,' said Dylan. He swivelled round to the mixing desk. 'Now, I thought if we added a bit of bass...'

'Yes, why not?' said Alex.

His mother smiled. 'Good idea.'

This was great. Love had made them putty in his hands.

By four o'clock, when Mrs Farthing insisted they stop for tea and scones on the terrace, they all agreed they'd probably laid down the best version of 'Angel in Red' they were going to get. The three of them managed to harmonise fantastically, plus Alex had come up with some of his amazing twiddly guitar bits to accompany Marie's rhythm. Finally, Dylan had brought in one or two sampled drum loops to stop them sounding too Peter, Paul and Mary.

'You know,' said a cheerful Alex, putting his guitar to one side and flexing his fingers, 'I think we might be on to something here. If we're not careful we'll have to start planning a tour. Think up a name for our new band.'

'Hey, what about my house?' asked Dylan.

'My House,' said Marie, tapping at her mouth with a finger. 'Not terribly memorable. We need something sharper, I'd say. Something eye-catching for the posters.'

'And the CDs,' chipped in Alex.

'No,' said Dylan. 'I meant, what about my house? It's pretty time-consuming, you know. There's still the roof to get on the extension, and it all has to be done properly, otherwise the Planning Department makes you re-do it.'

His parents looked bewildered. Astonished

even. 'How could our son be thinking of Building Regs at the birth of something so creatively exciting?' they seemed to be saying with their crinkled brows.

'Can't you leave that to Gaz?' asked Marie.

'Baz. I'm not sure I'd want to.'

'He told me he'd been in the business since he left school at sixteen. I expect it's child's play for him now.'

'Mm, I just think he might turn into a bit of a bodger if I took my eye off him for too long. Do you know what I mean?'

She laughed. 'He certainly takes a lot of chocolate breaks when you're not there.'

'I can imagine.'

'Ha!' said Alex, clapping his hands then kissing the top of Marie's head as they all trooped out of the studio. 'That's it, you clever girl.'

'What?' she asked.

'Child's play.'

'Sorry?'

'Our name. Child's Play. The three Childs playing together. Get it?'

'Oh, yes! You're right. That *was* very clever of me.'

'Perhaps we should make it one word,' said Alex. 'Childsplay.' He turned to Dylan. 'What do you think?'

Dylan decided to humour his father. He nodded, said, 'Yep, good,' and wondered what Coldplay would have to say.

With Mrs Farthing's high tea over, they were considering going back into the studio when

Fluffsky came trotting out to the terrace with the lead in his mouth. He dropped it in Dylan's lap.

'Oh dear,' said Alex. 'You're lumbered now. He can be very insistent once he decides on a walk.'

'But surely he can just charge around this huge garden to his heart's content?' asked Marie.

'He has to stay in this area,' said Alex, pointing at a wooden picket fence just beyond the terrace. 'Till all the holes are patched up. Or a new wall built. Once he gets the scent of rabbit, he's off, you see. Running across roads, over farmland.'

The dog was looking Dylan in the eye, cocking his head this way, then that. 'Maybe later,' Dylan told him.

Fluffsky took the lead in his mouth and re-plonked it in Dylan's lap. Everyone laughed and Alex said, 'See what I mean? He can keep this up for hours. You may as well just get it over with.'

'Go on,' said his mother. 'The exercise will do you good.'

Ah, thought Dylan, they wanted him gone for a while. He attached the lead to Fluffsky's collar and set off on a circuit of the Child estate. The day was turning sultry, and as he walked alone through the beautiful gardens, he came over quite emotional, miserable almost. In this perfect setting, on such a gorgeous evening, he would have forgiven Natalia everything just to have her here. Well, almost everything. Not Mark and Matt, the twins. Most definitely not. OK she loved to experiment, and they'd meant nothing to her she said, but surely a threesome of that nature was incest of a sort. Jesus, what a woman.

He let Fluffsky off his lead for a while and they

149

played fetch with a stick. Actually, it was quite fun having a dog. It had been fun having a girlfriend, too, in a hellish sort of way. Never a dull moment with Natalia, that was for sure. The problem was, how could he now settle for a nice ordinary woman who spent her weekends visiting National Trust sites or something. If only Natalia hadn't felt the need to tell him everything – 'Dylan, you know I'd love to screw your dad' – they might have still been together.

'Is she always that emotional?' asked Richard, after Ellie had flown from the room in tears because, at the end of Trivial Pursuit, she'd only got one segment.

'I'm just hopeless at these stupid games,' she'd sobbed on her way out.

Fliss sighed. 'Not usually. But I think she's tense about her A-level results and...' she lowered her voice, 'she's got a bit of a thing about the boy next door, but he doesn't seem interested.'

'Ah.' Richard was helping her pack the game away. 'Well, I can remember how that felt.'

'Oh yes?' She still wasn't sure she believed he'd been sweet on her at school.

'You know, one time I actually plucked up the courage to speak to you.'

Fliss raised her eyebrows. 'Do you mean the, "Is Watkins in his office?" time?'

'You re*mem*ber?'

'Of course.'

'That's incredible. So you must also remember snubbing me? Just walking off without answering? Leaving me standing there feeling like the lowest form of life. I didn't even have any reason to see Mr Watkins.'

'Oh dear.' Fliss tried to convince him she'd been in shock.

'Really? God, the pain and humiliation stayed with me for ages.'

'Oh, *I'm* sure. You were going out with that trollop from the convent before I knew it.'

'Only because you started seeing Steve the folk freak.'

She shook her head. 'Oh my, it's all so tricky at that age, isn't it?' She leaned back in the kitchen chair and her eyes drifted upwards. 'Perhaps I should go and see if she's all right.'

Richard looked at the cuckoo clock. 'And maybe I should head home. Come and see me next weekend?'

She nodded. How could she not? In fact, she wanted to go back with him now and help him lay patios for the rest of her life. How odd and unexpected all this had been. They just seemed to click, which was a weird thing to happen to someone as reclusive as herself. But somehow, in spite of the shambolic weekend – or perhaps even because of it – Fliss felt completely relaxed with him. She could look frighteningly knackered, as she had last night when he arrived, or she could have uninvited and rather demanding visitors roll up or a daughter having a strop, and it didn't seem to faze him. She could even fall out of bed in the night without him going off her. And what's more he was a dream to look at, as cuddly as a puppy and, like her, enjoyed playing board games. 'Love to,' she told him.

151

He stood up and shoved first his arms and then his head into a cotton jumper, the way men do but women don't. 'And you never know, you might even make it into the house this time.'

'If anyone's home, that is.' She reached for the ringing phone. 'Hello?'

'It's me,' said Ellie.

'Hi. Are you all right now? I was about to come up and—'

'Yeah, yeah, I'm fine. Can you just say sorry to Richard from me?'

'Why don't you say it yourself? Hang on, Ellie.' She handed Richard the phone. 'She's on her mobile.'

'Hello,' he said. 'Oh, that's OK. Don't worry about it. Listen, I'm just about to leave, so I'll see you again soon, I hope, yeah? Hey, and don't fret about your A-level results, will you. I did really badly in mine and had to resit them. But if I'd passed the first time, I would have studied the wrong subject altogether at college and had a miserable life as a geography teacher... Oh, I just got distracted by this girl I had an enormous crush on who barely knew I existed. Sorry?... Mm, yeah, we did get together.' He slipped an arm back round Fliss's waist. 'Took a while though.'

After waving him off, Fliss surveyed her garden in the fading light. Richard had given her one or two tips about her borders: what to fill the gaps with, what to move around because that will grower higher than that, or those colours will look better together. Of course, he'd be right. He seemed to have great tastes in everything. Try as

152

she might, Fliss couldn't think of a single thing she didn't like about Richard. Was it possible for a person to have no faults at all?

TWELVE

It was a typical summer's day – overcast, threatening to rain and cool enough for a coat – as Dylan and Alex crossed county after county on their way to Norfolk.

'It's Raining in My Heart,' said Alex.

'Summertime.'

'In the Summertime.'

'Springtime for Hitler.'

They were thinking up season and weather songs. It whiled away the time and seemed to keep Chuffsky, who just liked the sound of human voices, happy in the back of the van.

'Ain't No Sunshine When She's Gone,' said Alex, his thoughts instantly turning to Marie. She'd returned to London that morning, leaving him strangely bereft, even though they'd since spoken twice on their mobiles.

'Raindrops Keep Falling on My Head.'

'Winter Wonderland,' said Alex, yawning loudly.

'Shall we stop for coffee when we get to Cambridge?' asked Dylan.

Alex shook his head. 'Never heard of it.'

It was when they finally slotted into a Norwich parking space that Alex started to think about the needles. Would they be long? Would Fliss leave them in and twiddle them? He'd seen elderly oriental practitioners doing that on TV. Great long things. He shuddered and looked at his watch. Twenty minutes till his appointment. Enough time to grab a snack. He suggested it to Dylan and they went into the first sandwich bar they came to, where a girl's voice called out a surprised, 'Dylan?' from across the room.

'Ellie. Hi,' said Dylan. 'I didn't know this was where you worked. How are you?'

'Fine.'

'How's my house?'

'Oh, OK. Been watering the plant for you.' She was holding a tray of filled rolls, baguettes and paninis and was heading for the counter.

'This is a coincidence,' said Alex. 'I'm just off to see your mother for a spot of torture. Got an appointment.'

'Yeah? How funny.' She lifted the tray. 'Hang on, let me put these out.'

A large muscular woman behind the counter was giving both Alex and Dylan odd looks. When she'd finished serving she said, 'Alex Child, isn't it?'

'Yes.'

'I'm a big fan,' she said.

Alex laughed. 'Yes, I can see that.' He heard Dylan groan beside him. 'I mean...'

The woman turned to Ellie. 'And this is *the* Dylan, is it?'

Ellie nodded and looked a bit worried. 'This is Janet,' she told Alex and Dylan. 'The boss.' She laughed nervously.

'Right,' said Janet, removing her apron. She told Ellie to take over at the counter and then

155

crooked a finger at Dylan. 'I'd like a word with you, if you don't mind. This way.'

'Sorry?' he asked.

'Come.'

As she was such a big woman, Alex could perfectly well understand why his son meekly followed her through to the back, turning and shrugging his shoulders then frowning at Ellie, who suddenly had the look of someone witnessing a car crash. Her eyes were bulging, her mouth contorted, and before Alex had even perused the sandwich selection, she was heading for the street saying, 'Oh, *God!*'

Alex followed, and despite his age and the stiff back from the journey, managed to catch up with her several shops along. 'Ellie, stop!' he said, grabbing her arm as gently as he could whilst breathing ridiculously heavily for such a short sprint. Perhaps he should take the dog for longer walks. 'Please.'

The poor girl was crying and her hands flew up to her face. 'What's she saying to him? What's she *say*ing?'

'Can't help you there, Ellie. I haven't a clue what's going on. Look, maybe we should go back, eh? There's no one manning the counter, for a start. Come on, you don't want to lose your job, do you?'

'Oh, I don't care. The conditions are crap, they pay minimum wage and you have to buy your own sandwiches. Can you believe that? Oh, *shit*,' she said, as though suddenly remembering what was going on. 'I'll never be able to face Dylan again. Never.'

'Why?' asked Alex, watching her eyes produce tear after tear, like two tranquil but relentless water features.

'You all right, dear?' asked a woman trailing a bag on wheels. 'Is this man bothering you?'

Ellie shook her head. 'No, he's not.'

Alex scratched his chin. Should he go and rescue Dylan? But what about his appointment? He took his wallet out and looked at the vouchers. The address was on them. 'Come on,' he said. 'Let's take you to your mum.'

They found a taxi and within ten minutes the girl was being comforted in the waiting room of what appeared to be a very busy practice indeed.

'Five minutes,' Fliss mouthed at Alex, holding five fingers up to him then leading her daughter through a door with her name on it.

Alex nodded, found a seat and got out his phone to call Dylan, before remembering his son was one of the six people in Britain who didn't own a mobile. He put it away again, picked up a *Healthy Living* and tried not to worry about Chuffsky in the back of the van; all alone and bewildered and wondering where the BLT he'd been promised had got to.

'This just isn't like you,' Fliss was telling Ellie. 'You've always been so cheerful. So resilient. A bit of a toughie, even. When your dad and I split up, you were only upset for a day, then you decided it was great having two homes. Being able to say, "Well, *Dad* lets me..." or "Mum says *she'll* get me one if you're too stingy to" – that kind of thing.'

Ellie managed a giggle of sorts. 'Yeah, I did that a lot, didn't I?'

Fliss stroked her daughter's hair and took in the puffy eyes and downturned mouth. 'I don't understand what's happened. Is it mostly the results you're worrying about? Mm?'

'A bit,' she sniffed. 'It's just that I *really* like Dylan. Love him even. And now I've cocked everything up big time, 'cos I made out he was like my boyfriend at work. And Janet somehow got to think he treated me badly and oh God, now she's probably beaten him up for it and I want to die.' She sniffed again. 'The only *good* thing that's happened this summer is my spots have gone at last.'

'They have, haven't they, sweetie?'

'Yeah. Ever since I started taking the—'

Fliss leaned back in her seat and tilted her head. 'Taking the what? The pill?'

Ellie nodded. 'It was when I was with Rob, yeah? Towards the end. We got fed up with using ... you know, and he said it'd be like easier if I was on the pill, so, well... And then I was going to stop only the spots cleared up and I'd read in a magazine that can happen.'

Fliss's medical mind kicked in. Oestrogen sensitivity. She asked what the brand name was but Ellie couldn't remember. She'd got them from Family Planning, she said. Fliss was shocked at the thought of her little girl going to Family Planning, but managed to stay matter-of-fact. 'It might be an idea to stop taking it for a while,' she said, and told her that some women experience mood swings if a particular one doesn't suit them. She almost added, 'It's not as though you're in a relationship now,' but stopped herself in time. 'See if the depression lifts?'

'OK,' said Ellie. She wiped her cheeks with her arm and managed a weak laugh. 'You're the doctor. I've just finished a pack, so I just won't take any more, yeah?'

'No, don't. Then, hopefully, you'll be back to the old Ellie in a week's time. Look, I'd better see Alex now. He's got an appointment. You could go in one of the empty consulting rooms and have a bit of a rest if you like?'

'May as well. I can't go back to work and I can't face home.'

'I'll collect your things from the café later,' said Fliss. 'And maybe have a little chat with Dylan. Let him know you've been under a bit of a strain recently.'

'Don't tell him about the pill thing, will you? He'll think I was taking it, you know, hoping him and me might…'

'And you weren't?' Fliss smiled and winked. 'Maybe when Mum was away for a weekend?'

Ellie jumped up. 'No! Absolutely *not*. God, you must think I'm such a slag.'

'OK, OK, Ellie,' urged Fliss. 'Keep your voice down.'

What had *that* been about? wondered Dylan as he emerged from the sandwich bar, dazed.

'I wonder if you appreciate,' the woman – Janet? – had begun, 'just how important it is for my staff to have a cheery disposition. A welcoming and interested smile for customers. A kind word and a bit of a bounce to their step.'

Had she mistaken him for a job applicant? 'Yes, I'm sure, but–'

'I've had to keep Ellie out in the kitchen for the past few weeks, with her sour face and that pout and those red eyes. She wasn't like this when she first started here. Not at all. I don't suppose you've noticed this, Dylan, being a man, but she's *very* unhappy about things.'

No, not a job applicant, but Ellie's therapist. 'Actually–'

'I think a bit more sensitivity and a spot of TLC from you wouldn't go amiss.'

'Oh?' he said. He began to wonder if Norfolk had its very own 'Neighbours' Code of Practice' that no one had told him about. 'Right. Well, I know she's been worried about her results.'

'Among other things, Dylan.' The woman's eyes narrowed. 'I mean, I don't know the ins and outs of it all, and don't particularly want to. But talk to her. Reassure her. You're the only one who can pull her out of this. Please try.' She stood up and put her apron back on. She looked like a woman who worked out a lot and might enjoy a few jars on a Friday night. 'For my sake as much as for yours and hers.'

Dylan didn't fully understand how he'd benefit, but he too stood up and said, 'I'll do my best.'

'That's my boy,' she said and whacked him playfully but painfully on the arm before leading him back along a narrow corridor. 'You know,' she added over her shoulder, 'you've been a very pleasant surprise.'

'Is that so?' Dylan forced a laugh. The woman

was obviously a few bricks short of a wall.

Out in the street now he pondered on the surreal encounter, but only briefly. There was lunch still to get, and perhaps more importantly, a father to find. He went to a payphone, called directory enquiries, and then got through to a woman who told him Mr Child had just gone into a treatment room. With an hour or so to kill, he bought two burgers and fries and took them back to the van where he was greeted like he'd never been greeted in his life.

At five-thirty, Marie was in her odorous corner shop selecting only very essential items, tutting at the prices then dropping them in the grubby plastic basket on her arm. Underfoot, the grey and one-time-white tiles were chipped and uneven. Next to her were videos, from *Barely Legal* and *Just Eighteen* on the top shelf, down to *Hot Wives Gagging for It* right in front of her. To Marie, the gagging wives looked barely legal themselves. She'd hoped for something like *The House of Mirth* to pass the evening with but ended up sighing disappointedly, one eye on the late-teens boy beside her slotting a video, and then another one, inside his jacket. A CCTV camera by the ceiling seemed to be pointing directly at him, but even if it wasn't a fake, who was watching? Some sort of fracas was going on at the counter. A diversion, no doubt. The boy beside her was twice her height and width and she decided against confronting him. Besides, she thought, removing this porn from sight was quite public-spirited of him.

161

'I've heard that one's good,' she said, pointing to *Booby Babes*.

'Yeah?' said the kid. He reached across for it. 'Cheers.'

Marie picked up a magazine, paid for her things and went out into the dull and quite chilly street, where she took a deep breath of fresh air – well, air that wasn't heavy with old greens – and made her way home, past front gardens that were either beautifully groomed or horribly neglected. She turned into her own neat-as-a-pin one – dustbin tucked tidily under a trimmed hedge, tiny lawn newly mown – and wondered why she bothered when next door's was adorned with pizza boxes and a double mattress.

She had a late lunch, took five minutes to get through the magazine, tried a programme on Egyptian tombs then rang her cousin in Wimbledon. 'Are you in this evening?' she asked. A silly question. With four girls under fifteen, Kathleen and Mike were always in.

'Oh Marie, you're so unworldly sometimes,' said Kathleen. Marie had been telling her about the shoplifter. 'They'll most likely copy the videos and sell them to twelve year olds.'

'Oh.' Marie accepted a glass of red wine. 'How stupid of me.'

Kathleen continued clearing away the things from a dinner Marie had deliberately avoided. She'd wanted a heart-to-heart, rather than an evening with all the O'Malleys, as lovely as they were. Mike was upstairs reading a bedtime story and, conveniently, had 'something important to

162

get on with' afterwards. He was a barrister. They'd moved to London from Dublin soon after marrying, and although they'd both retained an Irish brogue, their privately educated girls all spoke like Jenny Agutter in *The Railway Children*. Two evenings a week, Kathleen taught a very soft and lilting form of German to adults, while the school runs took up her days.

'So what's the problem?' asked Kathleen, cutting to the chase.

'I think I'm falling in love with Alex all over again.'

Kathleen stopped in her tracks. 'Heck,' she said, 'that was the last thing I was expecting you to come up with. *Alex?* Surely you remember all those years he rolled up only once every couple of months? That he was always high on something? That he missed most of Dylan's birthdays?'

'Yes, but he's different now. Honestly. So settled in his beautiful Cotswold home. Got himself a dog. And he and Dylan have become very close.'

'Isn't Alex seeing someone?'

'Annabel? No. All over. In fact, he's as keen on me as I am on him. I'm pretty sure he wants me to move in with him.'

'Golly.' Kathleen closed the dishwasher door and pressed a button. 'But that's great, isn't it? Why the long face?'

'Well, it may sound a minor thing, but he's got this housekeeper who runs his life and thinks I'm Lucrezia Borgia reincarnated. She takes every opportunity to undermine me. You know me, Kath, I'm not easily intimidated, but this woman

163

scares me.'

'Couldn't he "let her go", as they say?'

'I don't think he wants to. He seems very fond of her and he's come to rely on her so much. You know, I walked into a room the other day and found her dunking a digestive in his coffee then handing it to him. Apparently, he can never quite get the timing right.'

'Jesus,' laughed Kathleen. She sat at the chaotic kitchen table and pulled a band off her almost permanent pony tail, freeing her curly red hair. Marie and Kathleen's mothers had married men of very different colouring. 'You know,' she said, 'I'd *love* to have someone like that in my life.'

'I suppose he thinks if he let her go and things didn't work out between us, she wouldn't come back. Then he'd have to find out where the washing machine was and all sorts.'

The two youngest children appeared at the door, urchin-like and adorable in their nighties, asking very politely for a drink of water. Although the household itself was a wild, uncontrolled collection of belongings, knee-deep in places, disorderly behaviour had never been tolerated by Mummy and Daddy O'Malley. Even their fifteen year old was pleasant.

'Thank you,' both little girls said after Kathleen poured them glasses of bottled water. 'Night night, Auntie Marie.'

'Night night, you two,' Marie replied. She used to find this all rather nauseating, especially when Dylan was going through his early-teens difficult stage, but now she rather appreciated the family's civility and put it down to their having

164

kept up Catholicism.

'You know what you should do?' said Kathleen.

'What?'

'Play this woman ... what's she called?'

'Mrs Farthing.'

'No first name?'

'I'm not sure she was ever given one.'

'Anyway, just play Mrs Farthing at her own game until she gives in. Easy.'

Marie curled a lip. 'You mean cut up his meat and iron his underpants?'

'Whatever. Just be quick off the mark. How old is she?'

'I don't know. Mid- to late-seventies?'

'Good grief. Desperate to retire then, surely?' She leaned towards Marie and whispered, 'So tell me ... what's the sex like these days?'

'Mrs Farthing's?'

'Ho ho.'

Marie reached across for the wine bottle. 'May I?' she asked.

'Of course.'

'Thanks.'

'Well?' asked Kathleen, who tended towards an unhealthy interest in other people's bedroom lives.

'Rather dreamy, actually,' said Marie. Which wasn't exactly a lie. She often dreamed of making proper love with Alex.

Ellie was spending the evening in her room, plugged into her Walkman, just in case Dylan started singing. Her mum had given her some herbal pills that had made her a bit woozy, even though Ellie didn't believe they'd do anything for her. Two minutes ago she'd sent a message to Rob saying she missed him – how much easier it was to write something like that in a text – and now her tiny phone was telling her he'd replied.

Did she want to go out on the sixteenth when they got their results? he wrote in text-ese. To drown their sorrows, three exclamation marks.

It was the first time in weeks they'd had any contact and Ellie suddenly felt very safe and all warm and gooey inside just hearing from him. Or was that the passiflora tablets?

Who cared. *Cool* she wrote back.

Downstairs, Fliss was talking to Richard on the phone. They'd got on to former spouses, something they'd avoided up till then. He'd been telling her all about Carolyn's control problems. How she'd disapproved of his being a self-employed gardener when he had a degree in Business Studies. He'd tried to get across that he *was* sort of using his useless, third-rate degree and that one day he'd have a lucrative concern going, but she'd still harangued him incessantly.

'And is it?' asked Fliss.

'What?'

'Lucrative.'

'Very. But she didn't hang around long enough to see that. Married a top cosmetic surgeon.'

'Gosh. So, not only monied now but she'll have lifelong youth?'

'Mm. Last time I saw Carolyn, I don't think she blinked. Anyway, less of me. What went wrong with you and–'

'Colin. Oh, you know, usual thing. My husband didn't understand me.'

'What's to understand?'

'I'll have you know I'm a very complex person with a myriad of conflicting needs.'

He laughed. 'Have you tried acupuncture?'

In Dylan's cosily lit guest room, *The Alchemist* was telling Alex about the principle of favourability, or beginner's luck. A taste of success that encourages you to fulfil your destiny. Interesting. He'd certainly been blessed with beginner's luck, aged seventeen. Of course, it couldn't happen to everyone. Look at Dylan. Beginner's bad luck when it came to girlfriends.

Alex's eyes felt heavy and his arm began to droop, book still in his hand. He'd taken it easy throughout the evening, as per Fliss's instructions: watching a video while Dylan took Chuffsky on a long walk, drinking only herbal tea and then taking himself off to bed at ten-fifteen. Marie had been right, he hadn't felt a thing. Well, not much. Fliss had spent the first half-hour taking copious notes about his physical and emotional health, past and present, finally asking, 'Is there anything you're particularly concerned about at the moment?'

'Not really,' he'd lied. If only she hadn't been Dylan's neighbour. And with that, the needles came out. And then went in. And that unsettling business with Ellie all of a sudden felt very distant and unreal, and really not worth mentioning to his son. Once Alex knew the treatment wasn't going to hurt, he handed himself over

167

totally to Fliss's practised hands. He was fairly surprised at some of the more intimate places the needles were placed, but well … how very relaxed, almost spacey, he'd felt at the end of it all.

He flicked over a page and wondered what Marie was doing. Five to eleven. Still up, no doubt. Maybe in the bath. He imagined her soaking in a sea of bubbles, little bits of her protruding above the water … soaping one of her lovely tanned legs and…

Alex put the book down, stared at the ceiling for a while, then lifted the duvet, looked underneath and blinked. He reached for his mobile. 'Marie,' he said when she answered. 'You'll never guess what.'

'What?'

'*Well*,' he said, trying to contain his excitement. Then in a very low voice he told her.

'Alex, that's fantastic!' she cried. 'Listen, I've downed half a bottle of wine this evening with Kathleen, but maybe I could get a taxi to Norfolk? I mean, I'd hate you to miss this window.'

Alex laughed. 'It's a kind offer, Marie. But I'm sure it'll keep.'

THIRTEEN

On Saturday morning, a week and a half after Ellie's crisis, Fliss was waiting for Hazel outside Marble Arch tube station. She'd decided to let Ellie have the house for the weekend to celebrate her results with one or two friends; one or two that had rapidly become twenty-odd as word got around. Fliss had asked Dylan to keep an eye on things and wasn't unduly worried. They were all eighteen, after all.

Meanwhile, the plan was to make Hazel over, ready for a foursome in a Knightsbridge restaurant with Hal, an American divorcé in his mid-fifties who liked a woman with a bit of flesh on her bones. He was a friend of Richard's Aunt June, and Richard had been working on his enormous Surrey garden for years now. Hal's home – one of three he owned – was 'something else', apparently.

'Tell Richard *yes*,' Hazel had cried into the phone. 'Yes, definitely. I forgot to ask what he looks like. Oh, I don't care. I think I might go on a crash diet though. My son told me I look like China from the back the other day. They can be so cruel, but maybe I needed telling!'

'Well, don't overdo it.'

'London. Golly. What on earth do I wear? Shall I get my hair done? What do you think?'

'Why not?'

It was then that Fliss had come up with the shopping expedition idea. 'How about a trek down Oxford Street?' she'd suggested, guessing Hazel would be on a limited budget.

And now a woman who looked a lot like Hazel, but blonde, was approaching her with a smile. 'What do you think?' She said to Fliss, patting her restyled, ash-coloured hair.

'Wow.'

'Cost a bloody fortune.'

'But worth it. You look *great.*' Apart from that floral teepee you're wearing, Fliss wanted to add. 'Ready for some serious shopping?'

'You bet.'

Every time Hazel homed in on anything pink, Fliss gave her a sharp prod with an elbow. It was a bit like training a puppy with taps on the nose, and she soon stopped doing it. Fliss had watched enough *What Not to Wear*-type programmes to know that for pear-shaped Hazel, an inverted triangle outfit was called for, preferably in a light or a pastel shade to tone down her high colouring. 'No pinks, A-lines or patterns,' she kept reminding her.

They skipped all shops displaying only Barbie-sized clothes in the window, which basically left them with M&S, where Hazel bounced out of a cubicle for the fifth time in *the* perfect dress. Cream, almost off the shoulder, tapering down to just on the knee. 'Grace Kelly or what?' she said, pirouetting.

'And,' she whispered to Fliss while they queued to pay, 'if it gets chilly this evening, my rose-patterned cardie will go *brilli*antly.'

You couldn't help but like Hal. He was chubby, expansive, endearingly old-fashioned and had the saddest, thinnest comb-over Fliss had ever seen – too black not to be dyed. But what she liked best about him was the way he still said things like 'muffler', 'parking lot' and 'Nottingham', despite having lived in the UK for twenty-three years. His two other homes turned out not to be in New York and LA, as Fliss had imagined, but Devon and Scotland. How a person was able to resist assimilation so well, Fliss would never know. By the end of a three-week US holiday she'd taken with Colin and Ellie some years back, words like 'garbage' and 'sidewalk' were tripping off her tongue as though she'd been born and bred in Little Rock. 'Eat up your tomayto,' she'd told little Ellie in a diner one day, and saw Colin roll his eyes before going back to the *Guardian Weekly.*

Hal was winding up his story. 'And I said, "Son, if you wanna be a bal*lay* dancer, so be it. Ain't no rule says only faggots get to join the Royal Bal*lay.* Go for it, son," I said. "Go for it".'

'Good for you,' said Hazel, who seemed to have warmed to Hal but wasn't showing signs of being flummoxed by him. 'Do you know, I'm not sure I'd be that understanding if my Greg wanted to be a ballet dancer. Not that he would, ha ha. Two left feet and nothing in the least gay about *him.* Oh! I mean, I'm sure your son isn't–'

'How's your trout, Hazel?' jumped in Fliss. 'My chicken's delish.'

171

Hal shook his head. ''Course, if I'd put my foot down when he was twelve and wanted that darned tutu so badly...'

Everyone stopped mid-chew and looked Hal's way.

'Kidding!' he said and they all laughed and moved on to their favourite holiday places in Europe. Or 'Yerp' as Fliss was soon calling it.

At 2 Biddlefarm Cottages, Dylan was feeling a little left out of things. He'd just declined the spliff being passed around – memories of his father having put him off drugs for life – and he couldn't possibly manage a fifth can of strong lager. Not with a plasterboard ceiling to install the next day. More and more people were rolling up. Some to celebrate their results, others to drown their sorrows. Ellie had got the two Bs and a C she needed, so was in good spirits, and looking great. Really pretty, thought Dylan. But young. As they all were. He was here more to keep an eye on the proceedings than to throw himself into wild, school-leaver debauchery.

The other thing was that Natalia was coming tomorrow, to collect her plant and that old roll-top desk. She'd hired a van and was spending the weekend collecting things she'd stored at her parents' place in order to fill her new loft in Holland Park. Even in his slightly pissed state, Dylan's stomach churned at the thought of seeing her. Perhaps he could be out. Leave the door unlocked. But would she be alone and need a hand? She hadn't said.

'You all right, Dylan?' shouted Ellie, sliding

172

down the living-room wall to join him on the floor. Something hip-hoppy was blasting from speakers but no one was dancing yet. 'Having a good time?'

He nodded. She had a kind of glow he hadn't seen on her before. 'And you?'

'Sorry?'

He raised his voice. 'And *you? Are* you having a *good time?*'

'Oh yeah. It's *so* brilliant to be with people I haven't seen for like months.' She was almost screeching to make herself heard.

'Have they all been on holiday?' he shouted back.

'Sorry? What did you say about holiday?'

'Never *mind,*' he told her and she gave him a big smile and put her fingers in her ears.

Ellie was certainly much happier, more chilled than he'd known her before. All his concern and attentiveness since that chat with her boss had, it seemed, paid off. He popped into the café once when he'd been in town, and Janet had given him a secret wink and a thumbs-up. A couple of times, Ellie had come round for a beer and they'd talked about music and films and what was in the news. She was quite a bright kid, really. And nice with it. Two days ago she'd turned up with stuff for Natalia's plant, which had begun to go the miserable way of all the houseplants Dylan had ever kept. She'd fed it with something her mum had recommended, then painstakingly washed each leaf and applied this shiny liquid that they apparently find delicious. 'There,' she'd puffed at the end, wiping her forehead and screwing tops back on. 'Just don't let any more dust settle on it, yeah?' There'd really been no need for her to do that.

Dylan suddenly felt like putting an arm around her, congratulating her on her results and giving her a brotherly kiss, but the looks he was getting from a lanky bloke with *DJ Robo* on his T-shirt stopped him.

'You could've brought someone, you know?' she said in a pause between tracks.

Was she feeling sorry for him? Dylan drained the can he was holding, then crushed it. 'Look, I might pop out for a while. Come back later. Will you be all right?'

She kissed his cheek, said, 'Don't be stupid,' then went and joined the guy doing the music.

He walked the half mile to The Fox, where he sat at the bar and chatted with Emma again. They got on well when strange Joe wasn't around, in a kind of 'let's not discuss anything challenging' way. He wasn't sure they had too much in common. Emma had only been to London twice – a school trip to Tussaud's, then on the day of Diana's funeral. She put 'Let Me Entertain You' on the pub jukebox, over and over, and said that *Home Alone* was her all-time favourite film. Not that it mattered. When it came to Emma, Dylan didn't have long-term and meaningful in mind.

'So, what are you doing when you finish here?' he asked her.

She shrugged and went to serve a customer. When she came back she said, 'No plans. Joe's off on one of his pot-holing weekends again.'

Dylan laughed. That explained the complexion. 'Fancy going to a party, then? My neighbour's having one.'

Emma glanced sideways at him while she rinsed out some glasses. 'I dunno,' she said, half-smiling. 'Am I dressed OK for it?'

Dylan leaned over the bar and took a look. Emma was barely dressed at all. 'Absolutely,' he told her.

While Alex was mixing a couple of songs on the 24-track, Marie was in the kitchen taking advantage of Mrs Farthing's evening absence. Into the fliptop bin went the criss-crossed, horribly unhygienic wooden chopping board, followed by, among other things, tapioca, rusty cans of pilchards, malt vinegar, economy instant coffee powder, tinned marrowfat peas, tinned potatoes, semi-stale white sliced bread and a plastic squeezy lemon. From the fridge came a bag of what could have been liver, a bowl of stewed apples, an opened tin of evaporated milk and a pack of lard. From the sink area went a disintegrating sponge, three mangled scourers and a nail brush. When the bin was full, she heaved the entire thing out of the back door.

Then, old tarnished cutlery went into a large cardboard box, as did every cooking utensil and all the scratched and buckled pots and pans. Next, Marie looked in the crockery cupboard and groaned. So much of it. She'd planned on giving everything to a charity shop, but would they just say, 'Oh no, not another oatmeal dinner service.'

175

Once she had all the 'to go' stuff stacked in a corner, Marie washed her hands and brushed her hair in the cloakroom, then popped her head around the studio door. 'How's it going?' she asked.

Alex looked up from his guitar. 'Quite well, actually. Want to listen?'

'Maybe later.'

'What are you doing?'

'This and that.'

'Having fun?'

'Oh, yes.'

Back in the kitchen again, she cleaned cupboards and filled them with jars of herbs and spices, ground coffee, balsamic vinegar, packets of couscous, wild rice; things she'd bought that afternoon when she was supposedly clothes shopping. A new stainless steel bin was installed, and soon top and bottom cupboards housed simple, fresh white crockery and tasteful nonstick ovenware, and the fridge sparkled with colourful vegetables and exotic fruit juices. Finally, she placed the wok on the cooker, plugged in the juicer and the cappuccino maker, and tried out the microwave with a cup of water and an Earl Grey teabag. Ready in forty seconds. Fantastic. She looked around her and grinned. What a lovely surprise Mrs Farthing was going to have.

Fliss couldn't sleep. The bedside clock said 1.04. Then 1.05 ... 06.

'But what do we know about this Hal?' she asked Richard, curled around her and lightly snoring. 'He could be into S & M or anything.'

'Mm.'

And we just allowed her to go off with him. How do we know she's safe?'

'Mm.'

'All her stuff's in your spare bedroom. She hasn't even got a toothbrush or clean knickers with her. Unless she slipped them into her handbag, of course. Just in case. And why isn't her mobile working? Do you think she's all right, Richard? Richard?'

Richard stopped the pretend snoring and took a deep breath. 'Well, she *is* a grown woman.'

'True.'

'And Hal loves hollyhocks.'

'Pardon?'

Richard turned on to his back with a quiet grunt. 'Well ... in my vast experience of clients, those who want hollyhocks in their gardens tend to be very nice people.'

'Really? And what about horrible people? What do they like?'

'Concrete mostly. Leylandiis. Can I go to sleep now?'

'Sorry.'

'Again?' said Marie, nestled against Alex and almost asleep. 'What do you mean, "again"?'

She wanted to giggle but couldn't manage it. All in all she'd had quite an exhausting day, topped off with an hour of very welcome, but terribly athletic lovemaking. The old chemistry was definitely back and she was so full of love for Alex, she couldn't quite believe it. How secure and happy she felt lying there in his strong arms, feeling his warm breath on her neck. 'Could we just sleep?' she asked him nicely.

Alex kissed the top of her head. 'Can't keep up with me, eh?'

'Not really. No.'

'Ellie,' said Rob, beside her in her mother's double bed.

'What?'

'You know that Dylan geezer?'

'Mm?'

'I reckon he fancies you.'

Ellie's eyes sprang open. 'Do you?'

'Blokes can tell these things.'

'Yeah, *I'm* sure,' she said. Could they? Did he?

'You haven't shagged him, have you?'

'Of *course* not. And try not to be so crude, would you?' She shook her head and tutted to herself. Dylan would never come out with something like that.

Next door, Dylan was telling Emma what a great fuck she was.

'Am I?' she panted, astride him.

'Oh God, yeah.' It was like watching a page three girl on a non-stop bucking bronco. Vice-like grip, hair tossing wildly and randomly, breasts bouncing like two firm jellies. Who cared if she called the letter H a 'haitch'?

FOURTEEN

Alex jumped awake at the sound of the alarm.

Marie leaned across him, switched it off and said, 'Wakey wakey, Alex. I'll take the shower, you take the bath, OK?' Then she was gone.

It felt very early. Alex looked at the clock. It *was* very early. Mrs Farthing usually called him for his Sunday fry-up at around ten. Why would Marie want to be leaping out of bed at this hour?

'You up yet?' he heard above the water in the en-suite bathroom.

'Almost.'

Better go along with this, he thought, what with things going so well between them, sex included. He lay for a little longer and smiled stupidly. He'd been smiling stupidly a lot over the past couple of days. Had the acupuncture been responsible for things working again? Or was it just that he and Marie were so physically familiar and comfortable with each other? Liked one another too. Annabel had been on the angular side, and scared him a little, truth be told, with that sharp tongue of hers.

'Oh Marie, Marie, Marie,' he whispered, just as she appeared brushing her wet hair and telling him she was going to make them a fabulous breakfast, and that it would be ready in fifteen minutes.

'But what about Mrs Far—' he asked before the

179

hairdryer went on.

Who'd have thought such a tiny person could produce such a loud scream? Alex dropped his croissant and ran, as fast as the hour would allow, from the dining room to the kitchen, where he found half the cupboards open and his house-keeper dangling, apparently frozen, from one of them. The dog, hot on his heels, began barking at whoever he thought had done his beloved Mrs Farthing harm.

'Quiet, Chumsky,' said Alex.

'What...?' asked Mrs Farthing, glaring at the cupboard. 'What...?'

'What?' asked Alex, who could make no sense of her hysteria. 'What?'

'Oh, I've made a few improvements,' said Marie, now at the kitchen door.

Mrs Farthing slowly turned around. She let go of the cupboard and her hands went to her hips as she returned Marie's rather confrontational stare. Alex flashed back to the mud-wrestling he'd been to in the States. His money would be on Mrs F.

'I thought you'd be pleased,' continued Marie. 'Look,' she said, pointing, 'a microwave oven. It'll save you masses of time.'

In an act of male solidarity, or possibly cowardice, Chumsky slunk over and sat himself beside Alex, who said, 'Well!' because that was all he could think of. He saw the packet of best back bacon Mrs Farthing turned up with every Sunday and began to salivate mildly at the thought of a full English. Marie's croissants and

180

strong coffee had felt all wrong, somehow. As though they were weekending in Normandy.

'And where's the lard gone?' Mrs Farthing was now demanding, her head in the fridge. 'How am I supposed to fry Mr Child's breakfast without lard?'

'No need to worry about that,' said Marie jauntily. 'We're just eating, aren't we, Alex? A light, simple and delicious breakfast.'

'Um ... actually I wouldn't mind...'

'Shall we go and finish? Alex?'

He couldn't speak. His worst nightmare was coming true before his eyes. Mrs Farthing was putting her summer coat back on, visibly shaken, poor thing. She picked up her bacon. Well, his bacon. Always done to perfection and served with fried bread, an egg, mushrooms and tomatoes. Lashings of butter on the toast. He swallowed hard. 'Oh, Mrs Farthing, please don't...'

'*Alex?*' said Marie, slightly more insistently.

His head swivelled from one woman to the other, then back again. All eyes were on him. Even Chumsky's. Alex looked down at the dog, and could have sworn he heard him say 'Walk,' in a breathy, doggy way. 'Walk, walk, walk,' he repeated. Or maybe he was just panting hard, owing to all the tension in the air. Alex bent right over, rubbed the dog's head and whispered very quietly into his ear: 'Lead, Chumsky. Go fetch your lead.'

'Thought I'd see the li'l lady all the way home,' said Hal. He wore a lightweight checked jacket and was standing behind Hazel with a protective

181

hand on her shoulder. Hazel herself was beaming from ear to ear. Either she'd had a good time or she was thrilled to be called little.

'Hello,' said Fliss, hiding her relief. 'Come in, come in. Come and have some coffee.'

Hal frowned apologetically. 'Rain check?'

'Oh, right.'

'Got my daughter and grandkid coming. Would've loved them to meet Hazel. What a woman, hey? But she tells me she's gotta shoot.' He eased Hazel round and planted a noisy kiss on her mouth. Then, with a tender pat of her bottom said, 'See ya Friday, sweetheart,' and headed for a sports car with its engine running.

'You all right?' Fliss asked the strangely glazed Hazel as they made their way down the hall.

'Mm.'

'Morning,' said Richard, sipping coffee at the kitchen table.

'Hi, Richard,' said Hazel, sounding a little tired, or maybe dreamy. She eased herself on to a chair and reached for the coffee-pot.

Richard said, 'You'll be needing a cup for that.' He leaned across to the cluttered plate-rack for one. 'Here.'

'Well?' asked Fliss, unable to contain herself. 'How did it go, Hazel?'

'Fan*ta*stic,' she exhaled.

'Oh good.'

'*Amaz*ing house.'

Richard nodded. 'Certainly is. But did you see the Scottish castle?'

'Mm, yes. Hal showed me all his home videos.'

Oh well, thought Fliss. So much for manacles

and pain in a black-walled cellar.

As she sipped at her coffee, Hazel came to life. 'Such a charming man. And good fun. And quite a lot like Paul Newman in a certain light, wouldn't you say? Oh dear, we did have a laugh. *And* he's treating me to the Wigmore Hall on Friday. This Czech quartet he says he's crazy about. A second date! Can you believe it? But how I'm ever going to have him over to my modern semi in Bedford, I'll never know.'

'How did you say he made his money?' Fliss asked Richard.

'I didn't. And neither did he. He once mumbled something about inheriting well and investing wisely.'

'Ah.'

Hazel got out her mobile and said, 'Oh dear, dead. Can I use your phone, Richard? Give the kids some warning that I'll be back soon.'

'Sure.'

Fliss shuddered at the thought of what she might be going back to herself: condoms in the bedrooms and so on. She prayed Dylan had kept a sensible eye on things.

'Why a person needs four bathrooms and two Jacuzzis is beyond me,' chuckled Hazel, phone at her ear. 'Still, at least I know he's clean! Greg? Hi, it's Mum. Just to – who's that I can hear?... Oh, is it?' All the joy seemed to fade from her features. 'Right. Well, say hello to her from me. No, no, don't worry about tidying up just yet. I won't be back until, oh ... five, sixish.'

Richard shot Fliss an oh-no look. It was only eleven, and they'd planned a walk along the river

183

and a pub lunch.

Hazel put the phone down. 'Right. I'll be off soon if that's all right?'

'Er, yeah,' said Richard.

She jumped from her chair, knocked back the dregs of her coffee and sped towards the stairs. 'I'll meet this bloody Karen if it kills me.'

Later, as Richard walked towards her with their drinks, Fliss caught her breath. Not for the first time. Although slowly adjusting, she still couldn't quite believe she was having a thing with Richard Honeyman. A woman's head turned when he passed. Did he notice these things?

'I couldn't remember if you wanted ice,' he said.

Even the way he spoke excited her. 'No. No ice.'

'Oh, good,' he said, handing over her change.

She often found it hard to take her eyes off Richard, but today, as she was feeling particularly warm towards him, it was even harder. Last night, in the throes of passion – delicious, other-worldly, *douze-points* passion – he'd used the L word. She'd said, 'Really?' and he'd said, 'Yes, really,' and she'd reciprocated. But then she'd kept him awake half the night wondering out loud about Hazel, so he might well have had a change of heart.

Well, whatever. She was having a wonderful time, anyway. Ambling arm-in-arm with him, listening to his eccentric-client anecdotes, having a lazy lunch. How she *so* didn't want to go home to a thousand empty beer cans and a Monday

184

packed with patients.

Of course, Richard wasn't totally perfect, she'd discovered. It was almost a relief. Aside from not parting all that freely with his money – never having cash on him, buying mostly two-for-ones then poring over that supermarket receipt on Friday evening – he tended to be a bit casual around the home. Clutter everywhere. Left the washing up a day or two too long, didn't shut cupboards or put lids back on. And forgot to pay bills, it seemed, from the number of final demands she came across. There was even a summons for non-payment of Council Tax. It wasn't as though Richard didn't have the money – she'd spotted a five-figure current-account balance – so it was either absentmindedness or a general reluctance to pay. Still, these were all things she could deal with, should they ever...

'Do you think you could live with me?' she asked him as she put her change away. Richard looked shocked and she laughed. 'It's not a proposal,' she added. 'Just a question. Hypothetical.'

'Yeah, I think I could. But...'

'What?'

'But I might have to gag you at night.'

Fliss coughed mid-sip. 'Not in a kinky way?'

'No. Just in a shut-the-fuck-up way.'

'Ah. Sorry.'

'Hal's been a client for six years. You get to know if a persons a serial rapist in that time. Anyway, I just had this feeling he and Hazel would hit it off, although I wasn't sure they'd have the same musical tastes. Hal's strictly classical. The louder the better.'

Fliss told him about Hazel and her violin playing, and how even Alex Child thought she was good.

Richard said, 'Yeah, but he'd hardly tell her she was crap, would he?'

'Oh, I think he might.'

The silence and emptiness of the house was almost palpable as Alex wiped the muddy paws of probably the only friend he had left in the world. The four-hour walk through fields and villages – and in Chumsky's case, streams – had exhausted them both; more and more as the post-midday sun had grown hotter. When he felt they were both clean, Alex led Chumsky through to the dining room, where they fell upon orange juice and half-eaten croissants before making their way to the sitting-room window to see if Marie's car had gone. Which of course it had. Should he look for a note? No, too knackered. He flopped on the sofa and stared into space for a while, Chumsky stretched full-length at his feet. So tired ... not enough sleep, that was the problem. It was great having a sex life again, albeit shortlived, but it did cut into the recommended seven hours.

After a couple of minutes, he hauled himself up and headed for the kitchen. First he found Chumsky's unexciting dried food and poured him a bowlful and, while the dog crunched noisily and ravenously, he went to the fridge and took out grapes and cheese and anything else that didn't look as though it needed cooking. Everything went on to a tray, as did a couple of rustic French-looking rolls. Then Alex, the tray and the dog made their way up to the master bedroom, where clothes were wearily tugged off, *The Alchemist* was found, and the bed was entered with a prolonged but satisfied groan. Lovely, he thought as he reached for a grape. With his other arm he elbowed the dog.

'Out you get,' he whispered. 'There's a good boy.'

But Chumsky didn't move. His eyes were very firmly shut and Alex could almost hear doggy heels digging into the mattress.

Oh, what the hell, he thought, lifting the book. Now where had he got to? Oh yes. Reading the omens strewn along life's path.

Dylan hadn't got round to putting curtains up at the little attic window, tucked between the eaves at the front of the house. But now, as he lay in the bright light, facing Emma's blotchy cheeks, open mouth and closed, mascara-smudged eyes, he wished he had. He turned away from her and remembered how delicious Natalia always looked first thing. That Mediterranean complexion no doubt helped. He reached down to the floor for his watch. Twenty-five to eight? Surely not, he thought, turning the watch around. Five past two, that was more like it. He stretched his arms towards the ceiling and froze mid-yawn. Five past two! Shit. And was that the sound of a large vehicle pulling up at the end of the garden?

He jumped from the bed with an, 'Aaargghh.'

'Wossgoinon?' mumbled panda eyes, pulling the duvet back over her.

Dylan flung open the window and there she

was, coming up his path with her long, catwalk legs. *Fuck.*

Emma appeared to have gone back to sleep, so Dylan grabbed some clothes and crept from the room. He dressed in the bathroom, splashed water over his face and reached the front door before Natalia did. She was still negotiating the cement mixer he'd strategically placed to keep last night's partygoers out.

'Hi, Natalia,' he puffed. God, he needed coffee. Did he look a mess? 'Sorry about this. Here, let me move it.

'Hi,' she said. She stood still while he inched it over, and took in all the building material. 'Jesus, Dylan. What's going on?'

She looked sensational. As usual. Thick, dark and very shiny hair. A trace of red lipstick, but no other make-up. His eyes wandered up the path and checked that no one was following her.

'I've been building a breeze-block extension,' he said, but she seemed baffled by his words. Out of her frame of reference, no doubt. 'Making my house bigger?'

'Really? You mean your*self?*'

'Mm.'

'Huh. Fancy. Well, are you going to invite me in?'

'Yeah, yeah.'

Dylan gestured her towards the door and she squeezed between him and the mixer in her pale blue jeans and deep pink short-sleeved top. Clothes that would have passed unnoticed on any other woman, but which seemed to say, 'Peel me off, slowly,' on Natalia.

'Oh, by the way,' she said. She turned around and pointed. 'There are two people sleeping in your garden.'

He nodded. 'Right.'

She seemed pleased with the plant, anyway. Together they carried the huge wavy thing down to the hire van, and put it in the back alongside the things she'd picked up from her parents' place. Once it was wedged in, there was almost no room left and Dylan asked if she was really going to get the desk in there too.

'I doubt it.' She closed the van's doors and locked them. 'Maybe I'll come back for that another time. I'm kind of aiming for modern, crisp and functional in the new place. One or two old pieces, perhaps. But I'll see.'

'Well, OK. I'll hang on to it, then.' Did he want her to keep coming back for stuff? It was definitely unsettling.

'I've missed you, Dyl,' she said, a hand coming up to his face. With her flat shoes, their eyes were level, which he was pleased about. He'd never been that comfortable with Natalia overtaking his six feet in her heels. She began stroking his cheek with her thumb.

Dylan swallowed hard. 'There's a woman in my bed.'

'I'm not surprised,' she said, smiling. 'Is it serious?'

'One-nighter.'

'Ah.'

A scruffy head suddenly appeared over the hedge and they both jumped. Male or female?

Dylan couldn't tell. 'All right?' it said. It was a boy. Then another popped up, rubbing its eyes. A girl with long matted hair.

'Don't suppose you're going into Norwich?' asked the first one, rubbing the back of his neck.

'Maybe,' said Natalia. 'Only, I'm not sure we can fit you in.'

Dylan frowned. We? Was she expecting him to go with her?

'Hang on,' she said. 'I'll just ask Chris.'

'Chris?' said Dylan, who still hadn't had that coffee. He pictured tall, tanned and blond. He followed her round to the driver's side and saw that he was right, apart from the fact that it was a woman. Early- to mid-twenties and pretty, in an unthreatening young-Meg Ryan kind of way. She was leaning against the van and swigging mineral water.

'This is Dylan,' said Natalia.

'Hi,' he said with a half-wave.

Natalia moved towards her friend, put an arm around her and kissed her wet lips with a degree of relish. 'And this is Chris,' she told him, giving the girl's bare shoulder a gentle nibble. 'Who, incidentally, is *not* a one-nighter.'

'Hi,' said Chris with a hint of Antipodean. 'It's spelt with a K, by the way.'

Dylan nodded. Did she think he'd be sending them Christmas cards?

'Coffee?' he asked calmly. 'Tea?'

It was a wrench, turning the key, easing up the clutch and accelerating away from Richard Honeyman, but Fliss also felt oddly elated.

Shakespeare's 'sweet sorrow', perhaps. She watched him grow smaller in her rearview mirror and sighed. They'd decided to give themselves a two-week break, to mull over things, do the stuff they might normally do at weekends – he should really visit Aunt June, he said – and see if their feelings were sustained over a whole fortnight. How very mature of them, thought Fliss. But then, of course, they were very mature.

Throughout the journey, while her mind was going over the past couple of days, she also ran through all the little but essential jobs there were to do in the garden. Maintenance mostly. All the work she'd put in earlier in the summer was now paying off and the front garden, in particular, had become a glorious canvas of colour. The lawn had well and truly taken and, thanks to regular watering and lashings of food, was almost an emerald green. Yep, it wouldn't be so bad having a bit of a break from the whirlwindy events of the past few weeks and catch up on her real life.

She had a quick stop halfway for a coffee, then, after what felt like a relatively short time, she pulled up outside Biddlefarm Cottages, switched off the engine and gazed at her house. How lovely it was to be home. But what, she wondered, was a pair of small, lacy, cerise-coloured knickers doing on her gatepost?

FIFTEEN

Where on earth was Baz? Dylan had tried his home number and the mobile with no luck, and decided to get on with the roof tiling by himself. Last week he'd watched Baz doing it, so was fairly confident. It just would have been easier with two.

As he worked under the changeable sky he couldn't stop thinking of Natalia. How great she'd looked yesterday, how amusing she'd been over the mid-afternoon breakfast he'd made them all. Emma had eventually joined them, showered but still bleary, as he, Natalia and Kris-with-a-K discussed a range of topics.

Kris worked for an environmental organisation and held strong views which she expressed fairly fervently. She told Dylan off good and proper for not having considered solar panels. She thought it appalling that flat East Anglia wasn't powered entirely by wind turbines. Natalia said she had friends who lived near some and found them incredibly noisy. They moved on to space exploration and things got quite heated. He was for it, the two women were against.

'Why are we spending shedloads of money trying to find out where life started when billions are dying of starvation and preventable diseases every year?' asked Natalia. She tutted and shook her head. 'It's just criminal. And such a boy thing.'

'Yiahh,' said Kris, sounding more and more *Home and Away*. 'Loik war.'

'And all the rest of the shit that happens in the world,' said Natalia.

Dylan didn't really hold the view that if things had been left to women we'd be on the verge of discovering the wheel, but he came out with it anyway. Natalia laughed, bless her, but Kris took umbrage and ranted for a while on men's refusal to do their bit domestically over the centuries. 'Let's fyce it, Shykespeare wouldn't have had time to write a bloody shopping list if he'd had the kids all day.'

All three agreed on that one.

Emma, who spent a lot of time washing up and giving the cooker a good wipe, was mostly quiet, but just before Natalia and Kris left, said, 'Um ... are you two like lezzes?'

'Not entirely,' Natalia replied with a wistful glance Dylan's way.

That look had stayed with him, and he now found himself coming over dizzy at the memory of it. Perhaps he should get down off the roof for a while, he thought. Have some lunch. He'd been trying to decide whether to skip art class and get on with the job in hand. He wasn't that keen on facing strange Joe after shagging his girlfriend, but he was definitely growing in confidence as far as his art went. Lately, he'd been spending more and more time in what was to be the main bedroom, drawing and painting. At the moment he was trying his hand at watercolours, which he'd always considered a bit tame until the twins – who, when pushed, were very instructive –

193

taught him otherwise. Watercolour paintings could be bright, vibrant, daring. He'd never known.

Oh, to hell with Joe – and the roof. He'd go. He cleaned himself up, had a bite to eat, got his stuff together and went out to the van.

After unlocking the back doors and chucking his rolled-up paintings and new set of paints in, he heard a noise behind him – like hurried footsteps – and turned. Coming towards him at quite a pace was someone tall and thin in a black suit and a balaclava. Dylan's peripheral vision told him two other similarly clad men were also heading his way: one short and wide, the other big and wide. His immediate reaction was to hurry to the front of the van and speed off, which he started to do before the first guy grabbed his hand and yanked the keys off him.

'What the–' Dylan began, just as something was pulled over his head, blocking out all light and shocking him into silence.

'Giddin the back with him, Mr Pink,' said someone in a dreadful high-pitched American accent. He sounded very young. 'In the front with me, Mr Orange. And hurry the fuck up, both of you.'

Dylan was suddenly pushed hard and found himself horizontal, thankful for the mattress he'd installed for his father's dog. Someone began tying his wrists together, while noisily chewing gum. Dylan hated that. Many a time he'd had to ask Baz not to yack quite so loudly when they were working in close proximity. The back doors were then slammed shut and within seconds the

194

engine started up.

'Where are you taking me?' demanded Dylan through the scratchy material.

'Shut da fuck up,' shouted someone through the grill. The bloke who'd grabbed his keys.

'Yeah, shut da fuck up, dude,' said a very familiar voice beside him.

'Hey!' shouted the driver. 'You ain't supposed to say nothin, Mr Pink. Remember!'

'Sorry, Mr White.'

'So just shut the fuck *up*, then!'

'Ookay,' said Mr Pink.

Dylan had the wherewithal to start counting the seconds, and then minutes, of the journey. It kept his mind off what his abductors might do to him, but also let him know roughly how far he was being taken. After thirteen bumpy, noisy and very uncomfortable minutes – when he wondered if he'd ever see his mother or have feeling in his left arm again – the van came to a halt.

'Waddayawant?' came a new voice. Mr Orange, probably.

'Get me a number fourteen and a number fifty-seven,' said Mr White.

'And you, Mr Pink?' asked Mr Orange. 'Don't say nothin'. Just hold up your fingers.' He paused, then said, 'OK, that's a thirty-one ... a twelve ... and a fifty-seven. Jeez, no wonder you're a fat slob.'

Mr Orange got out, slammed his door and the three of them remained in silence until he returned and filled the van with the aroma of Chinese food. By process of elimination, Dylan worked out that they were in West Washam.

195

Unfortunately, the engine then started up and he had to begin counting again. But not for long. When he was finally hauled from the back of the van, he knew he was on the outskirts of the small market town, close to a busy road and – as a jet was taking off – the RAF base.

They led him through what he was told was a gap in a hedge and bits of twiggy foliage brushed against his arms. Then across a field of some sort. There didn't appear to be a path, as it was pretty bumpy and uneven, and several times he stumbled, despite being helped along by one of the Misters. Someone opened a squeaky gate and a little further on he was told to climb up two steps.

'I hope you purchased some plastic spoons, Mr Orange,' said Mr White, as Dylan found himself being led into a building of some sort. ''Cos I ain't eating with my friggin' fingers.'

Not a well-equipped building, by the sound of it.

Marie was at sixes and sevens. She knew she should have stayed at The Manor yesterday and at least tried to explain to Alex that she'd meant well. Even if she hadn't. But he was gone so long with the dog that she'd become jittery and restless and eventually just took off. Then, as soon as she'd arrived home she wanted to be back with Alex. After throwing her bag down in the knocked-through living room, she'd stood and looked around her. What had possessed her to buy this horrible little house, anyway? In this part-gentrified, part-slum street, with its disgusting corner shop. And how had she managed to be so happy here just a few weeks ago? She ran herself a scented frothy bath and spent the rest of the day in front of the TV, not really watching, just waiting for Alex to give her a call.

Today, she'd tried ringing him several times, but with no luck. At lunchtime she'd created a sad little meal based around tuna, but couldn't eat it. At one forty-five she'd tried Dylan but he was out. Was it his art class day?

At two-thirty she called Kathleen. 'Are you in?' she asked.

'I think I actually had something more subtle in mind,' said Kathleen from across her kitchen table. It was almost time to collect her girls from summer tennis camp, but not quite. 'Not your forte, though, Marie.'

'No, I guess not. But about half of me thought Mrs Farthing would be pleasantly surprised.'

Kathleen raised an eyebrow at her.

'OK, a quarter.' Marie let out a weighty sigh. 'A lot of effort went into transforming that kitchen, and I bet she's back there now with her monstrous pressure cooker and her rusty carving knives, making him Camp coffee with evaporated milk. Honestly, Kath, it's like a living museum.'

'You should have introduced the changes slowly.'

'I know.'

'But you've always been headstrong.'

'True.'

'Why don't you phone and apologise? Say you thought they'd both be chuffed.'

197

'I've tried several times, but the bloody thing just rings. Unplugged, no doubt. The answerphone's been switched off, so has Alex's mobile. I think he must be cross with me.'

'Cross?' cried Kathleen. 'He's not *cross*, Marie, he's weak. Weak, weak, weak. Always has been. He might be a genius on the guitar, but first he let drugs rule his life then he let his housekeeper do it. And as for not answering the phone to you, that's just pathetic. In fact, I've changed my mind, he doesn't deserve an explanation.' She got up from the table and gathered bag, jumper and car keys. 'Sorry, Marie, but I've got to dash. Now, promise me you won't go rushing back to Gloucestershire?'

Marie had never known Kathleen be quite so judgmental. Poor Alex. It almost made her want to leap in the car and head back to The Manor, give him a big hug and compliment Mrs Farthing on her gravy.

'Of course I won't,' she said.

She stayed in Kathleen's shambolic kitchen, making herself more tea and thinking about what her cousin had said. Of course, it was true. Alex had always been inclined to do a disappearing act in times of crisis, or any time really. Why had she assumed he no longer went in for head-burying, just because he was off the drugs and living like Bertie Wooster? She thought back to all the other times in her life – and Dylan's – that she hadn't been able to contact him, and how utterly frustrating it had been, not to say infuriating, hurtful... Sod him, she decided, as something resembling anger suddenly hit her. She went over to her bag and took out her mobile. 'Two can play at that game,' she said, switching it off.

Ellie got off the bus and walked up the gravel lane that led to Biddlefarm Cottages. She was knackered from being on her feet all day. Or maybe it was from clearing up after the party. Oh God, the state of the front garden yesterday morning. She and Rob had spent hours trying to prop up trampled-on flowers, sometimes using little twigs and things, but her mum had still screamed when she saw the damage.

Someone had built a small fire in the middle of the lawn; that was the worst thing. Well, quite a big fire. They'd all sat around it and played the 'something I've never done, that everyone else here *has* done' game. Ellie said she'd never in her life touched a rodent of any description, thinking all the others must have done, but it turned out Ben hadn't either. Couldn't stand the things, he said. Not even guinea pigs. Then Hannah bravely announced she'd never actually had full sex, so of course she won. Unless some of the others were lying.

Anyway, it was quite fun, but Ellie didn't realise at the time that they were making a big black circle in the middle of the lawn that was definitely going to have to be dug up and returfed. Her mum had practically sobbed into the phone to Richard and he'd offered to come and help at the weekend. Ellie said sorry a million times but there'd still been An Atmosphere, so she'd just spent a quiet evening in her room getting on with some preparatory reading.

She smiled as she let herself into the disastrous garden. Loads of people had come into the café today and said what a wicked party it had been, so maybe it was worth all the grief her mum was giving her.

As she turned to close the gate, Ellie spotted something lying in the road. She went to have a look and found it was a wooden paintbox, half open. Dylan's? Some of the paints had come out of their little slots and were scattered around. She picked them up and replaced them as best she could, and guessed he must have put the box on top of his van then driven off, forgetting about it. Idiot. Mind you, just the sort of thing she'd do. She'd take it round when he got back, she decided, rather than leave it on his doorstep.

She clicked the lid shut and looked at the smooth honey-coloured wood, running her hand over it and thinking of its owner. She'd pretty much given up on ever becoming Dylan's girlfriend, as he was still so hung up on his old one. She'd had a glimpse of the famous Natalia yesterday, and decided no way could she compete with that. And well maybe he *was* a bit old for her, like her mum said. He didn't exactly join in the party, just suddenly disappearing like that and not coming back.

As she was going back through her gate, a text message arrived. It was Rob saying did she want to go and see a film. Something she hadn't heard of. Suddenly, she didn't feel so tired. *No car. Mum wking late. Pck me up?* she wrote. *OK* he replied and she hurried to the shower. She'd take Dylan's box back tomorrow.

Alex had downloaded some recipes and was trying out lasagne, having found a chunk of meat in the freezer which he assumed was minced beef and not some nasty horse-derived stuff that Mrs F had got in for Chumsky. He'd taxied into Gloucester early afternoon for one or two other ingredients, and finally got cracking on it around four-thirty. It had taken him quite a while to arrive at where he was now – the layering stage – what with having to consult the dictionary for 'roux' and 'parboil' and so on. But no doubt he'd speed up in future.

Chumsky was watching his every move with a proud but slightly critical eye. 'No, no, Mrs Farthing would never add *Herbes de Provence* to an Italian dish,' he seemed to want to say. Alex would then have to point out that, unless you counted macaroni cheese, Mrs F didn't do Italian.

Ah yes, this was so therapeutic. Phones switched off, Leonard Cohen on the portable CD, no one telling him his sauce was much too thick. As he gave it a helping hand out of the saucepan with a wooden spoon he wondered if his sheets and pillowcases had finished their wash-cycle, and if they would really smell of woodland glade as promised on the bottle. He tittered to himself and shook his head. He'd never read so many instructions in so short a space of time: the cooker manual, the washing-machine manual. He thought he wouldn't bother with the dishwasher, just as Mrs F hadn't judging from the cobwebs inside.

Oh dear. Mrs Farthing. She'd snubbed him early that morning in the village shop. It had all been a bit awkward. Just the two of them at the counter, her in front with an overflowing basket and him with just a sliced brown. Could bread and milk be frozen, he wondered, then he wouldn't have to keep going back there. Maybe it would tell him on the packet. More instructions!

He'd wanted to say something to her: that he was sorry, that Marie had only tried to be helpful. But somehow the words wouldn't come forth. Something to do with the disapproving expression she was giving his wholemeal loaf, perhaps. According to Marie, Mrs Farthing had a strict colour code: bread should be white, tea darkest tan, and vegetables almost colourless.

And Marie ... what to do? She'd be livid with him for copping out yesterday. Not staying and defending her. He wasn't sure he could face that right now, and besides, she tended to calm down given a little time. He'd call her in a couple of days, try and gauge the lie of the land, ask her to come back. And if she didn't? Could he live without a woman in his life? Neither Marie *nor* Mrs F? It was an idea that would have terrified him only a few days ago, but now – hoorah! – he could make a lasagne, which somehow changed everything. Life was suddenly full of possibilities. He slipped the dish into the pre-heated oven and began the massive task of cleaning up after himself.

At nine-fifty, rather later than Alex had planned, he and Chumsky dug into their much-anticipated and really-not-too-bad meal in front of a gripping programme about a former accountant who moved to Portugal to get away from it all and open a top-rate, world-cuisine restaurant. It had been a huge success, apparently. Alex looked down and nodded approvingly at the plate on his lap. He didn't want to run before he could walk, of course, but thought it was definitely an option worth considering.

On Tuesday morning, Fliss put a hand either side of her eyes as she made her way down the path. Like a blinkered horse racing for the finishing line, she aimed for the car, determined not to be distracted, and therefore upset, by the devastation that used to be her garden. It would soon be Saturday, she told herself, and then Richard would come to the rescue and they'd have it looking right as rain by Sunday evening.

Maybe. She'd never in fact seen any of Richard's work. Only his own garden, which was surprisingly compact considering his chosen profession. Basically a patio. Occasionally, over the past two days, she'd feared he might be of the Diarmuid Gavin school of gardening, and that she'd return from a shopping trip to find Stonehenge had been installed. In cobalt blue. 'Look,' he'd say, unpadlocking a hatch to a soundproofed underground bunker, 'the perfect place for teenagers to hang out,' and she'd instantly forgive him.

On reaching the gate, Fliss noticed that Dylan's van was missing and wondered if he'd got himself a new girlfriend, and how Ellie would take it if he had. She seemed happy to be back with Rob again but, as Fliss knew well, huge crushes weren't easy to shake off.

Resisting the urge to take a quick, gut-wrenching look at her garden, she got in her car and headed off to Norwich to earn, in a day, enough to replace all the wisteria, ivy and trellises that had once covered the front of the house. Demolished by Ben, according to a distraught Ellie. 'Got completely mashed and thought he was Spiderman.'

SIXTEEN

By Wednesday, it had become clear to Dylan that Mr White, the boss, was having no luck whatsoever getting through to either of his parents to demand a million-pound ransom.

Mr Pink strenuously denied having written the numbers down wrongly. 'Ain't no way I coulda wrote *four* numbers down wrong,' he drawled.

'Shuddup, Mr Pink,' he was told for the umpteenth time. 'No talking, you asshole.'

'Oops, forgot.'

'Don't make no sense to me,' chipped in Mr Orange, 'that this mega-rock-star guy don't have his mobile on for like the record company or whoever to call him.'

'Cell phone,' snapped Mr White.

'Pardon?'

'That's what we call them in the States, asshole. Cell phones.'

'Oh, yeah. Anyway, the dude ain't even checking his text messages. We gotta have sent six.'

'No, seven,' said Mr Pink.

'Shuddup!' said the others.

Dylan was on a plastic moulded chair, blindfolded, and with his wrists tied together in front of him. They'd given him a couple of cushions, which was considerate, but hardly made up for the despair and general pissed-offedness he was feeling. Occasionally, they'd let him take some exercise, guiding him around the hut for ten minutes or so, but that was all. Otherwise he just sat. God, what a pain, he kept saying to himself. He didn't exactly feel in danger of his life or anything; mostly he just feared losing his mind and getting fat. He was growing desperate for a stimulating conversation. A plate of salad. Exercise.

All the sitting, that was the problem. When he needed the toilet, Bar and Co led him there and loosened his bound hands a little, but didn't take the blindfold off. Having a pee was therefore a bit hiss and miss. The only other exercise he got was eating. Chinese, Indian, Chinese, Pizza, Chinese. Sometimes fish and chips. All washed down with warm Sprite or similar. Dylan could see he was going to emerge from this ordeal the same shape as Baz.

If he emerged at all. The fact that his parents weren't answering either of their phones was not just something of a mystery to Dylan, but also extremely worrying. He had horrible visions of them both dead in a head-on collision. What other explanation could there be? He really needed to get out of this stupid situation and find out what had happened. And that meant getting Mr Pink on side.

'Listen, Mr Pink,' he whispered when the two of them reached the toilet. He knew it was Baz from the chewing and humming. It was mid-afternoon and hot, and the tiny room reeked. He guessed he wasn't the only one who missed. 'Help me get out of here and I'll pretend I didn't even see you.

Not that I have seen you, of course. Anyway, no questions asked. I'll even pay you a bit of ransom money. Just you, Mr Pink, not those other pricks. All you have to do is untie me, show me to a back door or window or something, then say I overpowered you. Simple. What do you say? Mm?'

'You want me to shoot him, boss?' said Mr Orange, and Dylan's heart seized. The others must have followed on tiptoe.

'Sure is tempting,' squeaked Mr White.

For the second day in a row, Fliss and Ellie were trying to call Alex and Marie. It was Wednesday evening and they hadn't seen anything of Dylan since Sunday, when he'd made Fliss recuperative cups of tea in his kitchen while Ellie had continued, fruitlessly, to repair the garden.

'Maybe he's at his ex-girlfriend's,' said Ellie. 'She came here last weekend. Perhaps they've like got back together?'

'That's a thought. I can't remember her name, though. Can you?'

'Natalia.'

'That was it.'

Fliss looked her up. Yesterday they'd let themselves into Dylan's house with his spare keys, scoured the place for a note, checked for phone messages – just one, from an 'Emma' – then taken his address book home with them.

She got through to Natalia. No, Dylan wasn't with her, she said, wanting to know why his next-door neighbour was calling. 'Is there a problem with the house or something?'

'No, no,' said Fliss. 'We just haven't seen him for a few days and he didn't tell us he was going away.'

'Have you tried his parents?'

'Yes. I've been trying since yesterday. No answer from either of them.'

'You know, it sounds to me like they've all gone away together. Abroad maybe? Dylan told me his parents were an item again, and that they'd all been spending time together. And not everyone wants to be bothered by mobile calls when they're on holiday. I know I don't.'

'Mm,' said Fliss, 'it's a possibility. Well, sorry to have bothered you.'

'Get him to give me a call when he's back, would you?'

'Yes, of course.' They said their goodbyes and hung up. 'She thinks they may all be on holiday together,' Fliss told Ellie, whose eyes suddenly grew bigger.

'Oh,' said Ellie, colouring up. 'Um ... he might have mentioned something about a holiday at the party. Only the music was dead loud and I couldn't hear. Oh God, I bet that's it. He thought he'd told me.'

'But what about the paintbox?'

'Yeah, that's a bit weird. But maybe they're having like a painting holiday. His mum's a bit of an artist, didn't you say?'

'Yes, she is.' Fliss pushed the phone to one side, now feeling relatively reassured. 'Anyway, I'm sure he'll turn up soon, all tanned and rejuvenated and apologetic for not letting us know properly.'

Ellie nodded. 'How long do you think we should leave it, though? Before we call the police or whatever.'

Fliss laughed. 'I'm sure there won't be any need for that. But maybe if he's not back in, say, two weeks?' She passed her daughter a pair of extra-thick gardening gloves. 'In the meantime,' she said, 'you can get that holly tied back up.'

Ellie pulled a disgruntled face and yanked the gloves on. 'Are you *ever* gonna forgive me?'

'Nope.'

After her daughter flounced out, Fliss called Hazel for an update.

'I don't think Hal could quite believe the size of my house,' giggled Hazel. 'When he arrived and we were in the living room and I said, "Let me hang your jacket in the cupboard," he said he thought we *were* in the cupboard! Only he said closet, of course. Anyway, he met the kids and they really took to him, especially after he got out a wad of twenty-pound notes, you know like rich people and criminals did in films before Switch cards came along, and gave them half each.'

You couldn't fault Hal's people skills, thought Fliss. 'Did you do anything nice while he was there?' she asked.

'Well, we flew to Paris for the evening. Hal keeps a private jet at Cambridge airport.'

'*He* flew you?'

'No, no, no. We had a pilot. Hal's got his licence, but doesn't fly any more. Something to do with blood sugar.'

Hazel was sounding amazingly blasé about it all. As if she hadn't spent every Saturday night

209

for years watching *Casualty* and *Parkinson*, wishing a man would come along and whisk her off to Paris.

'It was quite fun,' she added. 'We had *moules*.'

'Uh huh?'

'That's mussels.'

'Yes.'

On Thursday afternoon, prompted by a sudden yearning for Marie, Alex downed his rolling pin, washed dough off his hands and almost ran to the phone. But by the time he'd plugged the lead back into its socket, sunk into a chair and heard Callminder tell him he had ten messages, his courage had abandoned him and he quickly hung up. Ten? At least half would be Marie venting her spleen, he guessed. Fear gripped him at the very thought of it. Or would she be contrite? Full of remorse and missing him as much as he was missing her? Oh hell. If only the voicemail service could detect content and give him a warning: 'You have ten messages: six friendly, one businesslike and three you *really* don't want to listen to.'

Have courage, Alex told himself and his hand ventured towards the handset, but then fell back into his lap. Within a minute, the lead was unplugged and he was back in the kitchen having his first ever stab at rough-puff pastry.

Marie had been in Brighton with Gavin for six days. After her chat with Kathleen, she'd called him and offered twice his courier income if he'd take her away somewhere. 'Cool,' he'd said and they'd zoomed down the motorway on his bike to stay with a thirty-something couple he knew, Steve and Amanda, in their seafront flat.

Suddenly surrounded by holidaymakers, Marie realised she ought to have organised herself an August trip abroad. Although not fond of packing herself into airports, planes and hotels with legions of stressed families, it might have stopped her getting embroiled with Alex over the past few weeks. Summer definitely did odd things to people. How could she have imagined her ex-husband would be much more solid now?

She took Gavin's hand and led him down to the beach. It was littered with bodies – couples, English language students, young families – but they managed to find themselves a patch where they threw towels down on the stones and stripped off.

Marie popped her shades on and lay back. Lovely. And so hot today. Yesterday had been dull and nippy, the day before that was hot then wet. You could never rely on the weather in Britain. Maybe when she got home she'd look into Italian villas or similar. Alex had his place in Deya, but she'd hardly be asking to borrow that.

She'd thought about Alex a lot over the past week, and on waking that morning, the first thing she'd done was to lean over for her mobile and switch it back on for the first time. She had lots of messages, it told her, and her heart soared. Although desperate to read them, she'd quickly switched the phone back off. Let him stew for a little longer, she thought. Learn that he must confront his problems, not swim away when things hot up. Of course, an uncharitable person might accuse her of the very same thing.

'Do my back?' Gavin was asking. He'd finished smothering his perfect legs, arms and chest, and was handing her the sunscreen.

'Pleasure,' she told him, lifting her sunglasses on to her head as he rolled over. She pulled herself up, sat astride his also-perfect bottom and decided there was a lot to be said for ignoring your phones, leaping on the back of a young man's motorbike and crashing with his friends for a while in a city where no one knows you. Well, apart from the prematurely old-looking guy in the cinema box-office the other evening, who said he'd been a fan of hers when he was a teenager, causing Steve to whisper rather too loudly to Amanda, 'Christ, she must be ancient.'

It was funny, though, how she didn't feel ancient when she was with Gavin. In fact, it was when she was with Alex, looking up the 100 Share Index over breakfast with reading glasses on the end of his nose, or watching *Top of the Pops* and saying, 'Why do they have to perform in their bloody coats all the time?' that she felt she was entering her twilight years.

She flipped the top back on the sun cream and, with both hands, gave Gavin's back one last massage, starting at the shoulders and ending just inside his shorts with two firm squeezes.

Dylan wasn't sure he could take even one more day. He was worried sick about his parents and could feel he was developing a paunch. But worst of all, he was bored witless. The sound of inane banter was whittling away at his brain and he wondered if he'd ever be able to hold an intelligent conversation again. Mind you, even the most chatty of the chattering classes might flag after eight days holed up in a hut. Was it eight? His counting had gone a bit hazy after day four.

It had been decided by Mr White that they could do nothing but wait for Dylan's parents to return from their holiday – his explanation for the unanswered calls. 'Bad friggin timing, huh?' he'd said with a hollow laugh. 'But I guess we sit it out, fellas? Waddayasay?'

It seemed to Dylan that what the others said didn't really count for anything. Mr White ruled, in as tough a way as one could with the voice of a twelve year old. Mr Orange, not the sharpest tool in the box, was the muscle. And Baz – who'd now, strangely, become Mr Pink to Dylan – was there as a bit of a runner. Mr White sent him out a lot. First of all for some clothes for Dylan. How many outfits he'd been bought, Dylan didn't know, but every morning he was stripped, allowed to wash at the basin in the toilet, sprayed liberally with deodorant, then led back through to his 'bedroom' and dressed. Although his hands were untied throughout this procedure, his blindfold remained, and Dylan therefore had no idea what he was having put on him by Mr Orange or whoever. Each time he was led out, though, the other two would laugh a lot, and Dylan prayed daily that any rescue attempt wouldn't be accompanied by TV cameras. Not that anyone *would* be rescuing him, now he'd clearly been orphaned.

He'd gathered from his abductors' conversations that Mr White was a carpenter and Mr Orange an electrician, and that they were losing money every day their captive's parents weren't calling. One evening, Dylan overheard Mr White whispering into the phone for some money to be transferred to his account. 'Just till this aristocrat pays what he owes us for doing up his mansion. Yeah, yeah, any day now. Right ... thanks. Um, you couldn't make it *two* hundred, could you, Mum?'

As well as fretting about their lost incomes they, like Dylan, had become restless and bored. This had been alleviated slightly a few days previously, when Mr Pink rolled up with a borrowed laptop and what must have been a flatpack from MFI or somewhere. During a lot of bashing and clonking and screwing and swearing, Dylan gathered it was a table and four chairs; all the better to play computer games on, eat takeaways off, and sit around discussing films till the cows came home. Mr White, having realised he was fighting a losing battle, was now allowing Mr Pink to speak, while Dylan continued to pretend he didn't know it was Baz behind the American/Norfolk accent. And when it came to his favourite topics, Mr Pink had plenty to say, as usual. Although Mr White didn't know it, he couldn't have come up with a better form of torture for his hostage.

Most evenings now, and sometimes in the afternoons too, the gang sat silently watching DVDs on the laptop, providing Dylan with some welcome entertainment. Being blindfolded meant the shoot-outs and car chases were a bit of

214

a bore, but listening to genuine American for a while was a joy.

'What day is it?' he asked as something Chinese and rubbery was being shovelled into his mouth. During his imprisonment, Dylan had gone from indifference to Chinese food, to never wanting to smell or taste it again, to becoming pretty much addicted.

'Tuesday?' said Mr Pink. He didn't sound too sure. 'There's a nice big chunk of prawn in this next spoonful.'

Dylan swallowed. 'Great. And when did you last try my parents?'

'Er, this morning, dude. Open wide.'

Dylan took the food, chewed, then chewed some more, then swallowed again. 'I'm really quite worried about them, Mr Pink. It's been, what, eight days now? What if they've come to some harm? On ventilators in intensive care somewhere?'

'Mr White reckons they're on holiday. I mean vacation.'

'Yes, but Mr White isn't always right, you know.' Dylan bent forward and whispered, 'Strikes me he's not too bright, and that *you* should be running this show, Mr Pink. I mean, what's he accomplished so far?'

'Er...'

'Zilch. That's what. Maybe it's time for the brains to take over. Discuss it with Mr Orange, why don't you? Organise some sort of coup.'

'A coup, eh?'

'Yep.'

'Like in *Steel Battalion?*'

'Sorry?'

'X-Box game. Brilliant.'

Dylan groaned.

'You see, you're a Vertical Tank pilot, right? Sorting out the military unrest after a coup. Loads of hi-tech robot wars. Forty-button cockpit simulator. Wick-*id*.'

Dylan opened his mouth and waited for more delicious food. Perhaps Mr Orange would be a better bet.

SEVENTEEN

Fliss loved what Richard was doing to her long front garden. Apart from repairing party damage, he'd managed, by moving lots of shrubs and small trees around, to make the whole thing look half as wide again. So clever. Sometimes he sought her permission before doing things, but mostly he didn't. He'd regularly dash off to the garden centre for items, and a stack of receipts was mounting daily for her beside the kettle. 'Do you want to settle as I go along?' he'd asked. 'Or at the end?' She'd smiled rigidly and told herself not to be ridiculous; of course she should reimburse him.

Anyway, he was showing no signs of wanting to go home, which was nice. 'I've cancelled next week's appointments,' he'd announced when he arrived to the rescue on Saturday. 'Don't worry, I didn't have that many,' he added when he saw her face.

The first thing he'd suggested was a vegetable patch. 'You barely use the back garden, anyway. And just think of all the exercise you'll get.'

'Good idea,' she said, pulling her tummy in. Was he trying to tell her something?

By Wednesday they'd fallen into a routine, and when she'd kissed him goodbye in the morning, and yelled to Ellie to hurry up, she had this odd sensation that she and Richard had been together forever. Perhaps because the idea of someone like him – easy, reliable, attractive – had been in her head for as long as she could remember. Anyway, it just felt so right.

'Don't forget to unload the washing machine,' she'd called to him from the front path. He'd installed a rotary line, well hidden behind the shed out the back, which was a godsend after the clothes horse in the bathroom. Each day now, Fliss came home to clean dry laundry, as well as a garden full of new surprises and a man who told her she had eyes the colour of *centaurea cyanus*. Which she hoped was good.

She'd driven to work on cloud nine, half-listening to Ellie babbling away. Eight hours and seven patients later, she drove back home on her own listening to the radio, not quite so cloud-niney, owing to exhaustion, but still chirpy enough to sing along to 'Jolene' at full volume.

On arriving in the kitchen, she was greeted with a vodka and tonic and a shoulder rub. 'Mmm, lovely,' she said, unable to ignore the usual trail of debris: butter-covered knives, puddles of milk, dirty plates not even stacked, egg shell on the floor where he'd missed the bin. Almost every cupboard door was open, and was that a bag of compost on the table? It would take her at least an hour to clear up again, she thought, as he rubbed and kneaded and chewed on her neck and told her he loved her. He really was too much.

As soon as they entered the flat on Thursday

218

evening, after a lovely stroll along the beach, their host, Amanda, handed Marie her mobile.

'I'm sorry,' she said. 'I thought it was my phone. Over there.' She pointed to the corner where Marie and Gavin had stashed their things. They'd been sleeping on a sofabed in the living room. 'They're identical, you see. Anyway, I switched it on and it told me I had all these messages and I thought, *odd*, and started reading them ... and well, I think you should take a look.'

Marie dropped her bag, pressed at buttons on her phone and, at first, couldn't take any of it in. Whose son had they 'got'? She moved on to the next message and then the next. Dylan was mentioned. A million-pound ransom was demanded, otherwise they'd 'take him out', they said. There wasn't, it appeared, a single message from Alex. She dialled in to pick up voicemail and a boy who sounded vaguely American was telling her to get hold of her ex-husband and get him to organise the ransom 'pronto'.

'Jesus,' she said, her knees suddenly giving way. How long had they been trying to get hold of her? Was Dylan still alive? Surely, they'd managed to get through to Alex? She fell into an armchair.

'What is it?' asked Gavin, and Amanda took him to one side and explained, while Marie called Alex. But his phone just rang and rang as it had ten days ago. She then tried his mobile with no luck.

'Do you think I could have a drink?' she asked.

'Yeah, of course. Wine? Red?'

Marie nodded. After trying Dylan's home number in case it was a prank, she trawled through the rest of her messages. None of them told her they'd cut off an ear or anything, thank God. She took a pen from her bag and with a shaky hand wrote down the kidnappers' number on the edge of a magazine. After a couple of swigs of wine, she dialled it.

One of their phones rang.

'Norfolk Broads Escort Agency,' said Mr White, not for the first time. 'You got the dough, we got the broads.'

Some kind of zap-em game was being played on the laptop. Full volume. It was almost as though Messrs White, Orange and Pink desperately wanted someone to hear them, just to bring the whole débâcle to an end.

'Turn that fuckin thing off!' Mr White suddenly yelled, and somebody did. He then whispered to the others that it was an important friggin phone call and to keep the fuckin noise down. He cleared his throat and in a pleasant voice said, 'You say you're Dylan's ma, huh?'

Dylan gave an involuntary jerk. He still had a parent!

'Well, let me see,' went on Mr White. 'Wadda-yasay you prove you're his old lady before we begin any negotiating. Tell me something about him his ma would know, but some undercover policewoman pretending to be his ma wouldn't, mm?... Oh yeah? Is that right? One moment, please.'

Dylan heard the phone being placed on the table and before he knew it, Mr White was beside him telling him to stand up. 'What for?' he asked as he was lifted from his chair. He froze as his trousers were unzipped and pulled down; then his underpants. The other two tittered. 'Look!' he protested.

'Huh,' said Mr White, 'so you do,' and he returned to the phone, snapping at Mr Pink to sort Dylan out.

'OK, I found the appendix scar,' Mr White said. 'Pretty neat one. Anyways, we ain't bin able to get a hold of that ex-husband of yours. I'm taking it he's the man when it comes to the million?... Uh?... No, no, lady. You get to talk to your son when we get to talk to his dad. Comprendez?'

The silence in the hut meant Dylan could just hear his mother's voice, and as Mr Pink hooked his waistband together for him, Dylan felt a lump forming in his throat.

'You and your ex-old man gotta call in every four hours, OK?' Mr White was saying. 'Or the kid gets it.'

'Don't worry,' whispered Mr Pink, suddenly beside him. 'Like old Thingy – whassisname ... er, Baldrick, that's it, used to say ... I have a cunning plan.'

Dylan gave a miserable sniff. Was this good news?

Ellie had gone to spend a few days at her dad's place in Norwich. Partly because it was just so much easier, logistically, being in town, now that her friends were back. But mostly it was because she was feeling a tad excluded at home with the lovebirds. It was hard to believe people actually *did it* when they got to that age, but when it was your own mother it really wasn't pleasant to be around. Plus, when your own mother, who you'd had all to yourself for years and years suddenly wasn't listening to you because she was listening instead to Richard, or else busily clearing up after him in a way that she never would for her daughter ... well, it was all a bit insulting really. Mind you, Richard was sorting out all the mess in the garden. And, he was quite a nice person. And funny. Plus he was really good-looking for his age, so she could sort of forgive her mother. Sort of.

The only problem with being at her dad's house – a big modern place in a cul de sac, with lots of gold taps, air fresheners and thick carpets – was that Gillian, her stepmother of four years, tried too hard. Constantly asking Ellie if she needed anything, what she wanted to watch on TV, was she warm enough, too warm. Did she want to go and see a film, have her friends round.

Well, normally it was a problem, and Ellie was forever saying, 'No, I'm *fine* thanks,' with a fake smile. But this evening she was kind of wallowing in all the attention after days of neglect at home. Earlier, Gillian had shot out for a pizza the moment Ellie said that was what she really fancied, and now the three of them, at her request, were watching *Big Brother*. It was the last week now, and down to four housemates. Wayne, and three girls.

'She's a total bitch, that Selina,' Ellie was explaining. 'And always like lifting her top at the two-way mirrors.'

'Which one's that?' said her dad, coming round from his half-slumber. Gillian gave him a mock slap and they all laughed.

This was fun, Ellie decided. So far, she'd watched every *Big Brother* on her own because her mum called it 'puerile', which she hadn't got round to looking up yet but guessed it didn't mean pure.

'All the blokes hated Wayne,' she explained, 'because he's good-looking and went to university and he knows a lot. Well, compared to them, anyway. I *really* want Wayne to win.'

'Do you?' asked Gillian. 'Use the phone if you want to vote for him. Don't worry about the cost.'

Ellie said, 'Yeah, thanks. Maybe later,' while her dad's eyes began drooping again and the phone out in the hall started ringing.

Gillian got up, apologising to Ellie for the interruption, and said, 'If it's a patient, shall I tell them you're asleep, Colin? I mean, it's almost true.'

'Please.'

She went out of the room and returned with the phone. 'It's your mother,' she said, handing it to Ellie. 'Sounds important.'

'Oh, right. Er ... hello?'

'Hi, Ellie,' said her mum. 'Having a nice time?'

'Yeah, I am.' She kept one eye on Wayne, who was sunbathing in his tiny shorts just a bit too close to bitch Selina. Was her top undone? 'How are you?' she asked absently.

'Not brilliant, actually. I've just had a call from Dylan's mother and, well, I don't want you to worry too much, love, but…'

'What?'

'Well, some people have got him. They're asking for money.'

Wayne had turned on his side and he and Selina were as good as snogging. Where the bikini top had gone Ellie had no idea.

'Shall I turn it off?' Gillian asked, the remote pointed at the screen.

'Hang on,' her dad was saying. 'Not just yet.'

'Ellie?' she heard. 'Are you there?'

'Yeah.' Her heart had begun doing this odd thumping thing and the television screen was going blurry. 'Are you saying he's been … you know?'

'Kidnapped? Yes, it does look that way, love. I didn't want to call you tonight, but Marie asked me to ask if you might have any idea who'd do such a thing.'

'Of course not.'

'You haven't seen any odd-looking people hanging around the cottages? In the lane, or anywhere.'

She had a think. 'No. Not at all. How much do they want for him?' Her dad and Gillian were giving her concerned looks and mouthing things she couldn't understand at her.

'A million.'

'Shit.'

'I'm sure Alex can spare that. Marie hasn't been able to get hold of him, so she's on her way to his place now. Let's pray he's there.'

'I want to come home.'

'Oh, there's no need. Honestly. Stay with Dad

224

and Gillian tonight. You know they love having you.'

'All right. But let me know if you hear anything, won't you. Ring my mobile or whatever, yeah? Even if it's like three in the morning.'

'OK.'

They said goodbye and Ellie handed the phone back to her stepmother, who'd been hovering beside her all the while to take it back to the hall. Nothing stayed out of its place for long in their house.

'Everything OK?' asked her dad when they were alone.

'Yeah, yeah,' she said, her heart still thumping like mad. She'd better not tell them, or Gillian would be out scouring Norfolk all night in her Nissan. 'Nothing serious.'

Brighton to Gloucestershire was quite a way, but the taxi driver put his foot down and Marie was there by eleven-fifteen. The house appeared to be in darkness, so she did her usual thing of finding a gap in the hedge, discovering the doorbell didn't work, then throwing stones at Alex's bedroom window and shouting. No response. Perhaps a downstairs window had been left open, she thought. She'd asked the driver to wait, just in case Alex wasn't home, and could hear his engine idling reassuringly as she made her way around the house. Everything seemed to be firmly shut, but then, as she turned a corner, light shone forth from the kitchen and she hurried towards it.

What she saw when she got there was almost

more of a shock than news of the kidnap. Alex appeared to be baking. With the very tips of his fingers, he was taking a large round piece of sponge from a cooling rack and placing it on top of an impressive three-tiered affair. Marie could hear music. The Moody Blues? For some reason she couldn't move. She watched him reach for a sieve, pour icing sugar in it and tap at the side with the palm of his right hand, lightly dusting the top of his cake. 'That's enough!' she wanted to shout, but he stopped before overdoing it. She knocked hard at the window, making the dog bark furiously and a small cloud fly up in the air as Alex jumped and turned towards her.

Marie summed up the situation in a couple of sentences and Alex turned white. Or it could have been icing sugar. 'Maybe you should sit down,' she said.

She plugged in his phone and made him listen to his messages while she went off to the kitchen for a cold drink. What greeted her in the fridge was most worrying. Dozens of silver-foil dishes, each with a cardboard lid with Alex's writing on it. She pulled them out, one by one: *Salmon and Fennel Fish Pie*; *Char-grilled Vegetables with Couscous (Vegan)*; *Luxury Bread and Butter Pudding*... Surely he hadn't cooked all these? Alex had barely made himself a sandwich in his life. And who on earth was going to eat them? A plastic jug labelled *Raspberry, Orange and Rhubarb Smoothie* sat in the fridge door and she flipped it open, sniffed, then poured herself a glassful and went back to where Alex sat stupefied, phone in hand.

'If he's dead,' he said hoarsely, like someone who hadn't had a conversation for a while, 'I'll never forgive myself.'

EIGHTEEN

Alex had learned a lot about cookery in the past week or so, but little about storage and preservation, it seemed. Before they set off for Norfolk on Friday morning, Marie made him freeze most of the things he'd cooked in the previous couple of days, and all the older dishes went in the bin.

She said, 'Didn't they teach you about multiplying bacteria at your posh school?' and he told her he'd mostly opted for arts subjects.

It was nine o'clock and Alex had now spoken to the kidnappers twice. Once at eleven-thirty last night, shortly after Marie arrived, and then at half-three – a call that didn't go down that well with the sleepy 'Mr White', who'd clearly forgotten the four-hour rule. Alex was told not to bother with the seven-thirty and eleven-thirty calls, but to, 'Just get your ass over here.'

The initial order had been to make his way to Norfolk with the ransom money in cash. When Alex said it would take his bank days to get that kind of money together, and what's more wouldn't it look a bit suspicious, Mr White had agreed to take a cheque. 'Only I want your, you know, card number on the back,' he'd added. 'And no going and cancelling the cheque or nothing.'

'Of course not. I'm a man of my word,' Alex

228

had said, managing to hide his incredulity.

Marie was going to drive them to Dylan's place in a car of her choice from Alex's well-stocked garages. She said she fancied the old classic Aston Martin, but he talked her into the Volvo estate instead. 'Loads of room for Chomsky in the back,' he said. 'Plus they're the safest of cars – you know, should we crash.'

He was made to regret the last remark for a while, but once they were on the road with homemade *Assorted Samosas* and *Double Choc Chip Cookies* to dip into should either of them recover their appetites, all was well again, if a little tense, owing to their son being at the mercy of a deranged adolescent with the oddest accent Alex had ever heard.

Soon they were sailing down the A40 towards Oxford. Well, more like flying down. Had Marie always driven so fast? In fact, had she driven at all back then?

'When did you pass your driving test?' he asked.

'When I was nineteen, Alex. You gave me most of my lessons.'

Had he? He nodded. 'Oh yeah, of course.'

Marie said, 'So tell me again exactly what Mr White's instructions were.'

'Right. He told me we're to go to Dylan's house with the chequebook...'

Alex and Marie turned to each other and managed a laugh.

'To be there by three p.m.,' he continued, 'when he'd call and give further instructions.' Alex drummed for a while on the plastic

229

container on his lap. 'You know, I'm having second thoughts about not contacting the police.'

'But we've said we wouldn't.' Marie turned and looked at him with desperation in her eyes. 'I just worry about Dylan's fingers, and his ears and everything. They may sound ten years old but who knows what these guys are capable of.'

'True,' Alex said miserably. He lifted the corner of the container. Would a cookie help? He took one out, bit in, and realised it wouldn't. 'Here, Chomsky,' he shouted, flinging the rest of it to the back of the estate.

'Biscuit?' he asked Marie.

'Uh uh, I'd only choke on it.' She laughed half-heartedly. 'No offence meant.'

'None taken.'

'So tell me,' said Marie, 'why all the cooking?'

Why indeed. He guessed it had sort of come out of necessity to begin with, there being little in the way of prepared meals in the house once all the women had flown. Then he'd just really got into it. He liked the routine: ordering a taxi every morning to take him and his shopping list to Gloucester. And the methodical aspect: putting all the weighed-out ingredients into little bowls ready for when they were needed. There'd been the odd pleasant surprise too, like discovering Mary Berry's *Cook Now, Eat Later* in the superstore. Perfect, he'd thought, dropping it into his trolley. Of course, she hadn't told him not to cook too much now. Anyway, it was an activity that proved most therapeutic, being part-practical, part-creative – like making music. Ideal for someone wanting to block out the world for a while. No big life-altering decisions to make. Only whether to opt for olive or groundnut oil, butter or margarine. With hindsight, he could see that he'd become overly absorbed with the project; rather too tunnel-visioned.

'Good question,' he said. 'Good question.'

'I wonder why it is,' said Marie, overtaking unnecessarily, 'that men tend towards the obsessive when it comes to interests and pastimes. Geoff was like that about World War Two, until we signed up for cable, that is, and he got military-documentary overload. And Gavin's always banging on about–'

'Who's Gavin?'

'Oh, he's...' Her voice trailed away and Alex turned towards her and saw a warning light flashing above her head. Or perhaps it was the sun bouncing off passing trees. Either way, she was looking uncomfortable and guilty as hell, and had begun chewing her bottom lip as though trying to button it. She stared ahead and said, 'Just a friend.'

Gavin? He was pretty sure she'd never mentioned a Gavin before. All of a sudden Alex was thrown back to a hazy memory of Marie owning up to having an affair with Matt D'Angelo, bass guitarist with Damp Dream. The worst band in the world but they oozed testosterone, even in their poncey stage outfits. Was Gavin a boyfriend of some sort? Might that explain the Hugo Boss cologne and electric shaver he'd seen on Marie's bathroom shelf?

He lifted the top box and opened the one beneath. 'There are samosas if you fancy one,' he said. 'Lamb, chicken ... vegetable.'

'Oh why not.' She reached across and took pot luck. 'It's about time I got *some*thing inside me.'

Alex winced as he imagined her saying the very same words to 'Gavin' several weeks back. He put the lid back on, brushed crumbs away then watched the Oxfordshire countryside roll by.

Matt D'Angelo.

Huh.

How had he forgotten all about that until now? It had been a tearful confession, *that* he remembered. But when? They'd been touring. Damp Dream were the support band. So, if Marie was with them, it must have been before Dylan was born. A long, long tour, taking in Europe, the Far East. Then Marie had dropped out of Blue Plum at the end of it, knackered or ill or something. Pregnant maybe.

Pregnant.

A cold sensation started in Alex's face and worked its way down towards first stomach, then knees. Oh, surely ... if only he had a better memory for dates and times and the order of events... He turned to her. 'You know that tour we did with Damp Dream?'

'Mm. What about it?'

'I was just trying to recall when that was.'

'Don't you remember? It was the year Dylan was born. We finished the tour in Paris in May and Dylan was born in October. God, I felt *so* ill at that last gig.'

Matt had been dark-haired, like Dylan. Dark-eyed, too. People were always saying of his young son, 'He's got your nose, Alex,' or similar, but

232

Alex could never see it. Had they known all along, and were just trying to reassure him?

'Do I take the next turning off?' Marie was saying.

'Um, yeah. Follow the signs to Bicester.'

No, Alex told himself. No, no, no. He was being ridiculous. He chuckled quietly and shook his head at his foolishness. How, after all, could someone with Dylan's musical ability be Matt D'Angelo's son?

Earlier in the day, Mr Pink had been sent out for masks, Mr White having decided that they should take Dylan's blindfold off for a while, before his eyes became infected or damaged and they had to take him to hospital and then got sued. Although the blindfold had been coming off at night when he was led into his windowless and, unfortunately, locked room with the mattress from the back of his van in it, Dylan had only caught glimpses of the hut's half-light before and it had taken him a while to adjust to the brightness.

What had greeted his eyes, once they'd got used to it, was, firstly, Baz's body beneath a Darth Vader mask. Behind him stood a tall, skinny Winston Churchill in silver trainers, and a beefy overly tattooed Queen Elizabeth II. Lastly, he noticed the hideous outfit he, himself, was wearing: bright blue tracksuit bottoms and a screamingly loud short-sleeved shirt, all purple and orange and geometric.

'Hey, so now I get a good look at you, dude,' said Churchill, alias Mr White. 'Kinda Keanu

233

Reeves meets the young Warren Beatty.'

'Thank you,' Dylan said with a nervous nod, wondering if things were a lot less scary with the blindfold on.

The Queen said, 'Be a shame to mess up a purdy face like that, huh?'

Mr White laughed, then barked – well, yapped – a couple of orders to the others regarding tidying up, and everyone dispersed, leaving Dylan to take in his surroundings. Possibly an old disused Nissen hut belonging to the RAF. Were they on Ministry of Defence land, then? Bit risky. With luck they'd be rooted out by the Military Police some time soon. Christ, how worried must his parents be? And had anyone told Natalia? His eyes misted up at the thought of her greeting him on his release with a relieved and lingering hug. Saying that thinking she'd lost him forever made her realise how much he meant to her. That if he'd take her back she'd be a proper girlfriend and never suggest a threesome again.

He blinked away the tears and continued to look around. The main door was at the far end of the long room. Behind him was the short corridor that led to the bathroom and his bedroom. There were stacks of empty takeaway cartons piled high, a big table, a laptop, scattered playing cards and one, two, three camp-beds. He could see that, behind the masks, Mr White had fleshy pink-rimmed ears and sandy-coloured hair and Mr Orange was bald or shaved.

Mr Pink and Mr Orange spent most of the morning and the whole of a very tricky lunch complaining about having to wear the effing masks, and then, just as Dylan was about to volunteer to get back into his blindfold, the noise of approaching tank-like engines could be heard through the many broken window panes. Closer and closer they came. Dylan – heart jumping for joy – wondered if those MPs were, after all, coming for him and braced himself for a storming of the hut. If only he could quickly change his outfit.

What sounded like half a dozen or so vehicles seemed to be doing a lot of manoeuvring, loud voices could be heard shouting, and Mr Pink was told to go and check it out. 'Discreetly, yeah?'

'Sure thing, boss,' he said, making for the door.

'Take fucking Darth Vader off first!'

Dylan was slowly getting used to hearing Winston Churchill come out with such things.

'And go out a back window or something, not the front fucking door.'

'Ookay.'

Baz was gone five minutes, then reappeared in his mask. 'It's a funfair,' he reported breathlessly. 'West Washam's having its summer fête in the field next door. This weekend. Wicked, eh?' He rubbed his hands together.

Mr White thumped the table and made a long growling noise, the kind Winston might have come out with on hearing some war plan had been scuppered. 'You stoopid fuckin no-brain asshole!' he hissed, nodding towards Dylan. 'You've given our friggin location away now.'

'Oops,' said Darth Vader.

Ellie couldn't believe her mum had *gone to work* in the middle of such a crisis.

'There really wasn't much she could do at home,' Richard said loyally. 'And besides, we're here should anything happen.'

'Yeah, I suppose so.'

The two of them were in Dylan's house. They knew his parents were on their way, but she and Richard thought they'd check the place out for clues. It was something to do while they waited.

While Richard looked around upstairs, Ellie picked up the phone in the entrance hall and listened to Dylan's messages: the one from Emma – whoever she was – then an elderly-sounding woman called Fay, saying they'd missed him the past couple of weeks, and asking if he might be able to take over the class while she and May were in St Ives.

After putting the phone down, Ellie turned and thought back to throwing Baz over her shoulder that time. She looked at the spot where he'd landed and smiled, remembering his astonished expression and how well he'd taken it. He was quite a nice bloke really. It was a bit odd, though, not seeing him around these days. In fact ... why *hadn't* he been around these past couple of weeks? Surely there were jobs he could be getting on with. And, come to think of it, why had he been sneakily looking in Dylan's address book in his absence? And why had he behaved so guiltily, and hidden his car and everything...

'Ellie!' she heard from a bedroom. 'Come and look.'

Her heart skipped a beat and she took the stairs

two at a time.

Richard stood surrounded by Dylan's paintings in the front bedroom. 'He's good, isn't he?'

'Oh,' she said, breathing again.

'Look at this. Excellent.'

Ellie went and inspected. It seemed to be the girl who worked in The Fox, which was a bit of a surprise considering she was completely naked. 'Not bad,' she sniffed as her eye was caught by a nearby sketch of Baz. Dylan had captured him well: drill in his hand and a sort of vacant expression. She stood and stared, long and hard. Baz, she kept thinking. Baz. The notion that she should get in touch with him slowly filled her head. That she should look him up in the address book as soon as she got back home. She suddenly felt all fired up. Was Dylan sending her telepathic messages?

'Can I borrow the car?' she asked her mum, practically snatching the keys from her hand as they passed on the front path just after six. 'Thanks!'

Thirty minutes later, she was outside the kind of house she wouldn't have dreamed Baz came from. Large, detached, old. Big swirly cast-iron gates and a plaque saying *Elmside*. She knew Baz lived in a granny flat at his parents' place, but she'd always imagined a bit of an extension to a modern estate house, or a converted garage or something. Not a Kensington Palace-type granny flat.

Earlier, she'd phoned his mother, who'd said, 'Thass three days since we've seen Barry – sorry,

Baz – so he should be popping in soon for some clean cloothes. Got a big live-in job on, out in the country, you see. Who should I tell him called?'

'Er ... Gloria.'

'Ookay.'

'Oh, you couldn't give me your address?' Ellie had quickly added. 'I just need to settle a bill.'

'Right you are. Got a pen?'

What exactly she was hoping for as she sat outside his house, Ellie wasn't sure. Half of her would be relieved to find Baz really did have a big building job out in the country. Meanwhile, all she could do was sit there, running her CD-player batteries down and waiting for his crappy old car to appear.

But by five past ten he hadn't shown and Ellie was getting quite chilly without a jacket or jumper or anything, so she decided to give up and go home. She guessed Baz wasn't going to make an appearance this late, especially as his parents had gone to bed ten minutes ago. The surveillance would have to continue tomorrow. She'd tell her mum she needed the car to visit Jess who, like them, lived miles from anywhere.

Back home again, with everyone gathered next door and a note on the table saying, *Ellie, No news. Chicken in fridge. Mum xx*, she rushed to the TV and just caught *Big Brother* winner, Wayne, being cheered like mad and parading around for the photographers. 'Yes!' she cried, convinced all her phone calls had swung it. Her eyes filled with tears of joy. She knew it was stupid, but she saw this as a good omen.

His father had called regularly throughout the day. One time, Dylan had been made to read a message – written by Mr White – while the phone was held a short distance away. 'Hello, Dad,' he called out stiltedly, a lump in his throat. 'This is Dylan. Your son. I am being took good care of. Do as they say or that might change.'

He gathered that both his parents were at Biddlefarm Cottages with the ransom money and all was ready for his release. The sense of anticipation Dylan felt was on a par with that time a tall, stunning-looking woman invited herself back to his place after picking him up in the supermarket. 'I can help you unpack your goods,' she'd said, fondling a courgette. For a while after they'd got together, he and Natalia occasionally re-enacted their first meeting. Sometimes it was an aubergine.

The problem was, at twenty past midnight, Mr White hadn't quite worked out how to execute the exchange, what with the funfair being set up right under their noses. Dylan guessed Mr White's mask was hindering clarity of thought, irritating him and making him sweat. Every now and then he'd turn away, lift his Winston face and mop at his brow and cheeks. Dylan guessed that by tomorrow morning his kidnappers would have him back in his blindfold.

'So,' said Darth Vader, suddenly at his side. 'You want the bog, did you say?'

'Er...'

'Just say yes,' whispered Baz.

'Um, *yes*. Desperately.' He stood and let himself be accompanied to the toilet.

'Send your dad a text,' said Baz, loosening the knot on Dylan's wrists, but not entirely freeing him. He took a mobile phone from his pocket, tapped at it a few times and handed it to Dylan. 'Thass his number. Tell them where you are. Quickly. Put something personal in so's they know it's you, then press this one here to send. Ookay?'

'Oh. Right. Cheers.' Surely Baz could have sent a message? Worried about his spelling maybe. Dylan had occasionally thought Baz might be dyslexic. Sometimes turning up with the wrong things when Dylan had given him a DIY shopping list. That could explain his preference for Chinese food, maybe. No words, just numbers.

'I'll guard the door,' Baz said. He turned to leave then stopped and whispered, 'Can I still come and work on the house for you?'

It was a bit disorientating, having Darth Vader ask if he could help with your extension. Dylan said he'd think about it.

Fliss and the kettle were reaching boiling point at roughly the same time.

'Mmm, *Honey*man,' she could hear Marie Child saying in the next room. She seemed to be a bit drunk, which was odd as they'd all been on coffee in order to stay awake. 'Such a romantic name. Honeyman... Honey *Man*... Honey*moon*...

Yes *OK*, thought Fliss. Considering she'd got Alex's vital organ working again for Marie – who'd even phoned Fliss to thank her – this was definitely out of order. She hunted in Dylan's makeshift cupboard for Epsom salts or similar to slip in Marie's cup.

'All that gardening must be what keeps you in shape.' *Sexy laugh*.

'Grrrr,' said Fliss, while her eye was caught by the large brandy bottle on the worktop, set aside from the other drinks and half gone. Hadn't it been full earlier? The woman was obviously drunk.

Fliss hid the bottle behind the rubbish bin, poured water into Dylan's cafetière then looked through to the living room where Marie was recrossing her annoyingly tanned legs and asking Richard what his *very* favourite flower was. Hers was the red tulip, she told him. 'Beautifully clean lines, vibrant, and always a joy to see after weeks and weeks of tiresome daffodils, don't you think?'

Richard said he rather liked daffodils. 'The first real splash of colour after months and months of tiresome winter.'

Marie gave another throaty chuckle and tucked hair behind an ear. Why wasn't Alex doing anything about the situation? Giving her a good slap or something? He seemed to be oblivious to it, though. Far away in a little world of his own, by the looks of it. And so sad. Worrying about his son, no doubt. Well, who wouldn't be? Apart from Marie, of course.

She carried two mugs through and handed Alex one. 'Here you are,' she said. The others could get theirs themselves.

'Thanks,' he said and she joined him on the largest of Dylan's tatty sofas.

'You OK?' she asked, stroking his shoulder. Two could play at Marie's game. 'I'm sure

241

Dylan's going to be fine.'

'Yes,' he said with a nod. 'I'm sure he will be.' He put his cup down on a small table and leaned towards her. 'Fliss,' he said quietly while Marie babbled away, 'I don't suppose you know anything about DNA testing, do you? You know, to establish paternity? Being in the profession.'

Fliss was momentarily stunned. Why did he want to know? Did he have doubts about Dylan's paternal line? She looked over at Marie corkscrewing her hair with a red-nailed finger and could see why he might. Or perhaps it was one of those *'I'm having Alex Child's baby!'* claims by a seventeen-year-old actress/model. As softly as she could, she told him what she knew.

'Thanks,' he said, just as his mobile phone played its little tune and everyone in the room gasped. 'Text message,' he told them, getting his reading glasses out of a pocket and hooking them over his ears. He pressed at a silent button, read it, said, 'Oh, thank God,' then passed it to Fliss.

Hi dad. Gt hold of phone. Im ok. Right by w washam summer fete in hut by raf runway. See u v soon I hope. No police. Love to u and angel in red. Dylan. Ps dont reply.

Fliss scrolled back to the top and read it again, not because she needed to, but just to power trip for a while.

'Well?' urged Marie eventually. 'What does it say?' She unwound her arm from Richard's and reached across for the phone. 'Aargghh!' she screamed as she read. 'This means we have to go. *Now!*' She jumped up from the two-seater sofa and straightened her clothes. 'Come on!'

'Hang on, hang on,' said Alex, sounding almost forceful. 'Let's think this through, shall we?'

Marie sat back down.

'First of all,' he continued, 'what's double-u washam?'

Fliss smiled. 'West Washam. You played there, remember?'

'Ah yes. Well, so you tell me.'

'Not much point in going out there at this time of night,' said Richard. 'Hard to find the place and it would be far too quiet to take them by surprise.'

Marie nodded in agreement. She seemed to have suddenly sobered up, and was perched on the edge of the sofa, chewing a nail.

'Better to wait until the fête's in full swing,' Richard added.

'OK, well I suggest we sleep on it,' said Alex. 'Come up with a plan over breakfast.'

Good idea, they all concluded, before setting off for their respective beds.

'Jesus,' said Richard, once he and Fliss were outside. 'She came on a bit strong for a first meeting.'

'I'm sure you loved it.'

'Not really. Never gone for highly sexed women.'

'No?'

'Isn't that obvious?' he asked, kissing her cheek and leaving her borderline hurt.

Marie was in the guest room, while Alex was in the attic with Chomsky, who was sprawled where he'd been since they arrived, on Dylan's bed, nose buried in a T-shirt.

'I know, old thing,' said Alex. 'We're all missing him.' He kicked off his shoes and stretched out next to the dog with his book. It wasn't often that money saved a person's life, the alchemist was telling the boy. Alex's eyes rose to the ceiling. Not totally true. A million pounds might yet save Dylan's life. But no, money didn't necessarily equal happiness. Especially not when you thought your son might not be your son.

All that was needed was a drop of blood, apparently. Or a mouth swab. Fairly difficult to get either from Dylan without his knowing, though. Surely the lab could do the test with a strand of hair or something? He should have asked Fliss. He rolled on to his side and examined his son's pillow, pleased to see it was positively covered in hairs. But not Dylan's, he realised, picking one up as he grew sleepier. They were all more or less the same. About two inches long and a mucky brown colour. His last conscious thought was that you really wouldn't want to go genetically testing Chomsky.

NINETEEN

Ellie was first up; showered and dressed and out of the door by eight, with a bag of food, a change of clothes and a camera. En route she stopped and picked up magazines, bottles of water and batteries and, from a hardware shop, a roll of thick silver duct tape, just in case, and a penknife, just in case. But then she got worried about the penknife and thought she'd just leave it in the car.

By a quarter to nine, she was back in place, opposite *Elmside*, flicking through pictures of celebrities and hoping her mum wouldn't erupt when she found her note saying she'd borrowed the car to visit Jess.

Oh no, it can't be, thought Fliss, her eyes popping open. But there it was again.

'Yoo hoo! Anyone home?' Clonk, clonk, clonk.

'Hey, cute li'l cottage,' came Hal's equally loud voice.

'Not that little inside, actually. Wait till you see. Three storeys, goes back a long way. He*llo?* Fliss?' Knock, knock, knock.

Richard rolled himself over and said, 'What does it mean when you have a recurring dream?'

'It means it's your turn to entertain in your bathrobe while I have a shower.'

245

Marie hadn't slept at all well. She'd tossed all night and didn't very much like being in the spare room Dylan had so lovingly done up for guests. It just reminded her of him and his plight. But Alex, who'd been terribly withdrawn and almost frosty with her yesterday evening, had insisted on separate bedrooms, saying he really needed a good sleep.

So many questions had zipped around her head in the night. What if the rescue attempt, or transfer, or whatever they were planning, went wrong and Dylan ended up shot? Or they were all shot? Fliss and Richard had volunteered to come along, but should they take that risk? Would it be best to get the police in after all, now they knew where Dylan was? Had the kidnappers moved him overnight? Or discovered he'd sent a text and killed him? It wasn't like Marie to worry unduly, and she wondered if sneakily adding Dylan's brandy to her coffees had been such a good idea. She'd never got on well with spirits, and now, at 9 a.m., was feeling groggy and queasy.

God what a sight, she thought, peering in the bathroom mirror at her hungover, sleep-deprived face. She hoped Alex would be capable of clear thinking this morning because she certainly wasn't. She could hear him now, busying himself in the kitchen below – bang, clatter, swish – and prayed it wasn't *Monkfish on a Bed of Rocket* or similar.

Mr Pink was ordered to do a bit of a recce and to buy a wheelbarrow. Dylan, now blindfolded again, was growing more and more tense. He'd overheard enough to know that he'd soon be leaving the hut in the said barrow, under various bits of bedding – his own, he prayed.

Although not an ideal living arrangement, he had sort of got used to the routine and the surroundings of the hut. He'd always felt he wasn't truly at risk of physical harm and in a strange way had come to feel quite safe in this unreal little world. So far, his captors had been endearingly bumbling and hopeless. Sort of Reservoir Puppies. However, being pushed along in a wheelbarrow by the oafish Mr Orange, to a situation which might, if his parents had ignored him, involve the police, possibly armed, was an altogether different kettle of fish. But with a bit of luck, his father, the SAS and a small regiment of Gurkhas would arrive before Baz had time to get to B&Q.

'Plastic or metal?' Mr Pink was asking.

Mr White sighed. 'I dunno. Metal.'

'One-wheeled or two?'

'Two-friggin-wheeled, of course. He's gotta be eleven stone.'

'Pounds,' corrected Mr Orange. 'We say pounds in the States, remember, Mr White.'

'Yeah, and who gave you permission to speak?'

'Sorry.'

Mr Pink said, 'Traditional or flatbed? Two-handles or a T-bar?'

'Oh, for fuck's sake,' snapped Mr White, who was still Churchill in Dylan's imagination. 'Just fuckin *big*, right?'

'Right.'

Dylan heard notes being counted out. 'A hundred should cover it, yeah?' said Mr White, whose mum had evidently coughed up. 'A minor investment considering the return. There. And don't stop at the friggin Chinese. No time for stuffing our faces today. Gotta get this show on the road.'

'Sure thing, boss.'

'But, well, maybe some chips, yeah?'

'Ookay.'

'Gotta keep our strength up.'

'Definitely. Shall I get four pickled eggs as well?'

Mr White sighed again. 'You know what?' he said. 'You disgust me, Mr Pink.'

They knocked tentatively on Dylan's front door and Marie, who to Fliss's delight had aged twenty years overnight, let them in.

'Any news?' Richard asked her.

'Not really. We called Mr White, but he said he'd ring back later with instructions.' She gave an enormous yawn behind a hand and talked through it. 'Meanwhile, we thought we'd go and check out West Washam. Try to find the hut.'

Fliss nodded. 'Shouldn't be too difficult. It's just what to do when we find it that's going to be tricky. Have you thought any more about getting the police in on it?'

'I'd rather not,' said Marie, all of a sudden squeezing Richard's arm. 'Anyway, we'll have two brave and brawny guys with us, won't we?'

Fliss heard a noise and turned to the front door. 'Or maybe three if–'

'Oh, I *say*,' said Hazel, clomping on to Dylan's bare floorboards in her court shoes. 'What a building site!'

'This is Hazel,' Fliss told Marie. 'And Hal.'

'Pleased to meet you, ma'am!' shouted Hal from the rear.

Marie flinched. 'Excuse me,' she said, pushing past her guests and heading for the stairs. 'Feeling a bit... Go on through. Alex is scrambling eggs in the microwave.'

Ellie was halfway through an article on cellulite when Dylan's van came around the corner very fast and stopped right outside *Elmside*. She dropped the magazine and clutched the steering wheel, waiting for something totally ordinary to happen. Dylan coming to pick up Baz for a day's work, for example. But it was Baz who got out of the van. Ellie lifted the camera slung round her neck and quickly took two photos of him locking the driver's door then charging through his parents' big curly gates. She picked up the magazine and made a note of the time on it. 10.43. The exact times things happened always seemed to be important in police investigations. She smiled to herself at her thoroughness, then pulled a big floppy hat of her mother's on to her head and went to examine the van.

Nothing in the front except rubbish: chocolate bar wrappers, empty crisp packets, a crumpled tabloid. Nothing in the back either, as far as she could tell. There were no rear windows, so she crooked her neck and peered through the windscreen. It looked empty beyond the grill, but

249

she gave a quick knock on the side of the van and shouted 'Dylan?' above the traffic a few times, just to be doubly sure.

But then Baz was back and opening the gate again so she ducked her head and promptly strode away, hat pulled down. Please don't let him spot Mum's car, she kept thinking but, once she'd slid back into it, she could see Baz was far too preoccupied with the task in hand – hoisting a big shiny wheelbarrow into the back of the van – to notice. Oh dear. Could it be he really *was* on some big building job after all?

She watched him lock the back doors, double check them, waddle to the front and get in. When he started up the engine, so did Ellie.

The only thing they'd all fit into was Alex's Volvo. Marie declared herself too braindead to drive and Alex said he wasn't allowed, so Richard volunteered, which pleased Fliss, as it meant she got to sit in the front. 'OK,' she said, strapping herself in. 'I'll direct you.'

'One moment!' said Hal, jumping out again. 'I just have to grab some things from my car.'

He came back carrying a raincoat, mysteriously winking at Fliss on his way past.

'OK, stick 'em up!' he said, once back in his place.

Fliss turned to face the barrel of a small black handgun. Marie screamed, Alex held his hands up, Chomsky barked and Hazel said, 'Oh Hal, you're such a wag. Put it away before someone punches your lights out.'

It turned out to be Hal's grandson's toy gun.

250

Once everyone had calmed down, they were all rather pleased to see it.

'They make them awfully realistic, these days,' said Fliss, examining it gingerly then handing it back. 'Not like the ones I used to play with.'

Richard finally pulled away down the lane. 'You played with guns?'

'Two brothers.'

'Oh, yes. Of course.'

Fliss wondered if it was such a good idea, all of them tagging along like this, but got the impression Alex and Marie were experiencing a certain safety in numbers. She was just pleased that Ellie was dealing with it all so well, going off to spend the day with her friend, Jess. One less person to worry about. She looked over at Richard and hoped he wouldn't try anything silly, ending up scarred and broken-nosed with a lifelong limp or something.

'Left at the bottom,' she told him, while behind her, Marie yawned loudly again.

'Anyone for an Opal Fruit?' asked Hazel, half-propped on Hal's lap, the seat being somewhat crowded. 'I know they're Starburst now, but they'll always be Opal Fruits to me. Hal?'

'No thanks, honey. The big "D" remember?'

'Oh, silly me. Did you remember your pill this morning, love?'

'Sure.'

'And you did have a decent breakfast while I was showering, I hope? Don't want you coming over woozy, like you did in Lady Hangbourne's pool.'

Fliss blinked. Whose pool? She turned and saw

251

Hal ruffle Hazel's highlights. 'Hey, champion worrier. Still alive, ain't I?'

'Yes, but only thanks to my Girl Guide lifesaver's badge!' Hazel shook her head then chuckled. 'Incredible how it all came back to me.'

'You know, acupuncture can help with diabetes,' said Fliss. 'Not cure it, of course, but ... oh, left at these traffic lights, Richard.'

'Right.'

'No, left, ha ha.'

Hazel thrust the sweets forward. 'Opal Fruit, Alex? Marie? Fliss?'

Fliss leaned back and took one for herself and one for Richard. 'Strawberry or Lemon?' she asked him.

'Lemon, please.'

'Beaudiful day!' called out Hal.

'Yes, isn't it?' shouted Richard as fulsome hedgerow whizzed past.

It was almost as though they were all off on a daytrip to the coast, and for a moment Fliss had a mild panic about not having her cozzie with her.

'ONE, TWO!' came blasting into the hut, making Dylan leap out of his skin. 'TESTING, TEST-ING. ONE TWO, ONE TWO...'

'Summer fuckin fête,' whined Mr White.

Dylan heard a generator start up, possibly two. Loud voices called to one another. 'Got the jack, Ron?' 'Back a couple of feet!'

'ONE, TWO! ONE, TWO!'

'Yeah, we know you can fuckin count to two, asshole.'

Mr Orange guffawed and Dylan wriggled his hands. Mr Pink had secretly loosened them earlier, whispering, 'You did send that text ookay, didn't you?'

'I think so. I dunno. Haven't used a mobile in a while.'

'Maybe I'll give your dad an anonymous phone call while I'm out, yeah?'

'Good idea.'

'Mr White'd kill me if he found out.'

'He won't.'

Mr Pink had been gone quite a while and tension was definitely building, both in and outside the hut. Last night they'd spent an hour taping something over all the windows and it was now sweltering in there and decidedly unpleasant.

Mr White was growing more and more anxious – 'Where the fuck's that wheelbarrow got to?' – and Mr Orange needed a bath. Well, they all did.

To keep his mind off impending doom, Dylan tried to concentrate on all the things he'd do when he got home. Check on that cistern leak, for instance. It hadn't seemed worth worrying about at the time but, in his head, had grown into a potential disaster since his capture. Tell his parents he loved them. Pay his Council Tax. Compliment his neighbour on her garden more often. Find a new pub to drink in. Call Natalia. Buy nice bread. Shave off his new beard...

Dylan's van all of a sudden pulled into a parking space in West Washam, and Ellie swore. She couldn't see another space anywhere. All she could do was slow right down and stick her left indicator on to let others overtake.

Baz got out and shot into a fish and chip shop, so Ellie just stayed put beside a row of parked cars, engine running, indicator still on, tummy churning, guessing he wouldn't be long. And she was right. He reappeared with wrapped-up goods just a couple of minutes later, and before she knew it she was on his tail again – well, two cars behind, so as not to be too obvious. But then he pulled over and parked outside a mini-supermarket place and she had to do the same thing again, much to other drivers' annoyance as she was practically in the middle of the road, engine idling. How Baz found these parking spaces completely baffled her. This time he was a bit longer, but eventually came out eating a chocolate bar of some sort, a large bottle tucked under each arm.

By the time they both set off again, Ellie was fairly convinced he was just stocking up for the building gang and that Dylan hadn't been sending her telepathic messages at all. Oh well, at least she hadn't told anyone what she'd been doing, so no embarrassment factor to deal with. When Baz stopped for a third time, to use a public phone box, she was on the verge of giving up and *really* visiting her friend, Jess. But she didn't, and Baz got back into Dylan's van and drove to the outskirts of the town. Then, just past a field on their right where there seemed to be a lot going on – marquees and a funfair – he shot into a lay-by on the righthand side of the road, some way ahead.

'Shit,' she said, but then directly in front of her a man in a bright yellow jacket was directing her off the road to the left. *Car Park* said the notice beside him and soon she was in a field and bumping over grass. Another man in a yellow jacket waved her into the exact place he wanted her and looked surprised when she jumped out of her car without even locking it and ran back towards the entrance, weaving her way through stationary and non-stationary cars like a slalom skier. Sometimes she was so grateful for all that judo she'd done.

She got to the main road just in time to see Baz pushing his wheelbarrow through a gap in a hedge. He seemed to be heading for the funfair. Odd, she thought, while she waited to cross. Did he think he was going to win so many fluffy toys and goldfish he wouldn't be able to carry them?

Once over the road, she too made her way through the gap – Baz's way of avoiding the entrance fee? – and found herself in a whole other world. It was like stepping through the wardrobe into Narnia. Only not quite. Kylie Minogue was 'La, la la'-ing on the dodgems, a little girl was screaming over the ice cream she'd dropped, and the loudspeaker was announcing that the Dog Show would begin in ten minutes in the main arena. With her hat pulled down and her eyes on his broad bottom, Ellie followed Baz and his barrow through the crowds and the noise, wondering if she'd ever had such a surreal experience.

'Wake up, Marie,' said Alex, gently nudging her

heavy head with his shoulder then patting her knee. 'We're there.'

'Got your gun, Hal?' asked Hazel.

Marie came round and gasped, 'Gun!'

'Not real,' said Alex, helping her upright. 'Remember? Come on, wake up properly.' He brushed hair away from her face with his fingers. 'Let's go and rescue your son.'

Your son? Had he really said that? Oh dear. It was just that every time he looked at Marie now, he saw her, Matt D'Angelo and Dylan – all one unit. He wondered if Dylan would choose to change his name if all were revealed. Dylan D'Angelo. Sounded like an Italian Renaissance painter if you said it quickly. Dylandangelo. He looked at Marie and remembered *The Angel in Red with a Lute*. His ex-wife wasn't looking quite so angelic these days.

'Ready?' he asked her.

'Yep.'

He helped her out of the car then went round the back for Chomsky, who promptly jumped down, Dylan's T-shirt still in his mouth. 'Aren't you ever going to part with that?' asked Alex. He clipped the lead to the dog's collar and rubbed affectionately at his head. 'Eh?'

The car park was full, and Alex really didn't want people recognising him, least of all the kidnappers, so he put on the grubby baseball hat he'd found in Dylan's building rubble and pulled it as far over his eyes as he could manage. He was sure he looked ridiculous, and this was confirmed when Marie – still pale and groggy-looking – managed a laugh.

'OK, guys,' said Hal. In his crisp white shirt and dark grey jacket, with his mackintosh over one arm, he looked as though he were about to meet with Microsoft executives. 'Let's get this show on the road.'

'Tell you what,' said Alex as they made their way through the car park towards the fete, 'why don't I go ahead with the dog and see what I can find? I'll come and report back. Meet you, say ... by the Lost Children tent? There's bound to be one of those.'

'Why don't we make it the liquor tent?' said Hal, winking and nudging Richard.

Hazel rolled her eyes. *'Beer* tent, Hal.'

Alex was anxious to be off and began striding ahead of the others. 'OK. See you in the beer tent. Give me half an hour or so.'

'Here, take the gun,' shouted Hal. He pulled it from a pocket and the couple beside Alex made strangled noises and quickly scooped up their toddlers.

'No, no,' insisted Alex as he hurried on. 'You keep it.' The first thing he saw on emerging from the car park was Dylan's van further along on the other side of the road. This filled him with hope and joy, but also brought a whole new terrifying reality to the rescue mission. He waited for a gap in the traffic then approached the van with caution. It seemed to be empty. Hard to see in the back, though. He followed Chomsky around the vehicle, watching him sniff excitedly at all four wheels, then the driver's door, the passenger door and the back doors. When the dog dropped the T-shirt, gave a knowing 'Woof,' and with the

257

sudden strength of a packhorse made for a gap in the hedge, Alex found himself almost flying through the air on the end of the lead.

TWENTY

Ellie hadn't wanted to follow Baz through the gate immediately, for fear of being spotted out in the open. Instead she slipped behind a nearby hotdog stall and watched him plonk the wheelbarrow by the narrow front entrance to a long and crappy-looking hut. Its windows were metal-framed and broken in places, and as far as she could see, were all covered on the inside. She grabbed the camera slung around her neck and took a couple of shots of Baz. Then, once he'd gathered the fish and chips and bottles out of the barrow and gone into the hut, she looked around for a well-hidden vantage point. Over there, she decided. Behind some bushes to the right of the hut. Rather than expose herself by going through the gate, she looked over both shoulders to make sure the coast was clear then, taking a run at the barbed-wire fence, cleared it with a scissor jump. Which wasn't bad for someone whose legs weren't forty-four inches.

Of course, she wasn't going to charge into the hut all by herself and confront the kidnappers or building gang, or whatever she found there. No, she'd just stake the place out for a while. She found a good spot, where she couldn't be seen from the fête or the hut, then flattened the grass, sat down and stared at the door through a leafy bush. When, two or three minutes later, nothing seemed to be happening, she opened the big canvas bag slung across her body and took out her magazine. After fanning herself with it for a while, she flicked through to the article on cellulite and carried on where she'd left off.

Dylan was convinced he could hear drops of sweat splash on to the floor. His feet were bare, his shirt was undone, but still he boiled in the airless room.

'We're gonna need more liquids, man,' announced Mr White halfway through their lunch of tepid mushy peas and chips. 'Two bottles wasn't enough, Mr Pink. Go get us something from one of them noisy friggin stalls out there. And quick. Can't fuckin think about this exchange when I'm dehydrated.'

Mr Pink stopped feeding Dylan. 'Ookay, boss. Coke? Sprite? Slush Puppies?'

'Anyfuckinthing. Just *go*. You need more dough?'

'No, it's ookay.'

'Yee-aaahh,' drawled Mr White. 'That reminds me. Where's the receipt for the wheelbarrow?' Huh?'

'Er ... in the van, boss. Sorry.'

There followed a long, low growl and Dylan heard Baz's footsteps heading for the door. But it wasn't a furious Mr White he realised, when the noise repeated itself. It was Mr Orange snoring. How anyone could sleep in such heat was beyond Dylan. Had Mr Orange passed out? It occurred to Dylan that if Mr White went the same way, he could be down The Fox for his dinner.

260

Ellie chucked her magazine aside and called out a quiet but urgent, 'Help! Help me! *Hee-eelp!*' She'd made her voice high-pitched and pathetic and watched while a baffled Baz plodded her way.

'Hello?' he called into the bushes, and with that Ellie was up like a Jack-in-the-box and grabbing his right arm before twisting it round behind his back and dragging him into her little lair.

'Yikes!' he cried out and she told him to hush.

Her free arm was now around his neck. 'Is Dylan in there? In that hut?'

'Ellie?' he said.

She tightened her grip. 'Just answer the question.

'Yeah yeah, he is. Only I've been trying to get him—'

'How many are there with him?'

'Ouch. Er ... two.'

'Are they big?'

'Sort of'

'Oh.'

Now she didn't quite know what to do, but nevertheless let go of Baz's neck and took the roll of tape from her bag. While her left hand held his arms behind his back she taped up his mouth with the aid of her teeth. It was funny, but Baz didn't seem to be resisting half as much as she'd expect. In fact, when it came to taping his hands together he was almost co-operative.

'Right,' she puffed when she'd finished. She dabbed at her brow and dug into her bag for the mobile. 'Time to call the police.'

Not far from the beer tent, Hal was hooking ducks out of water. Fairly successfully, it seemed, from the number of items Hazel was now holding. 'Gatcha!' he exclaimed each time, in a voice they could use if the loudspeakers broke.

Marie had been pacing up and down but suddenly plonked herself next to Richard on the grass, and with a coquettish pout said, 'Where do you think Alex has got to?'

There were certain women, thought Fliss, who would always choose to address a man if one were available.

'I'm sure he'll be back soon,' Richard reassured her. 'Do you want me to go and look for him?'

'Oh God, *no*,' she said, lifting her hair with all ten fingers, then letting it tumble over bare brown shoulders. 'You stay here with me.'

Fliss sighed. Was this something she'd have to get used to? Women coming on to her handsome boyfriend? *Boy*friend. Such a silly word when you're starting to read the newspaper at arm's length.

'Here comes the dog,' said Richard, leaping to his feet in an agile fashion Fliss could only envy. She hauled herself up just as Alex reached them.

'I think Chomsky's found the hut,' he panted beneath his horrible cap. 'Where's Hal?'

Fliss pointed to *Sitting Ducks – Prize for Every Catch!* and said, 'You'll be lucky to get him away from it.'

Alex cupped his mouth and yelled, 'Hal!'

'One moment!' came the reply as Hal leaned so far towards the ducks it must have constituted cheating. Hazel held on to his jacket until he cried, 'Gatcha!' pulled himself upright and pointed at something purple and hairy on the prize-stand.

It would have been much easier calling the police if she hadn't left her mobile in the car. 'Stupid cow,' she told herself, rummaging through her bag one more time, even though she knew it wasn't there.

'Mmm mm mm mmm,' said Baz. He was nodding his head towards something.

'What?'

'Mmm mm mm *mmm*.'

'Oh for...' she said, yanking the tape off his mouth. '*What?*'

His eyes filled with tears. 'You can use mine,' he told her. 'Left shorts pocket.'

'Oh. Right. Well, roll over a bit then.'

She wasn't too keen on going into Baz's shorts but concentrated on the object of the exercise and closed her eyes and grimaced as she stuck her hand in.

'I've been trying to help him escape,' Baz was telling her.

'Yeah, right. We'll see if the police believe *that*.' She pulled the phone out and tried not to think of germs as she looked at its blank screen and attempted to turn it on.

'No, honest.'

'Nothing's happening,' she said, pressing at buttons with her thumb.

'Oh yeah. Oh shit. It's run out of juice. Forgot.'

Ellie took a long look at Baz and decided he

really was too stupid for words and that she ought to make sure he didn't mess up her mission. She took the tape from her bag again and redid his mouth. When she'd almost finished binding his ankles, something caught her eye. It was an old bloke in a light-coloured raincoat, collar up, standing with his back against the hut, right beside the door.

'Who's that?' she whispered to Baz.

'Mm mm mmm.'

'Looks a bit of a gangster. Are you sure he's not like your big boss, or something?'

'Mm mmmm.'

'God, Baz,' she said, eyes glued to the stranger. 'You're *no* help.'

When the man put his hand in an inside pocket and pulled out a gun, Dylan's life began flashing through Ellie's head.

He'd started to wonder if dying of heat, thirst and suffocation would be fairly painless – no worse than carbon monoxide poisoning or too many paraceramols. He also pondered on whether his parents would sell his house just as it was, or finish off the work their late son had begun. Whether Natalia would bring Kris-with-a-K to the funeral, hold hands with her by the graveside. But he was jolted from such thoughts by the sound of the door opening with a deafening bang.

'OK guys, *freeze!*' shouted a new voice. Definitely not Mr Pink. 'Special Agent McClusky,' continued the man. He sounded mature and was doing an amazingly good American accent. 'FBI,' he added.

'What the fuck?' said Mr White, his chair scraping back. Something clonked on the floor. His phone perhaps. 'And don't you mean CIA?'

'Shuddup, and move away from the hostage. Throw any weapons on the floor. *Quick.*'

Dylan heard some shuffling, more swearing and Mr Orange still snoring. He found himself wondering if people snore when they're in a coma.

'You OK, Dylan?' asked Agent McClusky.

'Er... yeah.' He began wriggling his hands inside the loosened rope, and before long they were free. He lifted his blindfold gently, bracing himself for dazzling light, but the room was pretty much in darkness. The only light came from the open door and it was creating a kind of heavenly aura around Dylan's saviour, who by now had turned his attention back to Mr White. 'Lie face down on the floor and put your hands behind your back!' he yelled authoritatively. Then more gently, 'You wanna use that rope to tie him up, kid?'

'Er ... yeah,' Dylan said again, shock and thirst making him inarticulate. He stood up, rubbed at the pins and needles in his buttocks then saw another ethereal vision in the doorway. A blonde one this time. It seemed to be almost flying through the air for a while before it wrenched at Agent McClusky's arm, swung him round, and threw him over its shoulder and on to the floor.

Dylan rubbed both eyes with his knuckles. Too much blindness was clearly making him hallucinate. *'Ellie?'* he asked, his voice a quiet shriek.

265

His neighbour was now sitting on top of her victim and panting. 'You all right, Dylan?'

'Fine, yeah. But I think you might have the wrong–'

'Stay where you are!' she shouted at Mr White, yanking the gun from Agent McClusky's hand as he lay groaning beneath her. Dylan tried not to think sexist thoughts about women with guns. 'You too,' she said, swinging the thing round to Mr Orange, who was slowly regaining consciousness, lifting himself and his tattoos from his chair with a thrusting chin and a hungry look in his eye. But then he let out a quiet, 'Fuuuuck,' flopped back and stuck his hands in the air. Not for fear of the gun, it seemed, but because a dog the size of a bus was bounding towards him with bared teeth.

On following Alex into the hut, Marie's hand flew straight to her nose. God, it was ripe in there – old food, bodies, socks and worse made for a staggeringly awful combination, not helped by her hangover. She flew straight past Ellie – what was *she* doing there? – towards her strangely bearded son.

'Dylan!' she cried through her fingers, and with mind over aroma gave him a hug. 'We've been sick with worry, sweetie.'

'I'm sorry,' he said, half-sobbing, half-beaming. 'But, hey, it's all over now.' He lifted her off the ground and spun her full circle, which was, Marie felt, the last thing she needed.

After ordering the dog to 'Stay!' on top of a man with tattoos, Alex came over and joined in the hugging. 'Thank God,' he said. 'Thank *God*.

Are you OK, Dylan?'

'Yeah, fine. I'm just a bit worried about Agent McClusky.'

'Who?' they asked.

Dylan pointed at what Marie realised was Hal, spreadeagled under Ellie and lying just a little too still.

'Ellie, I think you should–' she began, when Hazel, Fliss and Richard stepped into the hut and gave a joint gasp. The sight of Ellie with a gun, Hal's demise or the ghastly smell? wondered Marie. All three perhaps.

'Hal!' Hazel screamed, yanking a bewildered-looking Ellie off her boyfriend. 'Are you all right, love?' She flopped to her knees. 'Hal?'

Ellie was pushing hair from her face. 'Oh dear,' she puffed. 'He was on *our* side, wasn't he?' She turned to her ashen-faced mother. 'Trust me.'

Fliss opened her mouth to speak but nothing came out.

Marie released Dylan to go and help poor Hal. 'Shtarrburrr...' she heard him murmur as she approached and knelt down.

'What was that, love?' asked Hazel, lowering her ear.

'Shtarrburr,' Hal repeated.

'Ah,' said Hazel, sitting up and unzipping her handbag. 'Blood sugar's dropped,' she explained to the others while she unwrapped a lemon sweet. 'Opal Fruits to the rescue!'

'Oi!' Ellie shouted, a little too close to Marie's headache. 'Where do you think you're going?' She dropped the gun and ran towards the tall skinny kidnapper – the one the dog wasn't sitting on – who appeared to be tiptoeing along the edge of the room, shoulders hunched, eyes fixed on the door.

But then Ellie suddenly stopped in her tracks and looked back at the others. 'Er ... goodie or baddie?' she asked.

Fliss thought better of telling her daughter off for leaving the car unlocked and, worse, the keys still in the ignition.

'Oh, that poor man,' Ellie was saying. She was watching Hazel help Hal into a car two rows away. 'I didn't realise he was one of us. And diabetic and Hazel's bloke and all that. God, I feel so stupid.'

'Foolhardy was what you were, Ellie. Not stupid.'

Ellie grinned over the top of the car. 'And dead brave, yeah?'

'No, just foolhardy. Now in you get. Let's get you out of harm's way.'

Fliss started up the engine. How proud she was of her daughter really. She smiled to herself then and changed her expression to a scowl. 'Promise me,' she said sternly, 'that you will never *ever* jump on a man holding a firearm again.'

Ellie grinned. 'Yeah, yeah. I promise.'

Out on the main road, Fliss began to relax a little after the high drama. She wondered how the others were getting on with the kidnappers, a few cars behind her. They were well and truly tied up, so no chance of a hijack or anything. Poor Dylan. What an experience he must have been through. Why he didn't want to press charges, she'd never know. Had something else in mind for the villains, apparently.

'So,' she said. 'Tell me from the beginning how you got to be at the hut.'

Ellie was checking her phone for messages. 'Well, I just started having these strange suspicions about Baz, so I followed him and *ohmyGod!*'

'What?' asked Fliss when her daughter turned a stricken face towards her.

'Baz!'

TWENTY-ONE

'I've done you a nice shepherd's pie,' said Mrs Farthing, who'd managed to reinstall herself in Alex's absence. 'After your long journey.'

They'd had a tedious trip back from Norfolk. Dylan being asleep in the back plus he and Marie barely exchanging a word, had made it tense and extremely lengthy. He beamed at Mrs F and rubbed his hands together.

'Lovely,' he said, but then he started digging in and realised it wasn't lovely at all. There were lumps in the mashed potato and not a single herb adorned the minced lamb. The accompanying out-of-season and horribly overcooked sprouts – no doubt shipped thousands of miles from foreign shores – gave off jets of water when pierced with a fork. He ate slowly under her watchful eye. How was he to tell this wonderful little person that he wanted to do his own cooking from now on? That he'd like her to just pop in occasionally and give the place a once-over. And maybe iron a few shirts.

'Tell Dylan I've left his in the oven,' she said, tugging a white cardigan on.

'Will do.'

'Along with the jam roly-poly.'

'Great. Thank you. Um ... Mrs Farthing, I was wonder–'

'So,' she said from the doorway. 'I'll see you

first thing.'

Alex nodded and mustered a smile. 'Yes.'

He put his fork down, listened for the back door to slam, then slowly counted to fifty before putting his plate on the floor and calling Chomsky over.

Out in the freezer he found a vegetable and couscous dish, which he defrosted then cooked, all in ten minutes in the microwave. He took everything through to the dining room just as his son appeared, freshly showered.

'It's weird,' Dylan said. 'I just can't stop sleeping.' He sat at the table and grabbed a serving spoon.

'Yes, well, you've been through quite an ordeal. We all have.'

'Mm. Sorry.'

'Hardly your fault.'

'No, I know. How's Mum?'

Alex shrugged. 'I think she went out for a walk.'

'Are you two not speaking?'

'Not really. No.'

'I thought as much.' Dylan frowned and looked concerned. 'Why's that then?'

Alex wondered what to say. 'Because your mother attempted an overthrow of Mrs Farthing,' would sound pathetic and, come to think of it, did he really mind? 'Because your mother is seeing someone else,' would be tacky, and still unconfirmed. And 'Because I'm not sure I'm your real father,' was out of the question, of course.

'Bloody hell,' said Dylan through a mouthful of food. 'Mrs Farthing's really excelled herself here.'

271

He pointed at his plate and nodded. *'Really good.'*

Alex sniggered and wobbled his head proudly. 'Actually, you're not going to believe this, but–'

'What's that smell?'

Alex sniffed and caught a whiff of something burning. 'Uh oh,' he said and rushed through to the kitchen, where he grabbed a cloth and pulled charred and unrecognisable remains from the oven.

Dylan came up to him, laughing. 'You haven't been trying to cook, have you, Dad?'

Marie hadn't meant to frighten Mrs F quite so much, popping out of the hedgerow that way.

'Never do that again!' the woman gasped, a hand at her throat.

'Sorry, Mrs Farthing. I just wanted to catch you on your way home. Wondered if I might have a word.'

'If it's how to use that cuppachinko contraption, you'll be wasting your breath.'

'No, no. Nothing like that. It's about Alex. Mr Child. I'm a bit, well, worried about him.'

Mrs Farthing eased her work bag a little further up her arm and carried on walking. 'You'd better come and have a cup of tea, then. You can't say anything in this village without the world and its mother finding out.' She turned into a neat garden and delved into the bag for a key.

Once they'd settled themselves in the front room, Mr, and not Mrs, Farthing made the tea, then did the trip to the kitchen and back another three or four times with the things his wife told him he'd forgotten: teaspoons, the biscuits ... 'No, not those ones, the *open* packet ... and plates for our biscuits!'

Marie could see now that tyranny came naturally to Mrs F. Her husband wasn't a total doormat though, and grumbled almost continually before announcing that he was taking the princess to The Lamb and Flag.

'Which princess?' asked Marie when he'd gone, thinking maybe it was early Alzheimer's or something.

'His car.'

'Ah.'

'So, you were wanting a word about Mr Child, were you? Only, there's an old *Touch of Frost* starting soon.'

'Yes. Sorry.' Marie took a deep breath and began to tell, in as tactful a way as she could and without mentioning drugs, of Alex's dependency problem. And of how, in Mrs Farthing and Marie's absence, he'd actually taught himself to cook. 'And so well!'

'You mean all those meals I found in the freezer? I thought that had been you.' She shook her head. 'Almost threw them away,' she added with a twinkle in her eye.

'Anyway,' Marie ploughed on, 'I just think it'd be terribly good for him, if we–' she emphasised the *we* – 'allowed him a little space to, you know, take care of himself. Domestically, as it were. I also think the tension between you and me...'

'What tension?' asked Mrs Farthing, eyebrows raised.

Marie chose to ignore this too. 'I think it's been

273

getting to him.'

Mrs F took a sip of tea and looked thoughtful. 'Trouble is, we'd miss the money, you see, if I wasn't full time for Mr Child. Mr Farthing's pension from the dairy is laughable.'

'Well,' said Marie. How could she tell Mrs F she'd pay her *not* to work? 'I'm sure you'd be entitled to substantial ... er, compensation.'

Mrs Farthing placed her cup on the coffee-table and clasped her hands in her lap. 'What do you mean by substantial?' she asked.

Marie picked up her bag and took out her chequebook. 'You tell me.'

The three of them arrived at nine on the dot, surprisingly neat in blue jeans, white T-shirts and builders' boots; all brand-new-looking.

'Dylan's away,' Ellie told them, 'but he's left instructions. Here.'

She handed a sheet of paper to Baz, who immediately passed it on to Jamie Dobbins. Either Baz had reading difficulties or he was still thinking of Jamie as Mr White. Jamie whizzed through it quickly and passed it over to Wesley Stephenson, whose mouth moved as he read.

'What have we got to do then?' asked Baz.

Jamie Dobbins curled a lip and tried to look hard and scary, instead of like someone who couldn't organise a kidnapping to save his life. 'You name it,' he told Baz. He took the list from Wesley and tucked it in his jeans.

Ellie straightened her back. 'You're to come to me if you want money for materials. Until Dylan gets back, that is. I'll be here most days, so, for the time being, you can think of me as your foreman. If there's any like slacking or trouble of any sort, well...' She did a few judo poses and they seemed to get the message. 'And don't forget we've got all those photos and texts and things,' she added, just to ram it home.

Jamie saluted her and the three of them went off to do whatever it was that builders do – probably find a kettle and a radio – while Ellie phoned Rob to see if he was on his way.

'Just at the bottom of your lane,' he told her.

'Oh, OK,' she said casually, although inside she was feeling extremely relieved. Good old Rob. If she wrote down pluses and minuses, the plus list would be very long – solid, caring, clever, great fun in a group, not-bad DJ, good personal hygiene, completely besotted with her – while the minus list would probably only have 'sticky-out ears' on it.

'Did you get bread and milk?' she asked him.

'Shit. Forgot. Sorry.'

And maybe 'forgetful'.

'I'll turn round and go back to West Washam, shall I?'

Through the window, Ellie could see Jamie Dobbins sharpening something – swish, swish, swish – on a long metal rod. His carpentry tools, she hoped, rather than a knife to slit her throat with. 'Er, no. Don't worry.'

Mrs Farthing had phoned in sick, so the three of them were enjoying Alex's fluffy eggs with a dash of Tabasco, on slices of olive-oil-splashed bread, baked for three minutes in a high oven. Not bad at all, Alex told himself. Sometimes, with Mrs F's scrambled eggs, you felt you were working your way through an insole.

'When I bumped into her yesterday,' said Marie, 'she didn't seem at all herself. Thought she might not be able to come and help you for quite a while.'

Alex hoped he hadn't somehow brought this about through the power of thought. 'Oh dear, poor old Mrs F. Hope it's nothing serious.'

'Great eggs,' said Dylan.

'Thanks. I'll take her some flowers or something.'

Marie said, 'Good idea,' and gave him a lovely smile.

Matt D'Angelo was all he could think. Was he becoming obsessed?

After breakfast they made their way, at Dylan's suggestion, to the recording studio. He had a new song he'd written in his head in captivity. 'I've called it "Sweet and Sour, Sweet and Sour",' he told them, and Alex thought it rather poetic until Dylan explained why.

Fliss had switched to semi-automatic-pilot mode. One half of her brain was checking patients' pulses, unwrapping sterilised needles, finding the spot, checking the pulses again, while the other half was musing on the proposed new pond. Would kidney-shaped be naff? Fish or frogs? Or could you have both? She saw lily pads and irises and years of therapeutic pond-gazing. Richard had already started the digging, and was going to line it and advise her on planting. He'd know the correct dimensions, and all about oxygenators and pump sizes. Whether her soil had the right pH balance for the marginals. Richard said he'd spent more time making ponds than making love in his life.

Between patients she quickly phoned Ellie again. 'You all right?'

'*Muuu-um.*'

'Is Rob still with you?'

'He's just popped into West Washam for some milk and stuff.'

'What!'

'It's OK. Honestly, Mum, it's all under control. Hang on...' Ellie bashed the phone down and disappeared, then Fliss heard a whistle being blown and her daughter shouting, 'Chop chop!'

Fliss swore quietly to herself. Maybe she should go home.

'Sorry,' Ellie said, back on the phone again. 'Just letting them know their fifteen-minute break's up.'

Fliss tutted. 'Just promise me you won't provoke them too much. I know what you can be like.'

'Oh, here's Rob now,' said Ellie. 'Gotta go!'

'OK then. See you later. And be careful.'

'*Muuu-um.*'

Next, Fliss phoned Rob's mobile. 'Hi, Rob, it's Ellie's mum. Um, where are you?'

'In the Co-op,' he said. 'Why?'

The tension between his parents was worse outside the studio than in it – music being a great raiser of spirits – so Dylan suggested change after

277

change to his song until he'd run out of ideas and, besides, knew they couldn't get it any better. With his captors in mind, he'd borrowed quite a bit from Tarantino soundtracks, making 'Sweet and Sour, Sweet and Sour' more electronic and edgier than their other stuff. A lot edgier than 'Angel in Red', that was for sure.

Late afternoon they stopped for a break, and while Marie walked Chomsky and Alex went off to the kitchen to make a batch of flapjacks, Dylan headed for his dad's study and the computer. If they were going to make a success of their new band – independently of his dad's record company, who it seemed weren't interested – someone would have to come up with a decent album cover and inside blurb. Him, for example. Lyrics written out, odd doodle-type drawings, photos of them all. The usual stuff. The fact that they hadn't settled on a name yet was a touch annoying, but he could add that last. Once Dylan had convinced his parents that maybe they should keep a connection with Blue Plum, they'd brainstormed on a regular basis. New Blue Plum? Blue Plum Revisited? Blue 2? It had become far more of an ordeal than producing the songs.

He sat in the plush office chair, switched on the computer then plugged the digital camera lead into the port and downloaded the pictures they'd taken that afternoon. Hey, good photos. There was one of scruffy mud-coloured Chomsky in front of the Manor that would make an excellent cover picture. But would his father want to show the whole world where he lived? Then there were the individual ones he and his parents had taken of each other. Perhaps he'd fiddle with those using the Photoshop he was certain his father didn't even know he had. Apparently, a guy had come from Gloucester and installed everything – scanner, masses of software – some time back, but most of it was just never used.

Dylan chose the best shot of his mother and began erasing one or two tiny lines, the odd puffy bit. He wouldn't tell her. It wasn't as though she really needed digital enhancement, but no harm in making her totally perfect. As he trawled through other pictures and, for fun, messed around with them, he pondered on what had caused the rift between his parents. The kidnapping? Must have been pretty distressing for them. Put a bit of a strain on the relationship, no doubt. Bloody Baz. What a ridiculous thing to try and pull off. Once again, Dylan's mind rewound to Ellie throwing poor Hal over her shoulder, then straddling him, all wired-up and breathless and damp with perspiration. What an amazing sight she'd been. And so, well … *hot*. No other word for it.

After some time, once Dylan had finished having fun with his mother's image, Alex walked into the studio and said, 'Hey, you can do all that stuff, can you?'

'Took a course a couple of years ago. It's not that hard. Here, sit down and look at this.' Dylan pulled a spare chair over, then clicked the mouse and laughed. 'Check this out. I made Mum ginger with green eyes.'

'God, that's amazing. Makes her look like

Kathleen. Very Irish.'

Dylan watched his father go quiet on him for a while, deep in thought and rubbing at his chin with the tips of his fingers. He wondered if he was reminiscing about the young girl he'd met after a gig all those decades back, or perhaps he was mulling over their current problems. But then he turned to Dylan and said, 'Show me how to do this, would you?'

'Sure.'

'I know – why don't we alter a picture of you? Can you give yourself, say, blue eyes?'

'Um, yeah. All right.' Dylan got the best photo of himself up on screen.

'And maybe blond hair?'

'Yeah, that'll be a laugh,' he said and got to work. It took a while, even though he didn't have that much hair to alter.

Eventually, he called his father over from the window he'd been staring out of and said, 'There. All done. It's spooky, you know, I look just like–'

'Aarghhh,' he heard behind him, and turned in time to see a streak of pale blue denim disappearing through the study door.

Fliss was relieved to find Ellie curled up with Rob in front of *The Simpsons*, even though she'd only called her an hour ago. Perhaps it would get easier after the first day, and then Dylan was bound to come home again at some point. Still, her intrepid daughter seemed happy with the arrangement, particularly as Dylan was paying her far more than she'd ever earn at the café.

'Are you in for dinner?' Fliss asked them both. 'No,' said Rob. 'Going to see a film.'

Oh *yes*. The evening to herself. Heaven. How little time she spent on her own now, compared to LBR. She tried to think of how she'd filled her time in her Life Before Richard. Had she got bored? Lonely? She thought not. Was she just one of those people who readily adapted to change? Colin had been very much in the other camp, and had never really recovered from her defection to alternative medicine. Just as running out of muesli and having to have cornflakes could wreck his entire day.

'Richard just called,' said Ellie. 'Said to tell you he'd got something for you. Hang on, I wrote it down.' She unravelled herself from Rob and picked up a piece of paper. 'Yeah. He said he's got a two-inch spiral hose and a telescopic extension.' She started giggling and Rob joined in. *'With...'* Now they were both doubled up and laughing helplessly '... a one-inch *nozzle*.'

Fliss rolled her eyes. 'Pond pump, Ellie.'

Marie was a mile or so from The Manor, in a field of sheep baaing pathetically at a dog that was taking absolutely no notice of them, when she spotted someone on the horizon limping her way. The man, who gradually revealed himself to be Alex, was waving big waves at her, like a person lost in the desert flagging down a plane. Suddenly filled with consternation – there must have been some bad news – she and Chomsky galloped towards him.

'What?' she asked on reaching him. She was

281

breathless, but not as breathless as he was.

'Who's Gavin?' he panted.

'Alex, for goodness sake sit down. You'll have a seizure.' She found them a patch of ground free of sheep poo, and eased him on to it, then sat beside him and took one of his hands. Chomsky attempted a rough-and-tumble with his master but soon gave up and sloped off. 'Now,' Marie said. She wiped at Alex's forehead with the back of her hand while he recovered his breath. 'Gavin was someone I was seeing, in a *very* casual way, before you and I got back together.'

'And it's over now?'

'Yes.'

He leaned his head against hers. 'Oh Marie. I'm sorry I've been so distant. I just had all these niggling little worries, and what with the kidnapping...'

'Don't worry,' she told him. 'It's OK.' She gave him a reassuring smile and promised herself she'd definitely end things with Gavin once and for all. Particularly as he hadn't called her since she left Brighton that night. Sex for sex's sake was such a ridiculous activity anyway. 'Come on,' she said, when Alex's breathing had slowed. 'Let's get back, shall we?'

They found Dylan on the computer. 'I've got this idea for the CD cover,' he told them. 'Based on a Chinese takeaway. Well, that's if we call the album "Sweet and Sour".'

Alex pulled a face. 'I had "Angel in Red" in mind.'

Marie thought she'd stay out of this one and

began idly flicking through some of Dylan's print-outs until she came across a picture of herself with ginger hair and green eyes. 'Jesus,' she said, shocked. 'That's *so* weird. But not unattractive, wouldn't you say? Perhaps I'll try dyeing my hair red.'

While Alex insisted he liked her exactly as she was, Marie picked up the next picture in the pile. It was of the young and gorgeous Alex, and it made her heart lurch as she recalled her utter infatuation with him back then. 'It's funny,' she said, turning and frowning at him, 'but I don't remember you ever having your hair this short.'

TWENTY-TWO

It was almost two weeks before Dylan returned to 1 Biddlefarm Cottages. Driving up the lane on Sunday evening, he lowered his eyes to the dashboard, terrified of what might greet him should he look up. But when he did, he was surprised not to see the cement mixer, or piles of bricks and tiles. And no plastic sheeting or ladder, he noticed, once out of the van and peering over the fence. Had the bastards, knowing he was coming back and scared of facing him, simply run off with all his stuff?

'Dylan!' called a vision of loveliness from the next garden. 'Don't go any further. You've got to close your eyes.'

Oh Christ, it was that bad. Ellie had given him occasional but vague reports over the phone. 'How's the house coming along?' he'd enquire. 'Oh, OK,' she'd say. Or, 'Fine, fine. Yeah, they've been working hard.' It hadn't really told him much.

She ran up to him and kissed his cheek, then put a hand over his eyes and led him down his garden path, something that was now much easier to negotiate, he noticed. He could just see, in the gap beneath her soft sweet-smelling fingers, that someone had not only cleared the path, but swept it too.

'Right,' she said at the door. He sensed

excitement in her voice, but wasn't sure if that was good or bad. 'Mind the step,' she told him, and Dylan flashed back to being led into a musty hut and felt his stomach tighten. 'OK. Now down the hall, watch the table, and into the living room.'

When Ellie stepped back, he opened his eyes and took it all in: white walls; that woodblock floor he'd once casually mentioned to Baz; exactly the right-sized hole in the chimney breast and a beautifully tiled surround. His Bang and Olufsen all set up. Oh please, he thought, walking through the living room, please, please, *please* let the kitchen be this nice.

'Dylan?' Ellie was saying. 'You OK?'

He discovered the kitchen to be just as he'd pictured it from the start. It was incredible that Baz had listened to him all those weeks he'd rattled on about chrome fittings and pots dangling from the ceiling. About how he wanted one of those big Scandinavian cookers and an American-style fridge. Now here it all was, right down to the dimmer switch for his sunken ceiling lights. Who'd have thought Baz's head had room for such information?

'Jesus,' he said, surveying the room with hands on hips. 'This is incredible.'

'I'm afraid they spent all that money you left me,' said Ellie.

'I'm not surprised.'

'I made them give me receipts for everything, just to make sure they weren't like paying themselves.'

'Great.'

'So what do you think?' she asked, leaning against one of the units and looking totally in keeping with the place. 'Baz wanted to go for white wall tiles, but I said no, black.'

'Black's perfect.'

She stretched across and pulled open the fridge door. 'I stocked up for you,' she said. 'Fancy a glass of champers?'

He smiled and nodded and began investigating some of the cupboards. Handmade. Mr White's work, he guessed. Nicely finished off.

'You'll have to buy plates and things,' said Ellie. 'I boxed up a lot of your cruddy old stuff.'

'Oh right. Thanks.'

The bottle popped and she was soon handing him a fizzing glass, holding up her own and saying, 'To the house.'

'No,' he said, slowly hooking his arm round hers for a more intimate toast. 'To *Ellie*.'

She blushed. Brilliant Ellie. She'd put her life at risk to save him, and now she'd helped bring about his dream house. What's more, she was beginning to look like Cameron Diaz. Their cheeks brushed as they sipped from their respective glasses, which made Ellie giggle and left Dylan feeling heady and bold. Should he make a move?

'Any left for me?' boomed a voice from the doorway, and Dylan's heart sank.

'*God*, Rob,' said Ellie, coughing on her champagne, unhooking her arm then placing her glass on the worktop. She went over and draped a hand over his shoulder. 'Don't frighten me like that.'

Rob was followed by Fliss. 'Hey,' said Dylan, going over and giving her a hug. 'Nice welcoming party. Want some champagne? We seem to have six bottles.'

'Mm, why not.'

There was another jolly toast, then they all made their way to the back garden where Dylan discovered he had a new patio in burnt-sienna decking. Ah well, he thought, and gave them nine out of ten.

Alex and Marie were on the terrace with pen and paper, working out their set. Alex felt this was an area he'd had a bit of experience in, but tried not to make Marie feel bamboozled.

'Sometimes it's good to keep the mood,' he said tentatively. 'Rather than, you know, fast song, followed by a slow one, then back to fast. If people are dancing they get thrown.'

'I'm not sure we've got anything people can dance *to*.'

'True.' Alex threw his pen aside and gave Marie a smile. 'You know, I think we're giving this too much thought. Let's play it by ear.'

She looked relieved. It was that 'planning' thing again. 'I *always* play it by ear,' she said. 'Literally, when it comes to music.'

'I know.' Alex had never understood how she and Dylan did that. He clung to his sheetmusic like a toddler to its comfort rag. He stood up, grabbed Marie's hand and raised her from her chair. 'Let's go and cook,' he said. He'd had an exciting idea involving beef and shallots earlier in the day. He'd put Marie in charge of the green salad, though. Make her feel useful.

She smiled at him and moved closer. 'I can think of something that's much more fun than cooking,' she purred, caressing his shirt pocket with her cheek.

Alex wasn't sure he'd agree, but just managed to stop himself saying so.

'I've missed you this weekend,' she told Richard over the phone. She'd left the kids opening a third bottle of champagne next door.

'I know,' he said. 'It's awful, isn't it? What are we going to do?'

Fliss left a pregnant pause. She didn't want to be the one making dramatic suggestions.

'How's the pond?' he went on disappointingly.

'Oh, coming along. I thought I saw a newt.'

'Really? That was quick work.'

'Yes.' She took a gulp from the glass she'd brought back with her. 'No lilies yet.'

'Right. Have you been–'

'Scooping the leaves out? Yes. Every day.'

'Good. Any signs of algae?'

'No, not yet.'

'We could always live together,' he said.

Fliss drained her glass. Of course they could. But where? His clients were there, hers were here. Oh dear, such a huge issue to be suddenly confronting. 'But wouldn't you miss London?' she asked, grinning to herself.

'I see.' He laughed. 'I do have a lucrative business to run, you know. Look, if you moved here you wouldn't have to worry about working.'

Fliss's eyes widened. Was he proposing to make

her a Kept Woman? Ambling round Chiswick each morning with a wicker shopping basket, filling her afternoons with flower arrangements and a nap... It sounded heavenly.

'Well, not for a couple of weeks,' he added.

'But Ellie needs a base in the holidays,' she told him. 'She can't stay in halls.'

'We could keep your house going for that. And for weekends away for us. I'm sure Dylan would look after it.'

'But I enjoy my work.' It was almost true. 'And you'd easily find clients with huge uncontrollable gardens in Norfolk.' Another pregnant pause. 'Oh yeah, talking of Dylan, he's giving a concert next weekend in West Washam. With his parents.'

'Sounds good.'

'See?'

'See what?'

'We're not completely culturally barren up here.'

'I don't think I ever said that.' Richard was beginning to sound narked. How had they gone from almost a proposal of marriage to almost an argument so quickly?

'I cleaned out the pump nozzle, by the way.'

'Oh good.'

When the youngsters rolled up, Fliss was still in the armchair, phone in her lap. Her watch told her she'd been staring into space for ten minutes. Thinking about Richard and what it would be like to live in London again after twenty-odd years away. It had been fun when she'd been studying and training, but would she just find it

289

hellish now? What would it be like tidying up after someone all the time? And could she really give up acupuncture? Would she, in fact, need to? Then there was her lovely garden. She looked up as Ellie and Rob tumbled into the room and entwined themselves on the sofa in a tangle of annoyingly supple limbs.

Oh, to be eighteen again, thought Fliss. So much more flexible. In all respects.

When Marie entered her hot and airless house on Wednesday afternoon, it wasn't with the usual heavy heart; just the opposite, in fact. She found herself bouncing gleefully from room to room, humming and grabbing stuff from drawers and cupboards. She opened bills, wrote out cheques and sealed envelopes in half the time it would normally take, then phoned her cousin.

'Alex and I thought we'd give it a go,' she told Kathleen while she wandered about the kitchen, pouring stuff down the sink, chucking out-of-date things in the bin. She mentioned Saturday's gig in Norfolk. 'A long way for you, I know, but do come. Mike can hold the fort.'

Kathleen said she'd try, adding, 'If only to meet this reformed Alex.'

'Good. We thought we'd try our new songs out on the public before releasing a CD. Somewhere low-profile. Don't want the music press turning up and slating us.'

'Is it similar to the old Blue Plum stuff? I used to like that.'

'It's a lot quieter. More, you know, unplugged. Folk-country-rock, that kind of thing. Alex thinks there's something missing, but then his last two albums have been dreadful cacophonies. Don't tell him I said that. Anyway, I don't agree with him. Dylan adds bits of synthesised stuff and ... well, you can tell me what you think when you've heard us.'

'You'll have to email me directions.'

Marie said, 'Will do,' and began pulling things from her miscellaneous-items drawer: bus time-table, takeaway menus, kettle guarantee, large bulldog clip, photo of Gavin ... a rather lovely one taken in Hyde Park in the spring. He was sitting on the grass, leaning back on his hands, long legs crossed at the ankle, head cocked with an aren't-I-stunning grin. Afterwards, they'd gone to an almost empty arthouse cinema where they'd petted adolescently at the back.

'...be a nuisance,' Kathleen was saying.

'Sorry?'

'I said could Dylan put me up?'

Marie tucked the phone under her chin and tore the photo in two. All in the past now, she decided, dropping it in the fliptop bin. 'Yeah, yeah, no problem.'

Before long, she'd filled her car with all the things she'd need. She took a key to a neighbour who'd offered to keep an eye on the house and forward mail for a small fee, then went back to check everything was switched off 'Right,' she puffed, letting herself out for the last time.

But at the gate she hesitated, put the final box of things down and went over to the dustbin. It took her a while to find the second half of the photograph, and it seemed to have pickle or something on the corner and was quite creased. 'Damn,' she said. She gave it a wipe and ironed out both halves with the edge of her hand, before letting herself back in to find the Sellotape.

Ellie was teaching herself statistics from a book. She knew it was going to come up in her Psychology course, so thought she'd better prepare herself, not having done any maths for two years. She was a bit fearful to begin with, but when she did the tests at the end of each chapter and got everything right, she began to warm to the subject and thought maybe she had a flair or something. '*Yes*,' she said, ticking another correct answer and turning the page, just as Dylan's head appeared through the open living-room window.

'Hi, Ellie. Can I try something out on you?' He held up his acoustic guitar.

'Oh. Actually I'm a bit busy, Dylan. Sorry. Maybe later?' She returned to her book and chewed on the rubber end of her pencil. *Chapter Three.*

'What are you doing?' he asked.

'Mm?' She looked up. 'Oh, just learning statistics. You know, for my course.'

'Ah.' He nodded and began backing away. 'Well, I'll leave you to it then.'

'Yeah. Thanks.' *Standard Deviation*, she read, then called out, 'See you later.'

Dylan thrust his head back again, making her jump. 'Do you mean...' he said, 'erm, never mind.'

It was only when her mum crashed through the

front door and called out, 'Come and help, will you?' that Ellie finally tore herself away from the book. As she filled cupboards and the fridge and freezer with food for the weekend guests, she thought, with the odd nervous stomach spin, about going off to university in a couple of weeks' time and not knowing a soul there. She'd always made friends easily, but you never knew. And what would it be like in mixed halls?

Rob, who was taking a gap year to basically hang out in Norwich, was a bit worried about that. He said he'd come and visit her the first weekend, but she'd told him to make it the second or third and he'd looked a bit gutted. 'Just so I can settle in properly, yeah?' she'd explained.

Ellie opened a packet of choc-chip cookies and bit into one. It didn't taste as exciting as it looked, then she saw they were 'suitable for diabetics'. So too, she discovered, were the marmalade, chocolate bar and spicy fruitcake. And the cereal. Was Hal going to get through all this in twenty-four hours, or would she and her mother be living on sorbitol till she left for uni? She carried on emptying bags, wondering if any of the guys in halls would be able to cook for themselves, or if, like Rob, they could only do Pop Tarts.

Chomsky had chased a rabbit and got through a gap in the fencing. 'Not again,' seethed Alex, tensing himself for the screech of brakes and a loud thud. Still, he had to admit it was the dog's only fault, and something he, Chomsky, appeared to have no control over. The scent of a small bobtailed animal just made him lose all sense of dignity and decorum. Not to say self-preservation.

But then Alex did hear the screech of brakes. No thud, though. Only the thump of his heartbeat as he hurtled the thirty yards or so towards the missing fencing panels. He pushed his way through foliage to find his own Volvo in front of him.

'Jesus, I almost killed him,' said Marie, winding down the window. Chomsky was in the passenger seat beside her, avoiding Alex's hard gaze. 'Do you want to squeeze yourself in too?'

The car was chock-a-block with boxes and plants and stuffed carrier bags, and of course the dog, so Alex declined and walked the third of a mile home with a cheerful spring in his step. Marie was moving in! Just when he thought he'd be creeping into old age alone, here he was, back with the biggest love of his life. He surely was blessed.

While Marie unpacked her things and put clothes away and arranged the special ornaments she hadn't wanted to leave behind, Alex, rather sluggishly and reluctantly, got dinner organised. The onus to do so was well and truly on him these days. Cooking was great fun when you had the time and the inclination but, on the whole, he was slowly growing tired of the daily effort involved. The planning, the shopping, the washing and slicing and dicing, then all the mess to deal with. Not to mention the expectation there now seemed to be for him to produce something dazzling every single day. Hopefully,

294

when Marie got completely settled in she'd start pulling her weight.

Alex whistled one of his old tunes as he threw in garlic and five-spice and a bit of soy sauce, more carelessly than he'd normally do. Of course, he didn't really mind making dinner tonight. Marie must have had a knackering day. All the same, he'd have a word with her about maybe taking it in turns. When he finally called out that it was ready, she came and joined him in the dining room and chatted away about her house and her nightmare journey back, and how fantastic it was to have a man who loved to cook for her.

'Mmmm,' she swooned as she dug into the food. 'Totally delicious, as usual.' She reached across and stroked his face. 'Definitely five stars.'

'Thanks,' he said with a quick smile. Perhaps tomorrow he'd aim for four stars, then three...

Fliss was trying so hard not to think about Ellie leaving home that, in the end, that was all she could think about. Her daughter had been out and bought crockery and bedding and other items she'd need, as though it was the most normal thing for someone who'd only been born five minutes ago to be doing. How could almost nineteen years fly by so quickly? And who would Fliss moan about her clients to in the evenings?

Over the years she'd seen lots of patients with empty-nest syndrome, and had always secretly thought they should get a life. 'Take up windsurfing! Have an affair!' she wanted to tell them. 'While your hips are still intact.'

But it wasn't quite that easy, she was discovering.

As Ellie watched TV and sent text messages in the living room, Fliss was chipping ice out of the freezer with a bread-knife, imagining night after night of meals on her own. She'd be one of those heart rending people in the Sunday-morning supermarket queue with a frozen roast platter for one and an individual apple pie. Fliss had always seen herself as someone who loved her own company, but... She put the knife down and phoned Richard.

'I suppose I could take a long sabbatical,' she said. 'Come and live in London.'

'Hey!'

'Look, don't get too excited. It's just an idea. I mean, there's your untidiness to consider.'

'It'd give you something to do all day though, wouldn't it?'

'Ho ho.'

'Alternatively, you could be my assistant. I'll train you up. Put you on ponds and water features.'

'I'm not going bra-less.'

He laughed. 'You'll do as you're told.'

'And London's so ... eeurghh.'

'Pardon?'

'Noisy. Dirty. Squalid.'

'Interesting. Vibrant. Stimulating.'

'Mmm. Well, I'll give it some more thought. Sound them out at the centre. There is another acupuncturist there, but he's pretty busy.'

'You could always set up a practice here. In the front room or something.'

'Oh yes? And where would your thousand issues of *New Statesman* go?'

'In the loft.'

'And the Rotavator?'

'Oh, that can go in the lock-up. Easy.'

'Right.' Why wasn't it there already?

Fliss watched Mont Blanc gradually tumble from her freezer and told Richard she'd have to go. 'I'll call you back later.'

She threw the phone down. 'Ellie, come and help!' she wanted to call out, but then thought about not being able to shout for help when her daughter was a hundred miles away defrosting her own freezer. She took a deep breath, told herself to be strong and wondered if it was too late to have another baby.

By eight o'clock, Dylan was beginning to feel sorry for them.

'OK, you can call it a day,' he said, and his workmen instantly downed their Black and Deckers and grabbed their mobiles, keys and wallets. He then gave them enough for a hearty takeaway, plus five pounds each and petrol money, feeling this was plenty. Jamie and Wes had temporarily moved into Baz's granny flat in order to live a bill-free life and, as they were spending all day every day at Biddlefarm Cottages, they really had no need for cash. 'See you bright and early tomorrow,' he called out as they trooped down the path, muttering darkly.

'We need to get these stairs stripped before my parents come tomorrow,' he added.

'We?' he heard Jamie scoff.

With just three days to go till the gig, Dylan went back to the practising – guitar, keyboard, guitar – then later, beer in hand, he sat and listened to the set. Ten songs, all fairly quiet, country-rockish. Nice. Little bit of slide guitar here, a touch of harmonica there. Lots of good hooks and long American vowels. Music your girlfriend would like, kind of thing.

His parents were coming a couple of days early, so they could all rehearse together and get things as tight as they possibly could before the 'mini-gig' as his father was calling it. Something Dylan was really looking forward to. He knew the band wasn't exactly going to take the charts by storm, but occasionally playing live with his famous old man might be fun.

When the last track came to an end, Dylan took his guitar up to his bedroom, the house becoming more and more shabby as he ascended. He'd planned on using the boys for the bedrooms too, but it was seriously doing his head in having them around all the time. And maybe they'd paid for their crime now.

He put his beer down then propped himself up on his bed with his guitar and broke into a half-written song called 'Elusive Ellie', wondering, every now and then, if she was listening on the other side of the wall.

TWENTY-THREE

'Greg's with us,' said Hazel, stating the obvious. 'Hope that's OK? He's got into my old Blue Plum tapes recently and wanted to see them play. Don't worry, he's brought a tent.'

Greg, towering over his mother, held the palm of his hand up to Fliss. 'Hello again.'

Hal was to the rear with two bits of luggage and his usual cheery face. A breeze had lifted his comb-over into a small arch. 'Fliss!' he bellowed. 'Good to see ya!'

Kisses were exchanged and before long tea was being served by Richard in the front garden.

Fliss proffered a plate to Hal. 'Diabetic fruitcake?'

'Is it really?' he asked, scowling as he examined it. 'Maybe it should cut down on sweet things then.'

There followed much laughter until Ellie appeared with textbook in hand. 'Hi,' she said, looking dazed.

Fliss watched Greg almost slide off his seat. 'This is Ellie,' she told him. 'Ellie, this is Greg. Hazel's son.'

'Hi!' he said enthusiastically.

'Hi.'

'What's that you're reading, honey?' asked Hal. 'A potboiler?'

'Sorry?'

'You know, Jackie Collins. Or is it Joan? I never remember.'

Ellie held up the cover. 'It's about cognitive dissonance. You know?'

Hal said no, he didn't know, and Hazel and Richard shrugged. Fliss did kind of know but thought she'd let her daughter explain.

However, Greg cleared his throat and leaned forward. 'Well,' he said and everyone turned. Such a nice-looking boy, thought Fliss. 'It's like, say you wanted to buy a CD but you couldn't decide between two that you liked equally. Let's call them A and B.'

'OK,' said Hazel, proudly scanning the group for reactions.

'Why not buy both?' asked Hal.

Greg shook his head. 'You can only afford one.'

'Oh.' Hal looked puzzled by the concept.

'So,' continued Greg while Ellie slowly lowered herself on to the lawn at his feet, 'you finally decide on B and buy it. Right? What happens then is that B goes way up in your estimation, while A goes down.'

'Oh, I say,' said Hazel. 'That happened to me last week at the Savoy, didn't it, Hal. Do you remember? With the hors d'oeuvres?'

'Anyway,' continued Greg, 'it's about the way we adjust our thinking and emotions, particularly in connection with decision-making. That was just one example.' He leaned back in his chair and got on with his mug of tea. Fliss couldn't decide if he was attractively knowledgeable and self-assured, or irritatingly cocky. Ellie was clearly going for the former, and while the two of them got into a quiet conversation about things cognitive, the rest of them moved on to pond maintenance.

Hal was shaking his head. 'Got so many darned trees in my garden, Richard here has a helluva time in the fall, keeping the pond clear of leaves.'

'It's more of a lake, really,' explained Hazel. 'We sailed on it last weekend.'

'Got a coupla ketches down there. Little boat-house.'

'And a *fabu*lous lakeside summerhouse.

'Gosh,' said Fliss, adding 'Hal's Place' to the reasons-to-move-to-London list in her head.

For the life of him, Alex couldn't recall playing in West Washam Corn Exchange. But maybe if he'd had to fetch the key from the Town Clerk, organise tickets and booze, and shift the band's equipment first time round, it would have stayed with him. What a drag all this was. Still, at least he had Dylan and his slaves helping. Later on, Baz would be on the door, selling/checking tickets, Jamie would be behind the bar, and although they hadn't come up with a job description for Wesley, he looked good bouncer material. In the meantime, the three of them helped with lugging and shifting, until everything was more or less where Alex thought it should be on stage and it was time for a sound test.

Around six-thirty, Baz was sent out to the Chinese. When he arrived back half an hour later with bags of steaming food he said, 'You should see the queue. Massive.'

'The Chinese is always busy Sat-dees,' said Wes.

'I meant outside this place.'

'No!' everyone said.

'Yeah. Seems like they can't wait to see Blue Plum.'

'Oh dear,' sighed Alex. 'Trouble is we're not Blue Plum, we're Little Blue Plum. Haven't they seen the posters?'

'Oh, I'm sure they'll love us,' said the ever-optimistic Marie. She came over and rubbed his back. 'Come on, let's take a look.'

The three of them went to the Ladies and took it in turns to stand on a toilet and peer through an open frosted window. Alex let the others go first, then saw for himself lots of balding heads, busty women and neat blue jeans. A handful of grungy kids. A man with a camcorder. He spotted the couple from the pub near Dylan looking excited, then overheard a guy talking about the last time he saw Blue Plum play at the Corn Exchange. 'Bloody brilliant,' the man said, twanging on his air guitar while Alex's stomach tightened a notch. What were all these people expecting? Shit. He swallowed hard, stepped off the toilet and joined the others in the kitchenette.

'So when's our community service, ha ha, gonna finish?' Jamie was asking Dylan. Chomsky quietly growled. He often did this with Jamie. 'Only I'm running up debts with my mum and everyone and it's not exactly making me popular.'

Dylan gave him an ah-poor-you smirk. 'Well, maybe we can call it quits after tonight.'

'Hallelujah.'

'For the time being, anyway.'

'Woof,' went Chomsky, in a kind of good-riddance way.

'Actually,' chipped in Alex, 'we could do with a garden wall being built, couldn't we, Marie? We'd give you food and shelter, of course. And a bit of pocket-money.' He grinned and bobbed his eyebrows at the boys. 'Pretty good food, actually.'

'A wall!' scoffed Jamie. 'All the way to Gloucestershire or wherever, just to build a garden wall?' The other two fell about over their dinners.

'There'd be around three miles of it,' Alex told them.

'Fuck,' said Baz. 'Oops, scuse my French.'

Hazel said, 'Just like old times, isn't it, Fliss?'

They were all – Fliss, Richard, Hazel, Hal, Greg and Marie's cousin, Kathleen – trying to squash into one car. Ellie had gone off earlier with Rob who, apparently, was the evening's DJ.

No, decided Fliss, it wasn't a bit like old times, when eight lithe bodies could get into a vehicle and there'd still be room for a hitchhiker. They gave up and took two cars, arriving in the centre of West Washam at roughly the same time only to find all the parking spaces taken and a queue of people a mile long snaking its way around the Market Square.

When they eventually regrouped ten minutes later, two lines of punters were moving into the Corn Exchange and the six of them joined the fast-moving ticket-holders' one.

'Gosh, I feel fourteen again,' said Hazel, breaking into a bit of Seventies' dancing. 'If I start screaming "Alex", do stop me, won't you, Hal?'

Greg looked as though he wanted a hole to open up, while Hal, wearing a tie for the occasion, gave Hazel a wink and a sneaky buttock smack and told her if she was a naughty girl, she'd be paying for it later. Fliss vowed not to let the image spoil her evening.

Once they'd all had their tickets clipped by big Wesley, Fliss and Richard went off to the bar and ordered drinks from another surly-looking former kidnapper. While Jamie took his time, Fliss stood on tiptoe and watched Rob up on stage, hand holding a headphone to his ear, head bobbing to something she couldn't categorise if she tried.

'Here,' said Richard, handing her Hazel's cider and blackcurrant – a drink they'd always enjoyed in their early teens for its fast-acting qualities, and because they were basically still Ribena drinkers.

'Can I change my order?' she shouted above the suddenly cranked-up music. People's fingers went flying to their ears. 'I'll have a pint of that too.'

'OK,' he said, then started patting his pockets and grimacing apologetically in that way Fliss was becoming all too familiar with.

She handed Hazel's drink back to him and got out her purse.

'Sorry,' he shouted.

Dylan had never seen his father so nervous, pacing up and down. Never seen him nervous, in fact.

'Oh Christ,' he was saying as he chewed on his

thumb. 'Christ, Christ. They *definitely* won't be expecting mostly acoustic, will they, Dylan? They'll want loud and electric and raucous. Hey, maybe we could start with "Sweet and Sour"? Mm? At least that's part electric. Yes, let's do that.'

'OK.'

Marie agreed and Dylan continued to strum on his guitar, humming to himself and not feeling at all nervous. But then he didn't have a monumental reputation to lose. His mother was slowly doing her make-up in the old Thirties' painted-white, dressing-table mirror, also looking tense but not in his dad's league.

'Ready to go on soon?' came Baz's voice through the door. 'We've sold all the tickets, and more. Now everyone's moaning 'cos it's hot and they can't stand the DJ.'

'OK,' called out Dylan. He held up two fingers to his parents and they nodded. 'Give us two minutes.'

'Ookay.'

Rob was going to introduce the band after he'd finished his stint so, with make-up applied, sweaty hands wiped on trousers and a guitar each, Little Blue Plum made their way to the side of the stage where, unfortunately, they were forced to hang around self-consciously while Rob tortured his audience for another five minutes.

It was during the third number that it became evident, to Dylan at least, that the audience was slowly disengaging from the music and turning instead to raised-voice conversations that even his flourishes on the synth couldn't drum out. When polite, but far from universal, applause greeted the end of song three, Dylan saw his father's face turn even whiter when people started yelling the titles of old Blue Plum songs. It was only twenty past nine and they were supposed to be playing till eleven. It wasn't going well.

From his stool, Dylan looked around at the sea of half-expectant, half-disappointed faces. There was lovely Ellie, looking concerned. She gave him an encouraging thumbs-up and he smiled back. Close to her was a tall good-looking bloke. A bit too close and a bit too good-looking. While his father introduced the next song, Dylan's gaze roamed on, catching Fliss and Richard, arms round each other, then Hal, then Hazel. Hazel was deep in conversation with his 'Aunt' Kathleen, talking about playing the violin it seemed from her gestures. He thought back to their fun evening in Fliss's kitchen.

'...take a short break and be back with you in twenty minutes or so,' his father was saying.

What? What was going on? When his parents left the stage Dylan felt he had no alternative but to follow, particularly as Rob came bounding back towards his decks.

'You all right, Dylan?' asked Ellie as he stepped down. 'I think it's brilliant, but some people are just being so rude.'

He ran his hands through his hair and nodded. 'Listen, Ellie,' he said. 'You couldn't do me an enormous favour, could you? One last one?' He whispered in her ear and handed her his van keys.

'OK,' she said with a shrug.

306

'As fast as you can, but don't drive like a maniac, will you?'

'Promise.'

They went outside with the smokers, even though none of them smoked.

'Gee,' chortled Hal, fanning himself with a large hand. 'Haven't been to a hootenanny like this in years.'

Richard laughed. 'I can't say I've *ever* been to one where the break comes after three songs.'

Fliss heard a passing woman say, 'It's a bit dull compared to Blue Plum. Good as background music, I expect.'

'If the peasants would only shut up,' someone else was saying, 'maybe we'd be able to hear their new stuff properly.'

'...wanted singalong folk, I'd have gone to see James Taylor.'

'...first song was OKish.'

'...no drummer even.'

Hazel was pushing her way towards them with two pints. 'Here you are,' she said to Fliss. 'Got you another cider and blackcurrant.'

Fliss's stomach was beginning to complain about the first pint, but she thanked her nicely and pretended to take a sip.

'I'll just pop back and fetch the boys' drinks,' Hazel said, but Hal protested.

'You wait there, sweetheart. Don't want you jostling with those hoodlums in there.' He rolled up his shirt-sleeves, loosened his tie and puffed himself up, obviously expecting something far rougher than West Washam had ever seen.

'The pints are on the far end of the bar,' Hazel told him. 'By the kitchenette hatch.'

When Hal returned a couple of minutes later he was followed by Baz, who called out, 'Which one's Hazel?'

Hazel stuck her free hand up. 'Me. Why?'

'Alex asked me to come and get you. Wants a word.'

'Ooh er,' she said. The blackcurrant had given her a red moustache. 'Are you sure he said me?'

'Yep.'

She handed Fliss her drink – just what Fliss wanted – and pushed her way back through the crowd.

'Where's Mum going?' asked Greg, suddenly behind her. 'To the bar I hope, I'm gasping for a drink.' He laughed at Fliss's two pints. 'What's this, lushes' corner?'

'Here,' she said, handing him the fullest.

He winked and said, 'Works every time.' So he was a cocky devil, after all. 'Seen Ellie anywhere?' he asked. 'I lost her just before the break.'

'I expect she's with her boyfriend,' she said pointedly.

Greg grinned. 'I think you'll find that's *ex*-boyfriend.'

Around a quarter of an hour later, someone rang a dainty little bell to get them all inside again, making Fliss feel she was about to see the second half of *Rigoletto* or something. She looked for a place to pour her cider, and was heading for the road to find a drain when Dylan's van screeched to a halt beside her and Ellie jumped out with her violin and bow and handed them to her. 'Quick,' she said breathily, as though she'd been running not driving. 'Get these to Dylan.'

In the dressing-room, Marie was wondering what the future held for herself and Alex now. An idle-rich life in the heart of the country? Could be worse, she thought, then quickly brushed aside all doubts about the band's potential. It would just take time for people to appreciate what they were doing. And, after all, they were hardly trying things out on a discerning London audience, who'd maybe read an interview or two in the broadsheets on Little Blue Plum's direction and influences.

'Yes, I can improvise, of course,' she heard Hazel say from where she was poring over Alex's sheet-music. 'But are you sure?' She paused for a chuckle. 'I mean, golly.'

There was a loud knock on the door and Fliss burst in with a violin. 'For Dylan?' she asked, holding it out to him.

'Uh uh.' He pointed at Hazel and realisation seemed to fill Fliss's face.

'Dylan thought we needed a little oomph,' explained Marie. She wasn't too sure how Hazel of all people would bring that about, but Alex and Dylan seemed optimistic.

'Excuse me,' said Alex, 'but I think you'll find I've been saying that all along.'

Fliss, still looking shocked, was slowly backing towards the door. 'Well, break a leg,' she said quietly to her friend before disappearing.

'You know, I actually did that once,' said Hazel

as she tuned her instrument. 'Broke a leg at a gig.'

Marie laughed. 'Really?'

'Mm. Well, a sort of gig. And it was more of a sprain, really. Played at the primary school on one of those little chairs they have. One of the legs snapped beneath me. Can you imagine!'

Yes, thought Marie, she could.

'Ready, everyone?' Dylan asked, and before Marie had time to check her face and pick up her guitar, Hazel was first out the door with a, 'Come on then. Let's get them jigging and jiving.'

Ellie's jaw dropped when Hazel appeared on stage and was introduced as the newest band member. But she wasn't half as shocked as Greg, beside her with his arm around her and his hand in a slightly dodgy place.

'*What* the...' he cried as the music struck up. 'Oh fuck, no. Not Mum. *No*. Beam me up Scottie, quick.'

'Don't worry!' Ellie had to shout at him as the band got louder. But Greg stood stock still, just staring, with lots of white showing in his eyes. Ellie thought he might have gone into a catatonic trance and wondered if she should slap him. 'She's dead good, your mum,' she yelled in his ear. 'I've heard her and Alex play before.'

That shocked him back to consciousness. 'Yeah?'

'Yeah. So give her a chance, OK? And move your hand off my bum.' She wondered where Rob was, all of a sudden longing for him. 'Just going to the loo,' she shouted at Greg and went off to look for her real boyfriend.

She found him at the bar and tugged at his T-shirt sleeve. 'Come on,' she said. 'Let's start the dancing.'

Alex was beaming as he listened to Marie introduce the next song. This was going down so well. People were dancing and calling out for more. During the slower numbers they swayed and seemed enraptured. What a difference having one more instrument had made. And all credit to Hazel, she was doing wonders with it. Adding a splash of Cajun, or sometimes Irish or jazz. He wondered if she could join them full time, then realised he had no idea what she did for a living. She'd told him – at length, he recalled – but he hadn't retained. Typically self-absorbed of him, of course. Anyway, he'd get her out to his studio. And Dylan too, who had no excuse now his house was mostly done.

Marie was talking about the message of their next song. It was one she'd written. Marie's songs tended to have messages. He bent down and picked up his sparkling water. He'd stopped drinking alcohol during performances after the fractured-arm incident at the Albert Hall. Long time ago now. He looked over at Hazel and smiled. She winked and gave him a thumbs-up and wiggled her ample bottom. Quite a livewire, really. Just what they'd needed, perhaps.

Marie had finished talking and was staring his way, waiting for him to count them in. Alex put his glass down and did so, wondering, briefly, if Chomsky might lose some of his hearing, sitting

311

so close to that speaker.

'You were terrific,' he shouted at Hazel, giving her a hug after they'd all, rather formally, bowed once again to the applause and whistles. 'An absolute lifesaver.'

'Oh, I'm sure I wasn't.' She bowed again, slowly and from the waist. He guessed she was more used to giving her little classical recitals.

'What do you do for a living?' he asked her.

'Office manager for a firm of heating consultants. Solid fuel, gas, oil, electric. You name it we can supply it.'

'Ah yes,' he said. 'Full time is it?' They were leaving the stage now and he was close behind her.

She turned to Alex and pulled a face. 'And more. Have to pay the mortgage and keep the kids in chips and trainers. Know what I mean?'

Alex nodded sympathetically, as though he too had spent his life scrimping and saving.

They stepped off the stage and a guy in his thirties, maybe forties, was collecting autographs as the band filed past. After Dylan scribbled his signature, the man held out pen and paper to Hazel who said, 'Oh, really?' and giggled and grew red in the face.

'What's your name?' she asked, taking them off him.

'Charles. Well, Charlie. You know, as in Bonnie Prince.'

'Really?' she said with a lovely warm smile. 'One of my very favourite names.'

TWENTY-FOUR

Dear Ellie wrote Dylan. He'd found a nice card in Norwich. Didn't want to email her at her new ac.uk address and have the whole university reading it. *Hope you're having a great time at uni, making masses of friends and going out every night. Oh yeah, and doing some work. You wouldn't believe how quiet it is here now your mother's down in London. Just like it was when I moved in, only quieter somehow.* Was he coming across as sad? He read it through. Yes, definitely.

However, things have been a bit mad, what with toing and froing to Gloucestershire to make the CD with Mum, Dad and Hazel. Plus running Great Banwell School of Art while the twins are taking a late autumn tour of Italian cities.

'Running' was a bit of an exaggeration. All he did was carry out May and Fay's instructions and wander from easel to easel, offering advice that was basically ignored. Particularly by Joe.

Did I tell you I've applied to Norwich School of Art to do Graphic Design? he wrote, knowing full well he hadn't. *I'll have to do a foundation course but that's cool.*

He stood up and stretched his legs and looked through the window at the garden Richard had helped him knock into shape five weekends back, before Fliss moved. Late October seemed to be *the* worst time for gardens. Everything was

313

bedraggled and covered in leaves. Maybe he'd go and clear up a bit; have a go at next door while he was at it.

He went outside, grabbed the broom and swept the path, heaping soggy leaves in a pile that he'd burn once they'd dried out a bit. A combine-harvester droned in the distance. The sugar beet harvesting season had been underway for a month or so and a lot of the fields were down to stubble now, giving him whole new vistas on his local rambles. Solitary rambles. Once, during over-the-bar banter, he'd dared Emma to come along on one, but had ended up giving her a piggyback for the last half-mile. Who wore mules on a hike?

Back in the house – bored by the garden mess – he put some music on, then picked up the phone and tapped in again to Natalia's message. Things hadn't worked out with Kris, it seemed. Realised she wasn't really into girls, so if ever he was in London...

The nerve of the woman.

He went and turned the CD up, singing along with his namesake to 'Don't Think Twice, It's All Right', oozing irony, the way Bob did. He wished Natalia could hear him. If anyone had wasted his precious time, she had.

He made himself a coffee in the kitchen he still loved, and thought about all the work that he should be getting on with upstairs: the master bedroom, the landing, the attic room. Baz and Co were busy on other jobs, so he'd have to go it alone. A bit of motivation would come in handy. Trouble was, he hadn't given any thought to the décor yet. More white walls and wooden floors? He wondered what Natalia's loft was like. Chic, intimidating but extremely inviting, no doubt, just like Natalia. He picked up the card to Ellie but couldn't think what else to write, so listened to Natalia's message again. Then went back to the card.

Were you thinking of coming back for a weekend at all? He doubted it somehow, having heard from a friend of a friend of DJ Robo that Ellie had dumped him again. News that had caused Dylan's spirits to soar and a large round of drinks to be bought. *Let me know and I'll get some things in for you – or fill your fridge with champagne!*

Oh dear. Mistake. She'd most likely forgotten about that, all wrapped up in her new life. Dylan dropped the card. What the hell. Maybe a weekend in London would do him good. He could catch up with some friends, go clubbing and screw Natalia in a just-for-old-times way. After finding her new number, he was punching it in and turning the CD volume down, when he heard a car pull up and give three hoots at the end of the gardens. He took the cordless phone to the front door and saw it was Fliss.

'Hello?' Natalia was saying in his ear as he strode down the path. By the time he got to the gate, Fliss was tugging two suitcases from her loaded-up car. She stopped, turned to Dylan and shrugged.

'I just missed this place,' she told him, slamming the boot shut. 'Oh, and *look*,' she added, breaking into a smile. 'So much to do in the garden.'

'He-*llo?*' sang Natalia.

Another vehicle trundled up the lane and parked behind Fliss's. It too looked packed to the gills. The engine died and Richard stuck his head out. He wasn't looking quite as ecstatic as Fliss, but nevertheless smiled and said, 'Hope you haven't got too used to the peace and quiet.'

'Er, no,' said Dylan. 'Not at all.'

Did he mean that? He had kind of got used to it, really. Playing and singing loudly when creativity struck at two in the morning. The occasional bout of abandoned, and therefore noisy, sex with Emma. Now he'd have a permanent neighbour again. And was Richard moving in too?

'Dylan, you couldn't do us an enormous favour?' Fliss was asking him. 'If you're not busy, that is.' She hauled another bag from her car.

'No, I wasn't doing much at all. What's the favour?'

'It's just that Ellie's due at the station at four-fifteen, and Richard and I have got all this–'

'Yeah, yeah, of course I'll go.' He lifted the phone to his ear. 'Dyl, is that you, sweetie?' he heard before lowering it and switching it off. Did he have time for a quick shower and shave? Had he let his hair grow too long?

Fliss hoisted two bags, kicked her gate open and said, 'She's bringing her new boyfriend, apparently. A post-grad student. Quite a bit older than her, but I don't suppose that matters. Anyway, I'm sure he won't mind going in the back of your van, if that's OK with you?'

Dylan nodded and tried to keep up the smile while he digested the news. 'Sure,' he said. 'No problem.' New boyfriend? Where were White,

Orange and Pink when you needed an abduction arranged?

Fliss stopped, put her bags down and yanked a length of dead bindweed from a fence post. 'Thanks,' she said, picking everything up again. 'Only Richard's got to get home, you see.'

'Oh, so he's not...?' Dylan gestured with his head towards her house.

'No,' she said. It was almost a whisper. 'Definitely *not*.' She headed up the path followed by her inscrutable partner, or former partner. It was hard to tell if Richard was disappointed, relieved or ambivalent; he just seemed weary.

Dylan remained by the gate, looking from Fliss and Richard to the phone in his hand, and suddenly saw the whole thing as a perfectly timed message from the gods, saying *Leave Natalia well alone! It was hell, remember?* But while his head was thinking in terms of omens and warnings, his thumb was busily pressing 14713, to reply to the last caller.

'Hi, Nat,' he said when she answered. 'What are you up to this weekend?'

⚫ ⚫ ⚫

The publishers hope that this book has given you enjoyable reading. Large Print Books are especially designed to be as easy to see and hold as possible. If you wish a complete list of our books please ask at your local library or write directly to:

Magna Large Print Books
Magna House, Long Preston,
Skipton, North Yorkshire.
BD23 4ND

This Large Print Book for the partially sighted, who cannot read normal print, is published under the auspices of

THE ULVERSCROFT FOUNDATION